SILENT ALARM

ALSO BY
JENNIFER BANASH

White Lines

JENNIFER BANASH

SILENT ALARM

G. P. PUTNAM'S SONS
AN IMPRINT OF PENGUIN GROUP (USA)

G. P. PUTNAM'S SONS
Published by the Penguin Group
Penguin Group (USA) LLC
375 Hudson Street, New York, NY 10014

USA | Canada | UK | Ireland | Australia
New Zealand | India | South Africa | China
penguin.com
A Penguin Random House Company

Library of Congress Cataloging-in-Publication Data
Banash, Jennifer.
Silent alarm / Jennifer Banash.
pages cm
Summary: Alys, a Plaineville, Wisconsin, junior who dreams of
studying violin at Julliard, must deal with the aftermath of a tragic
high school shooting in which her older brother, Luke, was the shooter.
[1. School shootings—Fiction. 2. High schools—Fiction. 3. Schools—Fiction.
4. Brothers and sisters—Fiction. 5. Interpersonal relations—Fiction.
6. Family problems—Fiction.] I. Title.
PZ7.B2176Sih 2015 [Fic]—dc23 2014004462

Printed in the United States of America.
ISBN 978-0-399-25789-6
1 3 5 7 9 10 8 6 4 2

Design by Ryan Thomann. Text set in Legacy Serif.
Title page photograph © Getty Images/Bob Cornelis.

Excerpt from *Human Nature* by Alice Anderson (copyright © 1994
by New York University Press) reprinted with permission from the author.

For Story

"For there is no friend like a sister
In calm or stormy weather;
To cheer one on the tedious way,
To fetch one if one goes astray."
—CHRISTINA ROSSETTI, "GOBLIN MARKET"

"Come into the candlelight. I'm not afraid
to look the dead in the face."
—RAINER MARIA RILKE, "REQUIEM FOR A FRIEND"

Life changes in a second. In the time it takes to turn a page, to pull your hair back from your face, everything you think you know can vanish, wiped out in an avalanche, erasing everything in its path.

I was in the library, hunched over my laptop, history notes spread out on the table, the edges crimped from the pressure and heat of my own worried fingertips. Headphones streamed Schubert into the open pink shells of my ears, "Death and the Maiden," the vibrato hammering through my body, my limbs tingling with electric shocks. I longed to play it with a quartet, four of us working together in unison, the notes so sharp and clear they could punch a hole in the ozone, make you reel back in your chair. But now I'm too advanced of a player to subject my skills to the "corrupting influence" of my peers—or so says Grace, my violin teacher.

It was still technically winter, snow melting on the ground, but in the last few days the green buds had pushed their way onto the branches of the trees, insistent, and now I could barely concentrate. There was that feeling in the air that happens only at the cusp of spring, a kind of restlessness, a quickening of the blood that made me want to put down my pen and sigh. I had a project due in three days—a project I had, as usual, put off till the last minute because I had stayed up most nights that week trying and failing to master the second movement of Brahms's Violin Sonata in D Minor, the tricky mournful bit where the notes seemed to topple over one another like piles of smooth, slippery stones, one clicking against the next so melodiously that you could barely tell when one ended and another began. I'd been working on the piece for months—I had an audition coming up for the summer orchestra program at the University of Wisconsin, a program so competitive that only twenty students were admitted each June. I wanted it so badly, I was afraid to even speak of it aloud. I tilted my head to one side, stretching my cramped neck as I clicked through photographs of Thailand, hypnotized into stillness by images of mountaintop temples, a gold Buddha smiling benevolently before an altar, a series of copper bowls filled with colored powder in shades of vermillion, magenta, and ochre.

I bent down to scratch an itch on my calf, pulling out my earbuds in the process, the cord tangled in a mass beneath my chin. At the first crack, my head came up sharply, my gaze meeting that of the girl across from me. Miranda Stillman, blond hair waving against her pink sweater. What I remember of that moment was my own annoyance. I wasn't doing well in history to begin with, and I had to get this paper done or I could kiss what was left of my grade sayonara. In order to get into any kind of decent university music program (I wanted Juilliard, Berklee, days spent with my neck crooked into the oiled wood of my violin, shoulders aching, fingers stiffened and sore), I needed the grades, and so far this semester, I was failing miserably. I didn't see the point of history. What was past was past. Why not focus on the present? The future even?

"Cherry bomb," Miranda said authoritatively, but I noticed that her eyes darted back and forth nervously. A few kids got up and drifted toward the double doors of the library, but then stopped, hovering near the circulation desk. I remember feeling nothing but annoyance. The week before, someone had tossed a smoke bomb into the toilet of the girl's bathroom, sending clouds of gray haze billowing out the windows and door, and we had to stand on the football field in the rain until they figured out it was just a prank.

There was a sharp bang. Then another. Staccato. Allegro. A series of small popping noises, and a muffled scream coming from somewhere outside the set of large double doors that led out to the quad. I flinched, my body jerking as if I'd been hit. Reflexively, my feet felt for my violin case, stashed under the table, my pulse thudding as I made contact with the hard black plastic. Miranda and I just sat there staring at each other. I had never said more than ten words to her before that day. I was an orchestra nerd, and she was . . . who? What? I had no real idea. All I knew was that she was a senior, like my brother, Luke, and I was a junior. Close enough in age, but separated by a gulf of experience, friends, cheerleading practice—or whatever it was she did. A gap so wide that it seemed impossible to bridge on a daily basis. So no one did. We kept to ourselves, to our friends, our families, our small, tight circles of familiarity.

With the grind of metal against metal, Keith Rappaport came flying through the double doors, his face flushed tomato red, as if he'd been running a great distance. He was slightly pudgy, a freshman, glasses constantly sliding down the bridge of his nose. I remember he was wearing a soccer jersey—he must've had a game that afternoon. He knocked into the circulation desk, and the librarian, Ms. Parsons, looked up with no small degree of irritation. We were always running through the library to get to the other side of campus, perpetually late, always harried, and she despised the constant noise and disruption. It was only 12:30 p.m., and it was clear from the scowl on her face that her day was already ruined.

"Gunshots," Keith said, panting. "Somebody has a gun out there. For real."

Everything seemed to stand motionless, the room freezing into silence, the kind of numbness that creeps up just before terror. I was breathing fast, my fingers tightening around my laptop, which I closed and shoved roughly into my bag. Suddenly, it seemed important to gather my notes and put them back in my binder, to clear the decks. I reached under the table, pulling my violin case to my chest, holding it like a small pet. It was a Matsuda, made in the Cremonese style—which just basically meant that it was a very good copy of an Italian violin called a Stradivarius, which could sell for anywhere from fifty thousand to a few million dollars. Even though the Matsuda was a total bargain compared to a Stradivarius, I'd heard my parents fighting for weeks over whether or not they could swing it, clapping my hands over my ears to block out the shouts that drifted into my room every night. I'd been playing since I was six, and I'd long ago outgrown the violin my father had originally bought me at Sutter's, our town's only music store, the worn aisles lined with guitars, cellos, and violins hanging dejectedly against lime-green walls.

"I don't care *what* Grace says," my father had shouted. "The bottom line is that we can't afford it." I could almost see the cords on his neck standing out like taut strips of wire, his cheeks reddening. "Besides, Luke's off to college next year—MIT isn't exactly cheap."

"I'm well aware of that fact, Paul." My mother brushed him off with the dry, sarcastic tone I'd heard her use more and more frequently with my father over the past few years. "But I do know that if she's going to be a serious musician, then she can't afford *not* to have it." Her voice echoed through the house with a sharp sense of finality. And with those words, my father grew quiet and, in the days that followed, folded completely, taking out a loan of thirty thousand dollars to augment the cost—cheap for a performance-level violin, but still more than we could really afford. Every time I removed the Matsuda from its case, the guilt—along with my parents' expectations (concert violinist, Lincoln Center alight with applause as I bent forward at the waist in a graceful bow) hung on me like blocks of concrete until I had to lie down on my bed and close my eyes. It was hard, at moments like those, to separate their desire from my own.

Miranda was suddenly next to me, a glazed look plastered across her nondescript features, an almost blurriness. If you had asked me what she was thinking right then, I would have said nothing. If I was thinking at that point, I wasn't aware of it.

The cracks got louder and closer, moving stealthily toward us. And the screams.

People began running, pushing against one another, bodies flailing. It was lunchtime, and the library was always crowded then with kids rushing to finish homework assignments due that day. I watched bodies dive beneath the round tables, binders and laptops still open on table-tops, pages spilling over in a froth of whiteness. Ms. Parsons waved kids over to the fire exit, but I didn't move.

"What do we do?" Miranda had gone white, her lips barely moving. For the first time I noticed her fingers clutching my arm. She was wearing dark blue nail polish, her manicure precise, expert. I looked down at my own trimmed and filed nails, comparing them, the cuticles a bit ragged and fraying along the edges. A gold ring wrapped around Miranda's in-dex finger, a tiny ruby chip embedded in the center winking in the overhead light.

Before I could answer, the doors burst open again, and a figure dressed in black stepped through them. At that mo-ment, an alarm went off, the same one we heard at least twice a year for fire drills, the shrillness ringing in my ears. There was a rifle in his hands, and I stared at the long barrel, the way it parted the crowd without sound, the menacing weight of it. All I could see was the gun, the way it advanced into the room, a sinuous black snake waiting to strike. Miranda's grip on my arm tightened and she pulled me backward.

"C'mon!" she whispered forcefully. "We've got to move."

I knocked into the table, banging my hip, wincing as Miranda pulled me to the ground and we crawled under-neath, huddling together, her face buried in my shoulder, my violin falling to the floor. When the gun went off, it was deafening, a volley of thunder. My ears were ringing, a high-pitched whine obliterating everything. A guy named T.J., a senior who had said hello to me in the halls a few times, went down, his body hitting the floor with a thud. I watched helplessly as blood began to pool beneath his head. The muscles in his forearms were fairly developed from tennis, and as the blood seeped across the floor, the pool growing wider, my stomach turned sharply. He landed facedown, one arm flung up beside his head as if to ward off the attack. His fingers twitched spasmodically, then abruptly stopped. The air was clotted with the smell of smoke and scorched cloth, a scent I will always associate with panic and death.

Miranda sobbed next to me, her hand gripping my arm tight, her words meaningless and nonsensical in my ear, but strangely musical. She was crying so hard, it almost sounded as if she were stuttering, tripping over the insurmountable obstacle of words. The futility of them. A pair of black-booted feet walked by the table, and I held my breath. Then there was the sound of another shot and the screams began again, louder this time. Paper fell from the sky like rain. Loose leaf. An AP Chemistry test came to rest beneath the table, a large *98%* scrawled at the top in red ink. *Good Job, Tony* was penned in the left-side margin, and a stifled sob escaped my throat. I heard a small gurgling sound nearby, and crawled to the edge of the table, sticking my head as far out from underneath as

I dared without exposing myself entirely. I acted on instinct, blindly, before I could second-guess it at all.

"Don't!" Miranda's fingers clutched frantically at my shirt. "He'll see you!"

Ms. Parsons lay on the floor, one hand holding her chest, her white cardigan soaked with blood. Her mouth opened and closed repeatedly, her eyes staring blankly at the ceiling. The sounds she made were guttural and incomprehensible, a language I couldn't decipher. Ms. Parsons had spent hours helping me with my ninth-grade research project on *The Handmaid's Tale,* shown me where my locker was on my first day of freshman year when I was too nervous to ask anyone and risk looking like a loser, put aside the endless stacks of sheet music she thought I might be interested in. Brahms. Beethoven. Ravel. Debussy. The names themselves made me feel calmer, more centered, as if nothing could really be wrong in the world. To one day be good enough to play Ravel, to master those intricate chains of notes like beads on a string . . . My head swam with the thought of it, my hands aching for the bow, the faint pine-tree scent of rosin tickling my nose. Sure, Ms. Parsons was cranky and old, but she also kept butterscotch candies in her desk, let us stay after school to work on projects as long as we were quiet, and covered the walls of her small office behind the circulation desk with handmade quilts and pictures of her grandchildren.

I crawled over to her, my palms skidding away in the

slickness of blood, tears that I couldn't feel dripping steadily onto the floor. There were pairs of sneakers running swiftly by my head and jumping over my body, the sound of cries and high-pitched screams, but it was somehow far away, in the hazy distance. I took her slight hand, freckled with age spots, and held it in mine. Her skin was cold and slightly clammy, and I could hear the air moving through her lungs, labored, heavy, and filled with a thick, viscous liquid. I tried not to look at the broken blossom in the center of her chest, the deep red hole of it, the scorched fabric blackened around the stain. Her lips moved soundlessly, and I leaned closer, bending down to her mouth.

"Run," she whispered over and over again, the words melting together in a single entity.

Runrunrunrunrunrunrunrunrunrunrunrunrunrunrunrun . . .

There was a shadow suddenly above, the light dimming across her face, a sword falling between us, and I turned around and looked up. The fluorescence stung my eyes, wet with salt, and for the first time I saw him: that slightly pointed chin I knew so well, the cheekbones that protruded sharply from the planes of his face. His eyes, usually brown and warm, the color of wet sand, were flat and lifeless. His arms were the first I'd ever crawled toward, my knees wobbly against the kitchen floor, his hands now wrapped around cold metal. The fingers, long and expressive, resting on the trigger, had helped build my first sand castle. My brother, with whom I had always felt safe, falling asleep each night to the sound of music drifting from behind the closed door of his room, the soft, jangling guitars he loved creeping slowly into my dreams.

"Hey." He nodded his chin at me, his tone casual, as if we were passing each other in the hallway late at night, the house shuddering in sleep around us.

My mouth opened, but my words had vanished and I gazed up at him, voiceless, blinking slowly into the light. I couldn't hear my own breathing, my heart pumping away silently. He pointed the gun at me, and I fell into the darkness that stretched out inside the barrel. We stared at each other for what felt like an eternity. If he knew me, I couldn't tell. He was unmistakably my brother and not my brother all at once, his features twisting and changing from moment to moment like a bad radio signal. Him. Not him. Him. Not him. I closed my eyes. The fact that I was his sister suddenly didn't seem to matter. All I knew was the gun in my face, the enormity of it, the world shrinking to a black dot somewhere out on the horizon. I had never thought much about death, bones turning to dust, the body gone forever. I lived for the now, our lives portioned out into manageable segments, photos that disappeared in twenty seconds. Now death loomed above me, so close I could smell the sharp sweat emanating from his pores. The Grim Reaper, dressed not in a long black robe, but in the combat boots I'd helped him pick out at the mall last month.

Suddenly, I felt the molecules of air surrounding my body rearrange themselves in a cool rush, the shadow falling abruptly away. Even before I opened my eyes, I knew he was gone. I watched his back as he walked away, striding purposefully toward the table I'd hidden under just minutes before. I could hear Miranda's cries intensify as he came closer, advancing. He walked briskly, almost passing her before he turned around, bending at the waist and peering under the table. Miranda began to scream helplessly then. I was aware that my hands were shaking, that I was cold, so cold it felt as if I might never be warm again.

"What's up?" I heard him say in the seconds before the gun went off, his voice taunting and menacing, belying those innocent words. The screaming abruptly stopped, the wail of an animal cut short. If you had asked me to sit still, or even to get up and run, I couldn't have done it. At some point soon after, he must've left the library, the double doors clanging noisily behind him. I stayed where I was, rocking back and forth as if to put myself to sleep, my hands clutching my head. A lullaby my mother had once sung to me before bed repeated itself over and over in my brain. *Safe and sound. Safe and sound. Go to sleep, you little baby* . . . There was peace in the repetition of words, the sameness of the syllables. Then there were hands on my body lifting me up, voices cooing into my deafened ears, smoothing my clothes. I pulled away with a violent jerk, the sound finally released from my throat in a long howl that rose steadily up and into the hollowness of the room. The light blue hoodie and jeans I wore that day were drenched, the blood beginning to dry, stiffening the fabric against my skin. That night when I sat down to brush my hair, I would find tiny pieces of bone matted in the long strands.

After leaving the library, my brother walked calmly through the quad, stopping in a deserted science lab, shutting the door behind him. I imagine him waiting for a long moment, the clock ticking on the wall, before resting the long barrel of the gun against his forehead and pulling the trigger. I can almost picture the explosion, the force that propelled him backward so that he fell into a desk, then hit the floor, his blood discoloring the pale yellow linoleum in a dirty smear. By the time the SWAT team busted through the doors of the school (he had secured them with bicycle locks), my brother had killed fifteen people. His face would be plastered across the front page of every newspaper in the country, that half smile I knew so well grinning out from the stark pages, my fingers smeared with ink as I sifted through the wreckage.

WISCONSIN DAILY RECORD

WEDNESDAY, MARCH 11, 2015

High school senior kills 15 in Plainewood shooting

Plainewood, Wisconsin— A student killed 15 people and injured 4 in a deadly shooting yesterday at Plainewood High School. Police have confirmed that the shooter, Lucas David Aronson, 18, died of a self-inflicted gunshot wound.

A student who witnessed the attack said he heard gunshots coming from the parking lot before seeing Aronson entering the library, where he proceeded to open fire.

FBI officials would not comment on a motive. And Plainewood Police said authorities "have much work to do yet" in their investigation of the shooting, which sent students running for their lives during their lunch hour at 1,200-student Plainewood High.

"Everybody just took off," said 17-year-old Melanie Walker, who was studying in a classroom when she heard shots fired. "We were all running and screaming down the hallway."

Heather Adams, 17, said she was in the library when she saw Aronson enter and begin shooting. She said she and several other students immediately ran outside, while others locked themselves in a teachers' lounge.

Classmates and residents described Aronson as a normal boy who excelled in school and enjoyed skateboarding.

Bill Dunne, a next-door

neighbor, said he was "stunned," to hear of Aronson's involvement in the Wednesday shooting, describing Aronson as "an average boy, pretty quiet."

"The boy was a senior, had gotten into a good college. He had everything going for him," Dunne said. Reportedly, some months prior to the shooting, Aronson had been accepted to MIT, where he planned to study biochemistry.

Equally stunned are Aronson's classmates.

Eighteen-year-old Christa Conners, a senior at Plaineville High School, said that Aronson was known for his willingness to counsel others. "He always had time to listen," Conners stated. When asked about bullying as a possible motive, Conners stated that as far as she knew, "Luke was never made fun of or bullied. He didn't talk a lot in class, but nobody picked on him."

"Even though he was kind of quiet, he still had friends," said Tyler Rosen, 16.

Plainewood High School principal David Clarke, who was injured in the attack, released a statement expressing the administration's "deep grief for the victims and survivors of this horrific event," and vowed to "bring the community back together swiftly and securely."

On Friday, teachers and administration will return to the school for the first time since yesterday's fatal shooting, with grief counselors on hand. Students and parents are urged to return to the school on Monday, March 16th for counseling, with classes set to resume after the spring break holiday on April 6th.

Aronson is survived by his parents and a sister, 17.

ONE

———

"It's the human's nature to survive,
Welcome to the living."
—ALICE ANDERSON, "HUMAN NATURE"

ONE

There's blood under my nails.

No matter how many showers I take, how much I scrub with a coarse brush, the bristles scouring the damp pads of my fingers, I can't get them clean. I hold my hands up to the light and scrutinize them, squinting my eyes, bringing them to my nose, my stomach recoiling at the coppery stink I imagine still permeates my chapped flesh. In spite of all of my efforts there remains a faint line embedded beneath each nail. A shadow.

I hear muffled noises from outside the house, and I walk to my window, pull the curtains back. Reporters stand there patiently, lying in wait, their hulking white news vans parked at the curb. I can feel their eyes sweeping the perimeter of the house, searching for signs of life, movement, a story.

One woman lights a cigarette, and as she draws the smoke into her lungs, a look of relief falls across her face, her hair shellacked into a dark helmet. I close the curtains and look around. My room is the same: pale blue walls the washed-out hue of skim milk, a mirrored vanity table with spindly wooden legs that used to belong to my grandmother, a pair of long windows that look over the sloping front yard. My violin case propped at the foot of my bed like a discarded doll. But everything is different. I open the case, still imagining that it is streaked with blood and other bodily fluids I don't want to think about, and pull my violin from the velvet interior, my fingers skidding over the well-oiled mahogany. I run my hands over the satiny wood, the tips of my fingers hardened and rough, before tucking it back in the case where it will be safe, where it can sleep and forget.

I should be practicing now, warming up with scales in the music room at school, light falling weakly through the dusty blinds, the bow moving effortlessly in my hands. Afterward, gulping down a carton of orange juice in the cafeteria before first track, the shreds of sweet pulp tickling the inside of my cheeks, the halls, redolent of floor wax, strong, musky perfume, and the chemical stench of Dry-Erase markers. My face staring back at me in the girls' bathroom mirror, hurriedly brushing my hair before class—eyes the color of hot cocoa, a pointed chin, two dark slashes for eyebrows, the brush caught in my straight sandy hair.

I walk downstairs, pulling my hoodie around me in the morning chill. My feet are bare and cold on the polished wood floors. *What do people do in the morning?* I wonder as I descend, my legs moving mechanically. Without school, time seems slowed down, heavy and thick as a snowdrift. Just yesterday I was rummaging through the kitchen in the early morning light, grabbing a banana from a bowl on the kitchen counter, Luke waiting impatiently in the driveway, car keys jangling against his leg—but it already seems lost in the distance. *Some people won't be walking downstairs today,* I think, *or eating anything at all. Some people won't ever walk again, and you know whose fault that is, don't you?* Miranda's face flashes in front of my eyes. I stop at the bottom, my hand on the banister, the scent of freshly brewed coffee drifting through the air. Even though I'm not particularly hungry, I want the normalcy of routine, an illusion of order. *Breakfast,* I tell myself firmly, putting one foot in front of the other. *You should eat breakfast.*

My mother sits at the kitchen table, engulfed in a sea of newsprint, her eyes staring straight ahead. The phone, I notice, is placed on the countertop, off the hook. She's wearing the blue terry-cloth robe my dad gave her for Christmas years ago, the fabric now worn into softness. Her golden hair is matted in the back, one piece sticking up crazily on top. She doesn't hear me come in, and when I touch her, she jumps, grabbing my arm. When she tilts her face up to look at me, there are shadows beneath her eyes, deep craters. In her heart-shaped face, I see my own wide-set eyes, though Luke got her dimple, the slight indentation on her left cheek that only appears when she smiles.

"Alys! You startled me." She looks away before noticing the newspapers cluttering the table, the mess of them. Words swim before my eyes in a tangle of black and white. *Shooter. Casualties. Unstable. Tragedy. Rifle.* I take a deep breath in and hold it, a sharp pain filling my lungs. She pulls the newspapers toward herself, crumpling them, and the sound it makes is like fire, my nerves standing on end. She gathers up the papers in her arms and walks over to the kitchen counter, stowing them there, out of reach.

"Let me make you something to eat." She turns around, her eyes unnaturally bright, glittering from lack of sleep. There is a cadence to her voice I haven't heard before, a kind of superficial cheerfulness. For the record, my mother is a lot of things, but cheerful isn't generally one of them. She works at an art gallery and makes pots and small sculptures in her studio in the basement in her spare time, glazing them in metallic bronzes and cloudy grays. She devours thrillers with hammers and sickles on the covers and is partial to boring experimental foreign films with endless subtitles. "Cheerful" is not generally on her radar. When my parents met, they were college students at the University of Chicago, spending all their time at weird-ass pseudo-hippie gatherings where people sat around in parks doing lots of drugs and making out with each other, even though the sixties were long over. They should've been listening to Nirvana and Pearl Jam, hanging out in coffeehouses dressed in plaid, ogling pictures of Kate Moss modeling the latest in heroin chic. Instead they organized protests against major corporations until they were chased from the sidewalks like bits of paper blown by the wind. It sounds stupid now, but when I look at the old pictures of them my mother keeps tucked away in her underwear drawer, patched and faded jeans sliding down her skinny hips, my father wrapped in some kind of crazy wool poncho, his dark hair longer than my own, I almost believe that they're going to end up on a farm somewhere, growing vegetables and baking their own bread, a merry band of weirdos sharing their ramshackle Victorian, the paint peeling in a shower of flakes like so much dead skin. Pots of vegetable chili cooking on the stove, and the sweet clucking of chickens in the yard.

But my dad gave all of that up for the dream of a white picket fence and the financial security of a corporate job—something my mother never quite forgave him for. Moving to Plainewood from Chicago was just about the worst thing that has ever happened to her, and she never gets tired of telling us so. "We live in a town where I sell paintings of kittens, for God's sake," she'll grumble after a particularly bad day at work. My dad works as an insurance adjuster, the guy people call when their roofs cave in or their houses burn to white-hot cinders. Most of the time, he sits in his office, hunched over a calculator, spreadsheets and cost analysis reports littered across his desk. Rows of suits line the walls of his closet, his threadbare jeans and poncho thrown in the trash long ago. In spite of the bleakness of his job, the floods, the fires, the acts of God that can tear a house down to its very foundation, my father is unremittingly cheerful—something that irritates my mother to no end. "How can you do what you do and be happy?" she'll mutter as she stalks around the kitchen, banging cabinets and pulling a dense block of cheese from the fridge for a makeshift dinner. "Who the hell did I marry?" is another one she's fond of lobbing out as she exits a room, the smell of turpentine trailing her like vapor. I watch as she pulls open the cupboard now, her hand hovering over a box of cereal.

I think of the myriad possibilities waiting patiently to be consumed: the bagels on the counter, the cartons of peach and strawberry yogurt in the fridge, the cereal my mother is about to pull from its shelf, and bile rises in my throat. How can I go through the mindless act of chewing and swallowing like it's just a normal day when everything's been burned to ashes? I sit down, one hand over my mouth.

"Alys?" My mother hurries over and places one hand on my forehead as if to check for fever. She tries to pull me to her, but I am stone. Immovable. My mother does not fuss, as a rule, but now she is all over me. "You didn't eat last night, did you?"

"Nobody did," I mumble as her face falls slightly, tears welling up in her eyes. "I told you. I'm not hungry."

"You'll feel better if you eat something." My mother is always happiest whenever she has a project, and she moves purposefully over to the refrigerator and pulls out a loaf of bread. The last time she made me breakfast, I was probably six. I notice her hands are trembling slightly, a low-grade tremor. *You'll feel better.* As if something as small as eating could fix anything at all. I watch, hypnotized by the banality of toast as she places two slices of bread in the oven and shuts the door, pulls the butter from the fridge so it can soften on the counter. My mother doesn't believe in toasters—she thinks they're a waste of money.

"Can I have some coffee?" I want to feel the cup in my hand, the heat burning my palms, the solid heft of the porcelain.

"You know how I feel about you drinking coffee. It stunts your growth."

I'm five eleven. Without coffee, I would be the Jolly Green Giant. I already tower over most of the guys in my class, which is slightly humiliating. I look out the kitchen window at the bare branches of trees, a light rain trickling down from the sky. I wish things could go back to the way they were yesterday, Luke telling me to hurry up, Mom yelling from her studio for us to have a good day, Dad talking on the phone to some agitated client before he left for work, his voice calming as a tranquilizer. Not my mother bustling around as if she knows what she's doing when everything has so obviously fallen apart. Not this awful silence we have to fill with toast and morning conversation. Not this.

"We'll need to get you a dress," she says casually, as if we're talking about shopping for the prom. "The service is tomorrow. We can go to the mall later. In Madison."

I notice that she doesn't say the word *funeral,* though she and I both know this is exactly what she means. A dress. A stupid black dress I will wear once, and then stuff in the garbage cans out back when no one is looking. A dress I would rather douse in gasoline and light on fire than ever see again. I should be shopping for bikinis for the trip to Maui we were supposed to be taking next week, staring at my body in the full-length mirrors of the dressing room with a combination of fascination and dismay, my legs long and too skinny, my chest annoyingly flat. Perusing the aisles of Ray's Drugs in search of the one self-tanner that smelled like coconuts and somehow magically enabled my dead-white skin to develop a burnished glow that whispered of exotic locales. Bali. Antigua. Bora Bora brown.

"Is that . . . necessary?" I say slowly.

"Why wouldn't it be?" She stops and stares at me, holding a knife in one hand like a talisman, her face impassive but her eyes flashing a warning. Danger.

Because there is a group of rabid reporters camped out on our doorstep, waiting for us to so much as stick a toe out the front door? Because Luke killed fifteen people? Because leaving the house right now to go anywhere makes me feel like I'm going to die?

"Your entire wardrobe consists of sweats and jeans with holes in them, so yes, Alys, I think it's necessary." She puts a yellow plate with toast cut into precise triangles down on the table in a sharp clatter—I get it: *You will eat this toast*—and sits down in a chair next to me. The smell turns my stomach, but I force myself to pick up a slice, to consider the tiny bubbles of air in the dough before bringing it to my mouth and taking a bite. The bread has no taste whatsoever, despite being liberally spread with butter, and I chew mechanically, then swallow, a lump sticking in my throat.

"Where's Dad?" I ask, taking another bite.

My mother looks away, her expression distant.

"He got up early—to go down to the hospital, to see your brother's . . ."

The hospital is for sick people. Dead.

She doesn't finish the sentence. Can't.

"Anyway. He's resting upstairs now."

"Why didn't you go?"

She looks at me wearily, and for the first time I notice the sharp lines around her mouth and eyes. My mother has always been one of those moms who can pass for ten years younger than she really is. People are forever commenting on it, which gets kind of annoying, if you want to know the truth. Now, for the first time I can remember, she looks old, worn-out, her face crumpling in on itself.

"I stayed for you. Someone needed to be here when you woke up. The phone's been ringing all morning."

This may or may not be true. I cannot picture my mother kneeling down by the cold metal slab, her legs failing her, one hand buried in my brother's thick, floppy hair. She would not survive it, her only son, his

(—his dark eyes fixed on the ceiling, seeing nothing—)

"I haven't heard anything." I chew slowly, reluctantly, willing myself to eat.

"Your father took the phone off the hook. And we turned off your cell after you got home."

My iPhone is sitting on the kitchen table, where I left it last night, the screen cracked down the center. When I pick it up, I notice the dried blood streaking the display, feel the slight stickiness on my fingers, and I begin to cough, dropping the phone with a clatter on the tabletop, bending at the waist. Then there is the steady pressure of my mother's hand on my back, the sound of her voice as she whispers, "Shush . . ." slowly, quietly. She pats me at first, then rubs in circles, which makes me want to jump out of my skin, to start screaming and never stop.

"I'm okay, I'm okay," I manage to get out, coughing in

between the words. I wave away her hands, and stumble over to the sink, fill a glass of water from the tap, and drink greedily, crumbs of toast still sputtering around in my windpipe like dried leaves. The feeder hanging from the oak tree in the backyard is birdless, snow dotting the ground in patches. The garden is asleep, and looking at it, brown and bare, I long for spring, the sunlight that will bring the wildflowers my mother planted last year to the surface, dotting the landscaping in a rich, colorful carpet. The tree house Luke built when he was thirteen still hangs from the upper branches of the oak, the wood weathered from the last few years of snow, rain, and sun. I remember him working on it all of that summer, cutting the wood into precise planks, a pencil tucked behind one ear. I blink back the tears and refill my glass, the rushing stream from the tap drowning my memories. But suddenly he's there, slinking through the yard, the gold streaks in his hair shining under overcast skies. I blink once, dropping the glass in the sink with a crash, but he's still there, walking through the backyard in a long winter coat, staring up at me.

"Alys?" My mother's voice sounds worried, tense, but I barely hear her.

Her hands are on my shoulders as I raise my index finger and point, wordless, at the dark figure meandering around near my mother's prize rosebushes: Lincoln. American Beauty.

Damask. Following my gaze, her grip tightens, the nails digging in like claws.

"Paul!" She screams my father's name, spinning around, hand on her hips, a wild look in her eyes. "Paul, someone's in the yard again!"

Luke, is that you?

I mouth the words silently, afraid to speak them aloud, but when the figure moves closer to the window, holding up a large black camera, I see that it's not him, not Luke, that his blond hair is shot with silver and there are wrinkles around his eyes. I realize that I am holding on to the kitchen counter, holding on with both hands as if I might fall down entirely if I let go.

My father enters the room, his bathrobe wrapped around him tightly. If I've ever seen my father in a robe after seven a.m. on a weekday, I can't remember it. He walks to the kitchen window and peers outside, his face set and grim, then yanks open the back door so that the house shakes. I watch him stride over to the man and grab his wrist. My father, whom I have never seen touch another living soul in anger—we were never even spanked as kids—grabs him so roughly that the man's camera falls to the ground, bouncing once before lying still, the lens pointed toward the sky. And in that one moment, my mother's hands on my shoulders again, I know for sure that from this second on, my life will never be the same again. There will always be someone lurking behind the hedges, waiting to stun us with the glare of flashbulbs, our faces blank as paper. Our smiles utterly erased.

Before yesterday, we were a normal family. *Normal.* Camp in the summer and igloo forts in the winter. Icees made from the first snowfall, sugar and drops of food coloring melting on our tongues in a pink slush. Two parents, two cars. The low moan of a cello streaming from the speakers, the high-pitched burst of my violin punctuating the bustle and hum of our daily lives. Chocolate chip pancakes at IHOP on Sunday mornings. A white clapboard house with a manicured lawn, splashes of yellow roses lining the fence. Everything neat and tidy. Ask anyone. Of course, now after what Luke has done, people will say, *Oh, the Aronsons. I always thought they were weird.* But we weren't. We were just like you. Except we weren't. But we didn't know it yet.

But you knew it, Luke, didn't you?

Didn't you.

TWO

Just as I'm about to walk upstairs and get dressed, the doorbell rings, making me jump. A clanging of bells reverberates through the house announcing the arrival of who? What now?

What fresh hell is this?

If I were in English class right now, Mrs. Miller would be boring me to death with Shakespeare and Eudora Welty, and I'd most likely be staring into space, stomach rumbling like a garbage truck, thinking about what culinary atrocity lay in wait for me in the cafeteria. Not standing at the foot of the stairs afraid to move, to answer the door, terrified at what might be on the other side.

My mother brushes past me, placing her hands on my waist and moving me out of the way as if I am suddenly small again, underfoot. The smell of coffee, the salty scent of her unwashed skin mixed with day-old perfume envelop me, and I want to throw myself into her arms and sleep, hiding beneath the soft folds of her robe. She looks out the peep-hole and a long sigh escapes her lips. "It's the police," she says, her voice wooden. "Again."

The detectives were here yesterday after my father picked me up from school, but I went up to my room and straight into the bathroom, their suits and blue uniforms a shapeless blur, their voices a horde of insects, my mother's shrieks rising above them all as I lay on the floor, moaning tunelessly. Later, wrapping her arms around me, her grip tight as she rocked me back and forth against the white tiles, her hot tears soaking the back of my neck, my tangled hair, my mouth stretched into a distorted scream. "Play the Brahms," I yelled out at some point, inconsolable. "Play the Brahms." But even the sweet, low sound coursing through the speakers in my room, the soaring soprano of that single, mournful violin, did nothing to ease the fire in my chest or take away the pain.

Help me.

When my mother opens the door, two men stand there wearing blue Windbreakers, sunglasses covering their eyes just like in the movies. Just beyond the front porch, I see the TV vans; the reporters clustered at the end of the driveway, talking into cell phones, pacing back and forth, holding up their cameras before the front door closes again, hoping for a glimpse. The taller of the two officers removes his sun-glasses, and his watery blue eyes take in my mother's robe, my messy hair, the fact that sleep last night was little more than wishful thinking as I lay there for hours, terrified to close my eyes and relive it all: that seasick, earthquake feeling as kids stampeded though the library, the tremor of running feet, the room vibrating with a peculiar mix of terror and tears.

"Mrs. Aronson, I'm so sorry to bother you at this difficult time," he says, sounding apologetic enough. "But we have some questions for Alys, if you don't mind. It will only take a few minutes."

He pronounces my name Alice, not A-lise, the way it's meant to be said, and for the millionth time I wonder why my parents gave Luke such a simple name—easy to say, easy to spell—but decided to bestow upon me one that pretty much guarantees that I'll be correcting people in a mild but constant state of irritation for my entire life.

"Right now?" My mother puts her hands on her hips, ready for an argument, her face veiled in annoyance. When my mother doesn't like someone—for whatever reason—they know it instantly.

"We wouldn't bother you if it weren't absolutely nec-essary." His voice is quiet and grave, and my mother hesi-tates for a moment. I can see the emotions shifting over her face—sadness, regret, reluctance, acceptance—before she moves aside to let them in. They step inside the foyer, looking around uncomfortably. I watch as they take in the family photos lining the walls of the staircase: me at my first violin concert when I was seven, the framed drawings Luke and I both made over the years, scribbles of bright crayon and smeared paint. My mother has always been more than eager to foster our artistic potential with drawing classes after school, tie-dye workshops, modeling clay—anything she thought might spark our "creative sides," as she likes to call it. Too bad for her that she wound up with kids who could barely color inside the lines, much less take the Guggenheim by storm.

We file into the living room, which is the one room in our house we barely ever use, except for "family" holidays like Christmas or Thanksgiving. All the tables and chairs have tiny matchstick legs that look like they will splinter if you so much as lean on them. My mother refers to it sarcastically as her "grown-up room," which Luke always thought was pretty hilarious. "You *are* a grown-up," he'd scoff, rolling his eyes. "You don't need a stupid room to prove it."

I sit down on the love seat, and the detectives sit across from me on the long couch, unzipping their Windbreakers, leaning back against the pillows. The taller one, who's done most of the talking so far, takes out a pad and a pen. "I'm Detective Marino," he says, then points at the guy sitting beside him. "And this is Detective Rogers." Detective Rogers has white-blond hair that's balding slightly on top, and a roll of fat that hangs over his belt, straining at the buttons of his white dress shirt. He's incredibly pale, and when he removes his sunglasses, his eyelashes are so light, they are practically nonexistent.

My mother hovers in the doorway, arms folded across her chest. I can feel the nervousness, the tension coming off of her in waves. Just as she makes her way over to the love seat to sit beside me, Marino holds up one hand. "Mrs. Aronson, we'd really like to speak to Alys privately, if you don't mind." He mispronounces my name once again.

"It's A-lise," I say, unable to let it go, putting the stress firmly on the second syllable as the words leave my lips.

"Sorry," Marino says, his cheeks reddening noticeably. He clears his throat once, a half cough behind a closed fist, and averts his eyes from my face. "We won't keep . . . her . . . long." He pauses, deciding whether to attempt my name once again. "We just have a few quick questions."

My mother opens her mouth as if to say something, to protest, then presses her lips together so tight that her mouth resembles a straight line. It hurts me to see her like this: someone I have never known to give up a fight easily, reduced to wordlessness and sorrow. I hear my father moving around upstairs, the creak of the floorboards in their bedroom, then the sound of water gushing through the pipes in the walls. My mother glances quickly upward, her expression tense and worried, and nods her head at the detectives.

"If you need me, I'll be right upstairs, Alys." She points at the ceiling above her, as if I don't know where her bedroom is and need to be reminded. With that, she shuffles out of the room and walks upstairs, the wooden stairs shifting and groaning beneath her weight.

"Alys," Detective Marino begins, his blue eyes bloodshot but kind, "we won't keep you long. We just have a few questions about Luke."

My brother's name in his mouth sounds obscene.

"What can you tell us about Luke's demeanor in the days before the . . . incident?"

(shooting)

I look at my feet, how white they look against the pink-and-beige rug, like two fish pulled from the icy depths of the sea, gasping on land.

"He seemed a little depressed," I say, my throat filled with static.

"Was that unusual for him?" Rogers inquires, pen poised above his little white pad.

"Not really." I look up to find both detectives watching me carefully. "I mean, Luke could sometimes get into a mood, but so can everyone. If you're asking me if I thought that he would bring a gun to school and mow down fifteen of our classmates, I had no clue."

Anger wells up inside me. I know they're wondering the same thing I am—how could I have not known? How could

I have lived one room away from him for the past seventeen years and not even thought once that something was so wrong? So utterly unfixable?

The detectives exchange a look between them but say nothing in response.

"Had Luke ever talked to you about buying a gun?"

(—*the long barrel looming over me, Luke's face, his cocoa-colored eyes reflected in mine. "Hey," he said, as if everything was normal. "Hey," he said, like he was about to ask if I wanted to go and get ice cream the way we'd done countless times since I was small. He hated chocolate, but loved whipped cream. Rainbow sprinkles. These are the things I remember about my brother. This is what is left to me—*)

I cannot speak. I stare ahead dumbly and listen to the rustle of people lining our front walk through the windows, curtains drawn like a veil.

"Did Luke know how to shoot?" Detective Rogers tries again, his tone slow and pointed, as if I have brain damage. I wonder if he's asked my parents these same exact questions, the words hitting their mark like so many sharp knives.

"Yeah," I manage to say, clearing my throat. "My dad taught him a few summers ago on one of their trips. I think it was at some shooting range, but you'll have to ask him. I think he's upstairs . . ." My eyes drift toward the ceiling. I imagine my mother and father at night, each moored on their own side of the mattress, the distance between them growing even wider, a chasm splitting the bed in two.

"Did Luke ever talk to you about buying a gun or wanting to purchase a weapon of any kind?"

"No." My voice comes out in a squeak, and I stare at the wallpaper behind their heads, the flowers and leaves twining together, green and beige.

"Do you need a break, Alys?" Marino asks, his tone not unkind, careful, this time, to say my name correctly. He leans forward, places his pad down on the coffee table between us. "We can stop for a minute if you like."

Stop for a minute. I want everything to stop for a minute. Longer, even.

"No, I'm okay." I look over at Marino, my eyes snapping back into focus, and take a deep breath, letting it out slowly.

"Did you and Luke have a good relationship?"

(—*I remember Luke's broad back as he dove into the lake the summer I was nine. "C'mon, slowpoke! I'll catch you." The slap of cold water against my legs, my brother's hands holding me up like a buoy. Weightless. "Is this swimming or drowning?" I ask, quizzical and silly, spitting water from my mouth in a fountain. Luke's face is serious, contemplative, as he considers the question, his head cocked to the side, droplets of water glistening on his forehead.*

"Which do you want it to be, Alys?"—)

The room spins. It dawns on me that there is a very real possibility I will spew the two bites of toast I've managed to swallow all over my mother's Oriental rug. I imagine the detective's shocked expressions, my vomit, messy and stinking

21

of rottenness, cracking their professional poker faces, and I almost want it to happen. There was a darkness in him even then, on that perfect summer day, pulsing somewhere below the surface, waiting to emerge.

"Alys." Rogers jumps in this time. "We asked if you and Luke had a good relationship."

"I thought we did."

"But you think differently now?"

"I didn't say that," I answer, unable to keep the first flicker of irritation from my voice. It's like they're trying to catch me in a lie, trip me up somehow. "I said *I* thought we did. My opinion. I can't speak for Luke."

(because he's dead)

"Did Luke have a lot of friends? Would you describe him as popular?" Marino asks, scribbling something down on his pad. I have the urge to reach over and grab it, rip up the pages.

"No. He kept to himself mostly. We're both kind of like that.

(were)

"He had one close friend, I guess . . ."

Rogers flips through his pad, searching. "Are you referring to Riley Larson?" he asks, looking up from the page expectantly.

"Yes," I say, shaken slightly. Riley Larson. My brother's closest friend. Riley's sunny demeanor the perfect foil for Luke's broody darkness, the periods of depression that started after his fifteenth birthday and could fall over him and linger for months. The sullen moods we all tried to ignore, pushing them away. Riley. The only person who knows Luke as well as I do.

(did)

"Did Luke have a girlfriend?"

"I don't know," I stammer. "I don't think so." I'm aware, even as I speak, that it's insane, ridiculous even, that I know so little about my brother's life. Shouldn't I know if he had a girlfriend? If he had a crush on someone? What kind of girls he liked—blondes, brunettes? If he'd had his heart broken? I keep talking, hoping that if I keep going I can make some sense out of the thoughts swirling through my head, confusing me. *When did you stop talking to me, Luke? When did the silence begin?*

"But what I was trying to say before was that he wasn't especially popular, but no one

(hated)

disliked him. Not as far as I know." I stop myself. "I mean knew." My face burns with the correction. His shoes are still lined up on the floor of the closet in his bedroom, his baseball mitt is still in the garage, his hair in the bathroom sink from the last time he shaved—biscuit-colored bits of DNA. How can he be gone?

"Was he bullied? Picked on? Did he have any enemies?" Rogers asks without looking up, his pen scratching against the paper with a sound that sets my teeth on edge. Marino stares at me, sitting back against the cushions and waiting for what I might say next. I wonder how I must seem to him, hair uncombed, eyes wild.

"Not that I know of," I say, and it's true. No one really picked on Luke, but they didn't exactly seek him out either. He was just . . . there.

"Just a few final questions, Alys, and then we'll be on our way," Marino says, leaning forward. "Did you see your brother in the library during the attack?"

(—*Luke's eyes, there but not there, unseeing, the muscles in his forearms working as he lifted the gun to eye level*—)

I nod, unable to find words.

"Did he say anything to you?"

I close my eyes and the tears begin to fall down my cheeks, hot, my skin on fire.

"He said . . ."

"Yes? We're listening, Alys," Rogers says with an edge of impatience, or maybe even excitement.

"He said, 'Hey.'"

"He said, 'Hey,'" Marino repeats without inflection. "Was that it?" He raises one dark eyebrow.

"Yeah," I say, wiping my face with the backs of my hands, looking away, my body weak with the effort. "That was it."

Rogers lets out a sigh, one made up of varying degrees of exasperation and contempt. *Leave, leave,* I think, the words buzzing through my brain. If they don't get up and head toward the door soon, I will be completely undone. I will lose it, and I will not come back, my sanity dissolving in a puddle of tears and unanswered questions.

"One more question, Alys, and then we're done, okay?" Before I can answer or shake my head, Marino pushes on. "Did you have any prior knowledge that your brother was planning to conduct a mass murder at Plainewood High School yesterday?"

Mass murder.

I remember Luke at ten, playing in a teepee in the backyard our dad had gotten him that summer, the canvas rustling in the soft breeze. "Members only," he'd belt out if anyone came too close—our parents; our nanny, Elizabeth, whom he loved. "You can come in," he'd say to me, pulling back the flaps so that I could crawl inside, "but only because you're my sister." His impish face, that lopsided grin. The force and heat with which he threw his arms around my neck back then, hugging me close, his wiry body smelling of grass and dirt and little-boy flesh, sweaty and sweet.

I shake my head no, afraid to speak, afraid that I might start crying again. Instead, I look down at my lap, not wanting to meet their gaze, to see the pity that I know is there, written all over their faces like Braille.

THREE

After the detectives leave, I turn my phone back on for the first time since I left school yesterday. The minute I press the power button, it begins to buzz incessantly. A text from a number I don't know pops up on-screen, written in all caps, searing my eyes with its vitriol.

I HOPE YOUR BROTHER BURNS IN HELL!!!!!!!!

My thumb reflexively hits the power button, turning the screen to black. As I walk upstairs I'm shaking, sobs shuddering in my throat. I stop in the bathroom to wet a washcloth and rub it over the darkened display. The cloth comes back streaked with rust and I avert my eyes, throwing the damp rag into the hamper, where it lands heavily with a wet thud.

In front of Luke's closed bedroom door, I pause for a moment, one hand reaching out for the metal knob, cold beneath my fingers. I lean my forehead against the smooth wood, listening for what, I don't know, before I let go and move toward my room. *Please,* I am thinking again. *Please, please.* But I don't know to whom, exactly, I am praying, or why. Maybe myself. Maybe no one. Even with the reporters waiting on the front steps, the echo of car doors slamming, the click and whir of cameras, the house feels too quiet without the trill of my violin, the monotony of scales, the jostle and hum of Luke's music seeping from beneath his door. I can almost feel the walls sigh as they settle around me.

I scroll through my contacts and dial Ben's number. That goofy pic of him with the dumb sunglasses and baseball hat I took a few months ago fills the screen as the phone rings and rings in my ear. I sit on my bed, hugging a pillow to my chest as I wait for him to answer. Ben and I basically grew up together—our parents have been inseparable ever since we moved here just before I was born. There are a bunch of pictures of us in diapers somewhere, seated next to each other in a grimy, Cheerio-littered playpen, grinning our heads off, baby drool running from my mouth in a long, translucent string onto his bare leg. The caption above the photo reads *Pebbles and Bamm-Bamm*, a reference to *The Flintstones,* and the nicknames our parents had for us for as long as we could remember. There is not one memory, one event from my life that I can recall that does not, in some way, include him. Watching him race across the soccer field as he kicked the ball expertly into the net. His hands stirring a large vat of spaghetti sauce, the smooth skin of one cheek dotted with a constellation of red. His long fingers petting the keyboard of the grand piano hulking in the corner of their living room, as if it might be tamed by his touch alone. Music filling the halls of their sprawling Victorian, drifting up to touch the high ceilings like smoke. His head bent over the keys, brow furrowed in concentration. So last summer, when he kissed me, it changed everything—and nothing—all at once.

It was August, the still dead of summer, and there was nothing much to do. Even the humid air seemed wrung out and exhausted, the stars dipping low in the sky as if they too wanted some kind of relief. It was late. Ben had come over earlier to watch some stupid horror flick Luke had told us about. I was wearing cutoffs and a tank top the color of jade, my hair pulled into a knot, feet bare against the rug. Ben had on a pair of faded jeans, and had lost his T-shirt the minute the movie began, as was his style whenever the temperature rose anywhere above sixty degrees. He was tanned all over from two months of swimming at the community pool, his skin dusky and satiny as an old cello. For the first time I thought about reaching out and touching it, running my fingers over his arms, his chest. Luke and I always turned bright pink long before we'd ever brown, but Ben just got darker and darker, shaking off his winter pallor like slipping out of a heavy coat.

We lay on the floor of the living room, shoulder to shoulder, and I was sucking on a piece of ice, rolling the cube around in the heat of my mouth, feeling it evaporate, my eyes fixed on the screen, when he turned toward me, slowly pressing his lips against mine. I could hear the dim rustling of my parents as they turned heavily in their bed, drawing thin sheets over their shoulders. *You,* I thought, the word exploding in my brain as I wrapped my arms tentatively around his neck, his pulse beneath my fingers steady as a bass drum. *It was you all along.*

When he pulled away, his eyes held mine for a long, worried moment before his face relaxed into a smile, his teeth shining blue in the light from the TV. On screen, a dark-clad figure holding an axe walked through a deserted summer camp, a series of sharp, spooky notes on a piano tracing his path.

"This isn't . . . you know . . ." he said, propping himself up on one arm and looking at me intently, "weird or anything?"

My head was spinning, one thought after another racing through the suddenly cramped confines of my brain. The strange thing wasn't the kiss—not exactly—but how, for the first time ever, I couldn't think of what to say back, how to answer him. Until that moment, Ben and I had never needed full sentences in order to understand each other—in fact, we routinely *finished* each other's thoughts more often than not. And it *was* a little weird, but not in a way that made me want to run for the door or push him away. Weird in the way that all new, exciting things are strange and mysterious and ever-so-slightly uncomfortable. We knew everything about each other, and the sheer familiarity should have been enough to stop us. But it wasn't. Even then, staring at him, his lips parted and gleaming, I wanted to lean in closer, to press my mouth against his, my heart tripping over its own clumsy feet, clicking away in my chest like a metronome.

"No. It's fine," I said quickly—too quickly, almost stammering. "Fine." The word tossed like a boulder, heavy and careless. As usual, when it was time to open my mouth about something really important, I blew it. Getting a B on a history test was "fine." But kissing? Not so much. "I mean, no—it's *great*." I put one hand on his arm, feeling the heat rising from his tanned skin. "It's perfect." That smile again as he pulled me even closer, his lips finding mine in that same shock of recognition, that feeling that had maybe always been there, but that I'd never noticed. Maybe I'd been afraid to. His tongue explored the inside of my mouth, tentatively at first, insistently, hot then impossibly cool as the ice melted away. My arms wrapped around his back, pulling him down on top of me, blotting out the thoughts that told me to slow down, to think, to wait, the words drowned out by the friction of our own bodies, the heat of his kiss.

"Alys?" The low thrill of Ben's voice coming through the tiny speaker makes me believe, just for a moment, that everything is going to be all right, and I feel a weight lifting off of my shoulders before I remember that it isn't, that it won't be, that nothing could ever be all right again.

"Yeah. I'm here." My voice sounds small and tinny traveling through the air. Not like myself at all. An imposter.

There is silence on his end. Then an intake of breath. I can almost see him there in his room, the white walls and dark wood, his laptop glowing softly on his desk. I knew he was sitting on his bed, one hand absentmindedly pulling at his thick, dark hair, twisting pieces of it between his fingers the way he always did whenever he was sad or upset, his face tense.

"Jesus Christ, Alys. I've been going out of my fucking mind. Things are crazy over here." His voice is clipped, impatient. "I called you all last night. I didn't know . . . I mean, I hoped, but I wasn't sure if . . ." His voice trails off, and I knew—I knew without him having to say a word.

If you'd made it out.

"I'm sorry." I look down at the floor, at the navy- and sky-blue polka-dot rug my mother bought me at Target last year. We stopped for ice cream on the way home, mint chocolate chip, my tongue numbed from the cold. "I should've called. I just . . . there are reporters sneaking into my backyard, camped out on our doorstep, and my parents are basically losing it." My eyes fill with tears that splash down the end of my nose. "I saw him, Ben. In the library. Luke. I was there."

I could hear the sound of his breathing, the way it caught in his chest.

"Alys."

Never had my name sounded so ominous. A feeling of dread sweeps through me, and I grab the quilt on my bed in one hand, balling it in my fist until my knuckles turn white and numb.

"Katie's gone. She didn't come home from school yesterday, so we went to the hospital and waited there, but no one would tell us anything at first. We didn't know if she was hurt or . . ."

His voice broke, and a tearing sound came from his throat, echoing through the phone. "She's gone, Alys."

Katie. Oh, Katie.

Katie is Ben's younger sister. She has gobs of long dark hair that she ties back with colored ribbons (a different shade for each day of the week) and cheeks that are perpetually flushed. She's all pinks and whites, a walking strawberry sundae. Her life's goal is basically to make the varsity cheer team by next year. She wears TOMS shoes exclusively in bright red and blue, collects rocks, and still believes in fairies. She follows Ben everywhere as if he's her own personal god. She's also a freshman, and is thus highly annoying, and I love her unreservedly.

Was a freshman. Was.

My heart falters in my chest, a sharp, searing pain, and for the first time I wonder if it were to actually stop, give out, if it wouldn't be a relief, if it wouldn't be better for everyone.

"Are they . . . Are they sure? I mean, Ben, there were a lot of people there yesterday, and she looks a lot like Sarah Boyd, *a lot* like her, and—"

I hear myself and I am babbling. I know I am, but I can't stop. If I stop, something worse might happen, something might—

Oh, Katie, please don't be

(dead)

I can't say it aloud. I can't even think it.

"It was her, Alys." Ben's voice is resigned. I can hear the exhaustion in it, the grief. "They saw her. Late yesterday afternoon."

What's left of my hope surfaces for a moment, stretching its wings. "So she's okay? She's going to be all right?"

There is a pause, a long beat where I can hear the clock he always kept on his bedside table ticking. I can hear my own blood pumping, the thump of my own heart. Then that tone again as he says my name and the world falls away entirely.

"They had to go to the morgue. To ID her."

I close my eyes, tears running from the corners, snot dripping from the end of my nose. Ben and me and Katie running through the sprinklers in the summertime, the smell of freshly cut grass in the humid air. Luke blasting the hose and shooting it toward the sun, the prism of color trapped inside the wet diamond droplets. Katie's small, elfin face widening into a smile, her hands clapping at the magic of rainbows

33

and light. Katie helping Luke pour brownie batter into a buttered pan; fighting over the bowl, elbows jostling; the sweet, dense taste of the chocolate, dark and bitter as secrets.

My eyes snap open and I sit up, gripping the phone tighter.

"But he loved Katie! Ben, he loved her! He would never hurt her. I know he wouldn't."

"But he DID, Alys. He did. He—"

(killed her)

"Well, then it must've been an accident! She must've gotten in the way somehow! Luke would never—"

I am hyperventilating, the air in the room sucked out through an enormous hole in my head, my heart, a void of my brother's making.

"Yes, yes he fucking *would* and he *did,* Aronson. He did."

Ben has never ever called me anything except Alys for as long as I can remember. All of those syllables hit me in the chest like so much dead weight. Like a corpse.

"No. It's not true." I whisper these words even though I know they are lies, and that there is nothing, nothing I can do or say that will make the jagged pieces of Ben, or of any of us, for that matter, whole again.

Before I can say anything else, there is a rustling noise on his end of the phone, and I hear the creak of a door opening, murmured conversation, voices rising higher in pitch, a crescendo. Sweat breaks out beneath my underarms, cold and sour, and I am shaking uncontrollably. I feel like I've just drunk a hundred double espressos, my entire body vibrating at a frenzied pitch, a whine I can almost hear.

"Who are you . . . Her? Dammit, Ben, give me the goddamn phone!"

"Who is this?"

Arianne, Ben's mom, is suddenly on the line. At the sound of her voice, something inside me unfurls a tiny bit, relaxing, even though I know it shouldn't. I can't help it—Arianne has read me bedtime stories when my parents were out of town (I was always partial to *Goodnight Moon*), fed me innumerable dinners and lunches (tuna salad on toast was a real winner for a while), taught Luke how to drive and let him spin their old station wagon around the cul-de-sac at the end of our street until he got the hang of it, blasting AC/DC on the stereo, all the windows rolled down. She's listened to me practice for hours on end, a smile falling over her soft features as she watched the bow fly through my hand as if it had wings. If anyone will understand, it is Arianne.

But Luke killed her daughter. Shot her. How could anyone possibly understand that?

"It's Alys, Arianne. I don't know what to say. I'm so sorry, I don't know how to—"

"Alys, you need to stay away from our family. Just stay away. From *all* of us."

The voice coming through the phone is alien and clipped. This is not the Arianne of the makeshift s'mores assembled over the kitchen stove, melted chocolate coating our fingers like wax, the woman who taught me to shave my legs the summer I turned twelve, guiding my hand so that the blade slid over my limbs effortlessly.

"Arianne, I didn't—"

"Haven't you people done enough? Haven't you done *enough already*?" Arianne's voice grows shrill, then collapses into sobs that are so deep that it sounds as if she is drowning in a bottomless black pool, water reducing her lungs to gray, spent balloons.

"I *didn't*," I whisper, pleading now. "It wasn't—"

(me)

There is a wailing that shudders through the phone, jarring me to my core, Ben's voice in the background, a low mumbling, ripped and gravelly. Then the line goes dead.

FOUR

When we first get into the car, my mother reaches over and snaps the radio off the minute the engine sparks up. Still, there are seconds where I hear the announcer's voice booming through the cramped space, my eyes straining in the darkened garage filled with old, rusty bikes and my father's workbench, the tools that he cleans and organizes incessantly but rarely uses. Organization and order are more important to my father now than creativity. The neater things are, the happier he is. For most of my childhood, he spent hours here, sanding wood into supple softness, building first a chest of drawers, then a kitchen table for some friends of theirs as a wedding present. But lately it seems that the only reason he steps foot in the garage is to make sure that things are in their rightful place, tucked safely away. Sometimes, if I look at his hands and concentrate really hard, I can almost see his fingers splayed against the grain of wood, a piece of sandpaper clutched in his grasp, the tinge of wood stain tracing his skin like a henna tattoo.

"Lucas Aronson, eighteen, shot and killed a total of fifteen students in one of the largest mass murders in Wisconsin history yesterday . . ."

With every mention of my brother's name, I am shrinking down smaller and smaller. Soon there will be nothing left. A dot, a slick, greasy smear where I once stood. My mother, wearing a pair of dark sunglasses, nervously adjusts her mirrors, her hair pulled back into a messy bun. Her hand hovers over the garage door opener, and she turns and looks at me for a moment, her face an empty canvas. The car smells of the sickly sweet vanilla air freshener my mother likes to spray, the one Luke always said made the car smell like a fucking bakery. Sometimes, but not often, she would let Luke drive it instead of the twelve-year-old, hand-me-down Volvo my dad gave to Luke on his sixteenth birthday, and I wonder if his prints are still on the steering wheel, the whorls of his fingers imbedded onto the worn leather, if I will become one of those crazy, grief-stricken people I've seen in movies, crawling on the floor looking for a scrap of hair, looking for something, anything, left behind. My head is swimming with images: me, Katie, Ben, Luke. It's like the sadness in my body is so large that I don't know which part to acknowledge first. It all blurs together in an uncontainable heap, trash spilling out of a Dumpster. Yesterday, I was a girl on her way to school, her brother beeping the horn once, twice, before she slid inside the car, the door barely closed before his foot stepped firmly on the gas. Luke's car always smelled of sweaty gym clothes, motor oil, and inexplicably of popcorn, though he always said he hated it.

(—*Luke's face as he backed out of the driveway, one hand draped over the back of my seat, his ebony-colored jacket and heavy boots sucking the air from the interior. A black hole. "Going to a funeral?" I quipped, pulling down the visor and checking my face in the mirror, my lips twisted in a sarcastic grin. He stared straight ahead at the road, turning up his iPod so that music blasted through the car's speakers, buzzing through the seats. I closed my eyes, lulled into safety by the trees whipping past the windows, the sound of my brother's breathing, the heat coming through the vents. "Alys," he said as we pulled into the school parking lot and the car came to a stop, his hands tightening on the wheel. "Yeah?" I answered, rummaging through my backpack distractedly. There was a long pause, and I stopped digging and looked up at him, blinking in the morning light. I was tired, worried about my history project, anxious about being late, as usual. "Have a good day," he said finally, pulling his keys from the ignition and shoving them in the pocket of his jacket, his face empty—*)

The minute the garage door opens with a rumble, the reporters run up to the car, tapping their silver microphones against the windows, cameras rolling. I look into the eye of the lens, hypnotized, until my mother steps on the gas, throwing a hand in front of my face to shield me.

"Get down!" she yells. "Head down, Alys. Now."

I lean forward, place my head between my knees, trying to breathe normally, but there's not enough air, not enough air in the whole world, it seems, to satisfy me, and I gulp it down greedily as if it might run out at any second.

"Mrs. Aronson, do you have a statement you'd like to make?"

"Alys! What was Luke *really* like?"

The tires squeal as my mother pulls out of the driveway. I can hear her gasping so hard it sounds as if she's hiccupping. Tears flow out from beneath the glasses and down her cheeks. She's not wearing any makeup, and her face looks vulnerable and exposed without it. I reach over and put my hand on hers, almost pulling away when I feel how cold she is, how stiff.

(*—don't think about Miranda under the table, how her screams got louder and louder, then stopped altogether. The blood that seeped over the pages of fallen books that rained down, pages fluttering. Don't think about Ms. Parsons splayed on the floor, a starfish pinned to a board, her mouth opening and closing—*)

Don't think.

I turn to look out the window, taking in our street, a place I have always loved, with its rows of even lawns, garden gnomes, Victorian houses with long porches set back from the road, tall oak trees lining the streets. White picket fences, the paint flaking in some places. The lilacs blooming in the spring, filling the night with their impossibly heady, purple scent, the synchronicity of countless sprinklers the unwritten soundtrack to our lives. I sink down into my jacket, wishing I could disappear inside it entirely.

"Have you talked to anyone? What about Delilah?" My mother pulls off the sunglasses and wipes her eyes with the back of her hand. As always, there is clay lodged under her short nails from her nightly work in her basement studio, pots springing from her hands like alchemy.

Delilah and I have been best friends since we were in the fourth grade. Like Ben, she lives only a few streets away, and there has hardly been a day in the past ten years that I haven't seen or talked to her at least twenty times. I don't even have to close my eyes to conjure her image—I know it as well as my own. Waves of dark hair swarming around her face. Blue, almost violet, eyes that change color in the light—especially when she's thinking about breaking some kind of rule, which is most of the time. Her small, compact body that barely fills out her dance leotard, muscles as tightly strung as the strings on my violin, her legs corded and strong, her feet flitting across the floor, more glide than walk, toes pointed out. Duck walk. I remember the time she tried to teach Luke to dance, the only time I'd ever seen him flustered, his face reddening as she pulled his arms around her waist, smiling up at him. Luke's big feet tripping through the steps until they gave up, falling over in a heap, their laughter uncontrollable. That was two winters ago. Before my brother started spending all of his time in his room, away from us. Before he started speaking in monosyllables, then stopped talking altogether, his eyes growing flatter, deader as the months passed.

"What's wrong with him?" Delilah asked last Christmas. "Is he okay?" Her eyes, violet now, reflected against the white lights of the tree, fragrant and tall. I brushed it off, nodding my head yes with a snort as if to say, *Duh, how could you be so stupid? Of COURSE he's fine.*

But you weren't, Luke. Not really. I just didn't want to see it.

"When I checked my phone earlier, her number came up a few times from yesterday, but she hasn't called back. I talked to Ben this morning, though."

Tears blur my vision, and I concentrate on the street signs that flash by as we creep toward the edge of town. Ben's face appears, his wide smile superimposed on the translucent glass, and something in me shatters further, and so I look away, reaching over to flip on the heat.

My mother lets out a long sigh and pulls the car over on the side of the road.

"He told you about . . . about Katie?" My mother's tone is halting but matter-of-fact, and I wonder how she knew, who told her, and then I remember the paper crumpled in her hands this morning. Was Katie's name there, in stark black and white for everyone to see?

Katie Marie Horton. Fifteen years old.

"We have to go. To the service," I manage to say through a wave of tears. I have cried so much in the last twenty-four hours that my face feels abused, stinging with salt, my eyes swollen. I've blown my nose so repeatedly that there are actual scabs forming on the raw skin.

"Alys." She sounds so much like Ben when she says my name like that, so resigned that I want to clap my hands over my ears, open the car door and run as far away as I can. "I don't think that's such a good idea, do you?"

Arianne's words float back to me, and I take in a breath so deep that my chest aches.

Haven't you people done enough?

The engine hums quietly. Heat pours from the vents, but my fingers are icy branches shaking in the wind.

"Dad ran into Arianne this morning at the hospital, and . . ." She stops, exhaling loudly and turning away. "It didn't go well, Alys."

A small, dry laugh escapes from my throat, although nothing is even remotely funny about any of this. All at once I am angry with Luke, furious about what he's done to us, the rage bubbling up from deep inside me, my chest hot and tight with all I haven't said, everything I can't say. "Well, how could it? How could it when Katie's dead?" My mother flinches, her face blanched of color, but I can't stop. I am shouting now, the space between us constricting more tightly with every word that leaves my lips. "She's dead! And whether he meant to or not, he shot her!" I feel dizzy, dislocated, my face hot and sweating, my hands ice-cold.

My mother reaches out, palm open, and slaps me once, hard, across the face. I raise my hand to my cheek and it burns beneath my fingers. My mother has never hit me before. Not even when I was five and flushed all of her good jewelry down the toilet because I wanted to see what would happen.

I drop my hand to my lap and begin ripping off my cuticles. The pain feels good, right somehow. My nose is running and I reach up and wipe it on the back of my sleeve. My mother exhales loudly, cursing under her breath, and I cannot look at her.

"Honey, I'm sorry," she says, her voice breaking. "But you've got to understand something." She reaches over and cups my face in her hand, gently turning it toward her. Her eyes are bloodshot and so very tired that I can barely look at her. "Luke's not around anymore for people to

(hate)

blame. So they're going to blame us."

"But we didn't do anything," I whisper.

Did we?

Or maybe that was the problem. *Was that it, Luke? Did you want more attention? Well, you certainly got it, didn't you?*

Luke's face appears before my eyes, swaying there blur-rily. I don't know how to reconcile it, that face that's more familiar to me than my own, with what he's done.

"That doesn't matter, Alys." She says this slowly and with infinite patience, like I'm four. "It doesn't matter one bit."

The sadness in my mother's voice is stronger than the waves of heat filling the car, and even though I don't want to accept it, I know she's right, that people will hate us simply because we're the ones left behind to blame, simply because, unlike Luke or the fifteen other people he killed yesterday, we still exist.

FIVE

Later that night, I hang the dress on a hook behind my closet door. The best thing I can say about it is that it covers my knees, which I've hated ever since the fourth grade, when rat-faced John Mulligan called them knobby. The reporters finally left an hour ago, walking back to their vans and slamming the doors in exasperation, their breath hovering in front of their faces in dense white clouds. At the mall I stood in the dressing room facing my reflection, a pile of shapeless black dresses at my feet. My hair, the color of a wet graham cracker, pulled back in a ponytail, a scratch on my right arm that I don't remember getting. It's deep and red and throbs like a constant reminder. *You're burying your brother tomorrow,* I informed the girl in the mirror, but she just stared back at me with swollen, empty eyes. Somehow it still doesn't seem real. Like if I walked down the hall to Luke's bedroom and opened the door, he'd still be inside, surfing the Web or playing video games, yelling at me to get the hell out of his room without even turning around in his chair, his feet propped up on his desk, one boot tapping restlessly against the other.

Time feels interminable, the numbers on the clock barely moving although the day has somehow passed into twilight, then evening, a dark oblivion. I'm so tired, my legs and arms throbbing in unison, but I'm afraid to get into bed, to turn on the TV, to close my eyes. Luke on every channel, that same picture from last year's yearbook filling the screen, the one where he stares right into the lens, almost glowering, the face he always wore in the past few years whenever he was forced to have his picture taken. This went over screamingly well on family vacations, let me tell you. My mother would spend most of her time pleading with him in front of every rest stop or scenic vista to smile, to pose with his arm around me, to hold up a fish that he and my dad had caught. Luke would roll his eyes, cross his arms over his chest, and look off into the distance, as if he'd suddenly gone spontaneously deaf, as if he weren't there at all while my mother snapped away, determined to capture him on film. Finally, he'd turn toward the camera lens, his lips drawn over his teeth, his expression almost feral. The look in his eyes made me turn away each and every time. It was as if something had been taken from him.

"Why do you hate it so much?" I'd asked him last year on a road trip through New England, after our parents had finally gone to their room for the night, the door clicking shut with a sharp finality that gave way to a low mumble of voices, the rising crescendo of another argument. A sound we tried more and more to ignore as it became more frequent. "He's *fine*," my father would shout over my mother's many attempts to shush him, to make him lower his voice. "He's just finding his way, that's all. When he goes to college he'll snap out of it. I'm surprised you notice him at all considering how focused on *Alys* you are."

I felt my face turning red, my father's words echoing in the air between Luke and me.

How focused on Alys you are.

Was it true? I didn't know. My mother had high expectations for my future as a musician, but I'd always thought that my father shared them, wanted the same for me—glowing stage lights, gilded ceilings, the rustling of programs. All I did know was that my father's words made me feel exposed and uncomfortable. Guilty.

"Why do you hate it so much?" I asked again, trying to detract his attention away from our parents' closed motel room door.

"It makes me feel like I'm not real," he said, shrugging. "Like she's searching for evidence of . . . I don't know *what*. It's so fake. It's like she wants proof that we're all so fucking happy all the time, that we've had such a *nice* family vacation." When he said the word "nice," his voice rose to a falsetto, such a keen, cloying imitation of my mother that it made me flinch slightly.

"Well, haven't we? *Aren't* we?" I stuffed a handful of Sun-Chips into my mouth, chewing distractedly. We had just raided the vending machines in the motel lobby, and I was looking forward to a night of eating junk food and drinking Cokes in front of the TV. Luke didn't answer, just opened a package of peanut butter crackers, cramming two squares in his mouth. In the past two years, I'd grown accustomed to my brother's cryptic silences, his mood swings, how one moment he could be thrilled to see me, and the next he'd be just as likely to slam his bedroom door in my face, shutting me out completely. It never stopped hurting my feelings, but I had accepted it as just One of Those Things. "He'll grow out of it," my mother said consolingly in a voice that wanted to seem confident, but instead wavered slightly, unsure. So I tried to ignore those intermittent snubs, pretending they didn't matter, when in reality, every unkind word my brother hurled toward me burned its way into my brain, lodging there indelibly.

"So why don't you just say no, then? Why do it at all if it just makes you nuts?"

He reached over and grabbed my chips, popping them into his mouth one after the other.

"I don't know," he said after a long moment. "I guess it's too much hassle to say no, to make a fuss. And I don't care enough to bother. So I just give in and go along with it. The way I do with everything else—school, Mom and Dad, applying to college, whatever."

I wrinkled my brow in confusion, trying to understand.

"But I thought you wanted to go to college? Right?"

His face closed off the way it always did when he didn't want to talk about something, and he turned away from me, switching on the TV, his eyes flickering across the images on the screen. I knew enough not to ask any more questions. Even though in the past few years I'd seen these moods get stronger, occupying Luke's attention for longer periods of time, there were moments of grace, long stretches when the darkness would lighten and he'd be the brother I knew so well, the guy who pushed me on the tire swing in our yard until his arms were sore, who sat with me at the kitchen table working through a problem in algebra, his unfailing belief in the power of numbers, the logic of them somehow soothing, marching across a pristine white page. But once Luke was in a mood, there was no busting him out of it until he was good and ready. You left him alone until it broke, like a fever. Until he snapped out of it. And sooner or later, he always did.

Except for the one time he didn't.

I want to talk to Ben, to hear his voice telling me every-thing will be all right. It occurs to me that he probably needs the same thing right now, and that as much as I want to, I can't be the one to say it to him, can't wrap my arms around him and hold on tight. The thought makes my chest seize up like a car out of gas, the needle falling into the red. I pic-ture us in our separate houses, grief pinning us to our beds. I wonder what he's doing right now, if he's thinking about me or if he just can't think about anything at all, if he's pecking out notes at the piano, finding solace there in the music the way we always did, or if he's gone as mute as I am right now. Beethoven deaf at the keyboard.

Restless, I get up and walk down the hall, the muffled noises of my parents moving around in their bedroom echo-ing in the hallway, my father's voice and my mother's sobs, a sound that tears at my heart. I picture the tattered muscle in my chest unraveling further with every heartbeat. Hopelessly frayed.

Luke's door is ajar, moonlight peeking from inside in a strip of silver that falls across my feet when I push it all the way open. The room is eerily quiet. Clothes strewn across the floor, the pictures from the summer we spent at the lake with my grandparents in frames on top of his dresser. Maps of the universe on the ceiling, along with the glow-in-the-dark stars I stuck there when I was nine. A periodic table of the elements hanging over his desk, the earth broken into molecules. I switch on the desk lamp, sit down on the bed, pick up his favorite blue sweatshirt, hold it to my nose, and close my eyes. Dirt, shampoo, sweat, and that maple-syrup smell that seemed to seep from his pores when it had been a few days between showers. I hold the sweatshirt in my lap, petting it distractedly, hugging the soft, worn fabric to my stomach, aching all the time now.

When I open my eyes, Luke is sitting at his desk, his hands resting lightly on the varnished surface as if any moment he'll open his books and start reading. When I got home yesterday, I vaguely remember seeing the police combing through Luke's room, and my mother told me later that they'd confiscated his laptop, his journals, and anything else they considered relevant, which was pretty much everything.

He's wearing the same clothes he had on yesterday, the last time I saw him—jeans and a black V-neck sweater, black jacket, heavy boots on his feet. His hair shines in the lamplight, lit with gold. He raises one eyebrow, blinking slowly, as if to say, *What are you looking at?* His expression is slightly blurred, as if I'm looking at him through a foggy window. I rub my eyes hard with my fists, but when I look back, he's still there, patiently watching me.

"How many times have I told you to stay out of my room?" he asks, his voice lower in pitch than I remember. I shake my head in disbelief. It's barely been forty-eight hours, and I'm already forgetting his voice. What will I lose tomorrow? How much will be taken from me before this is all over? Which, of course, implies that it might be, someday. Over, that is. As he looks at me, waiting for me to speak, he doesn't seem angry the way he always used to be whenever I'd barge into his space without knocking, just vaguely amused and so Luke-like, so present and absolutely *there* that my mouth opens, but nothing comes out. .

You can't come back, Luke. You're dead.

"Always looking for a way to get in here and bug me," he snorts. "You're so predictable. Even now."

He opens a drawer, pulls out a piece of paper and a pen, and starts scribbling. I can see the hair glistening on his arms where he's pushed the sleeves up. When I find my voice again, it comes out in a whisper, like we're in church, someplace sacred, my throat raw.

"I wish I could say the same for you."

Luke stops writing and looks over at me, his expression unreadable. "You shouldn't be in here now," he says as if it's just another regular school night and I'm pestering him when he needs to get his homework done.

"Why not? It's not really your room anymore. Is it?"

I'm staring at my dead brother and trying to keep myself from losing what's left of my mind. He was always someone I could count on, and before yesterday, I'd always thought that, in spite of the moods that made him snap at me suddenly, without warning, he felt the same way about me. A given. Now I'm not so sure.

(—*the gun, a sinuous black snake, Luke's face blown apart by the blast. Unrecognizable. How long, exactly, had he been that way? A stranger*—)

"That's beside the point," he says, turning back to the sheet of paper in front of him, the intricate doodles and shapes he scratches into the paper in black ink. His skin looks spookily translucent, or maybe it's just the light, my exhaustion. Still, I have the unsettling feeling that if I touched him, my hand would sink right through his skin. "Shouldn't you be practicing, anyway?" He smirks, his face twisted, but not exactly unkind. Not yet. "The great *virtuoso*? Surprised you even have time to come in here at all and bother with us little people."

I recoil, leaning back on my hands, suddenly unsteady. My brother had come to every performance and recital, had helped me with my application to the summer orchestral program, patiently correcting my grammar on the essay portion and driving me to the post office to mail it, watching, bemused, as I kissed the envelope for luck. The idea that he was

(is)

resentful of me, my playing, is ridiculous. Laughable. But the anger in his voice is unmistakable. A slow burn. A smoldering.

He turns to look at me, the bookshelf behind his head shimmering through his skull, and I'm just about to answer him, the hurt coloring my face, the corners of my mouth turning down in anticipation of tears, when the doorbell rings, making me jump. I turn toward the door, startled, and when I turn back, he's gone, the desk clear and empty. The air smells strange and heady, lilies mixed with the scent of burning paper, leaves maybe, the smell of something dry and dead and charred all the way to ashes. My heart is skipping out of beat, out of time, as I get up and run downstairs.

SIX

My father is at the door before I can get to it. It could be the reporters, still, but at nine p.m. it's a little late—even for them. He stands there, one finger pressed to his lips, his normally neatly combed dark hair standing on end, the temples graying more than I remember, still wearing the same bathrobe he sported this morning. His expression is frozen, that glazed-over look I'm sure is pasted all over my own face, what we are wearing these days instead of actual feelings. He looks out the peephole, and I watch as his body relaxes slightly, the tension draining from his face.

"It's Delilah," he says, unlocking the door.

At the mention of her name, something dormant and still leaps up in my heart, and I motion frantically for him to move out of the way, fingers scrabbling at the nubby material of his robe.

The door opens and she's there, all five feet three inches of her, her black hair curling around her shoulders, blue eyes wide and startled and rimmed with red, her cheeks pink from the cold, the promise of snow on her clothes. She's wearing a red sweatshirt and the pajama pants printed with martini glasses that I know she sleeps in every night, scuffed Ugg boots on her feet. This tells me that, most likely, she's snuck out, that her parents don't know she's here, which is not a good sign. If she had to sneak out to come here, that means her parents don't want her in my house. Or around me at all.

"Hey," she says, coming toward me, arms open, and I fall into them, releasing the stress I've been bottling up all day, the fear that I'll always be alone now, no friends, no one who will talk to me or even bestow a kind glance. It's not as if I was so screamingly popular before the

(shooting)

Ben and Delilah were pretty much my whole world. But it was more than that. I didn't like drawing attention to myself in any way. I was wary of even raising my hand in class—even when I knew the right answer. Instead, I sat there, the unsaid words scalding the inside of my mouth. It wasn't that I had nothing to say, but that I didn't know where to *start*. I was a coward. Worried about being wrong all the time, terrified of failure. I watched my peers with barely contained fascination, as if they were exotic pets—how they spoke in class, their entitlement palpable. I was never so sure about anything. Except maybe music.

"That's a story you tell yourself, Alys. It doesn't mean that it's true, or that it will *stay* true forever," my mother would say when I questioned my inability to step outside of the life I'd made for myself and make new friends, stop relying so much on routine and habit. Practice. School. Home. Practice. Study. Repeat. In my sophomore year I wanted to try out for the cheer squad, but when I walked into the gym for tryouts, the minute the door opened and a sea of faces swiveled in my direction, I lost whatever strength and momentum I'd built up, just to get in the room. I'd stood outside the gym with Delilah, her fingers squeezing mine, my palms an ocean of sweat. "You can do this," she'd said confidently, sure I was so much more than the tentative face I presented to the world every day.

Girls milled around the gym, the members of the squad dressed in Plainewood's school colors, navy and gold. As I stood there, Simone Sanders, last year's captain, looked me up and down, then turned to the girl standing next to her, mumbling something low and unintelligible in the small space between them. Laughter broke out, turning me to ashes, my face crumpling like parchment. I could only imagine what she said, what everyone thought as I walked down the hallways, hurrying to class, my head down.

That's Luke Aronson's sister. I don't know . . . some kind of weird music freak? It's like a fucking mouse trying out for cheer. And I have no idea what Ben Horton sees in her . . .

And in my bleakest hours, I couldn't help wondering whether I was little more than just a collection of other people's thoughts and ideas. Ben's. Delilah's. My parents'.

Luke's.

Delilah's grip is strong and sure, all lilac soap and baby powder—she's addicted to anything with a powdery baby smell, and has been using Johnson's "No More Tears" since we were kids. It reminds me of nurseries, of tender baby skin and soft, knitted booties. "I wanted to come sooner . . ." She pulls away, sniffling, wiping a tear from my cheek with one finger, her touch tentative and featherlight. "But . . ." She shrugs, her expression bashful.

But things have been crazy because my brother is now a mass murderer and everyone in town thinks I'm a pariah?

My father is still standing there, his face creased with rough lines that I'm not sure were as deep before the shooting, dark stubble creeping in and obscuring the line of his jaw. He looks spent and colorless. My dad is the kind of guy who fills out a suit with aplomb, barrel-chested, solid as a tree trunk, his handshake firm and uncompromising. I've never seen him look so small, so fragile and unsure, like he might break apart at any second.

"Mr. Aronson," Delilah starts, turning to face my father, "I'm so sorry." She puts a hand on my father's arm, and I watch as he flinches, his eyelids fluttering uncomfortably. The last time Delilah was here, almost a week ago, her delicate hands were slicing cucumbers and tomatoes at the kitchen counter, my father adding olive oil and lemon zest to the dressing. At dinner, I tried not to notice that Luke just pushed piles of meat and scalloped potatoes from one side of his plate to the other, finicky as ever, his eyes trained on the white china plate in front of him, the swirls in the Formica table.

My father nods at Delilah and looks away as if he doesn't know her, has never seen her before, and shuffles toward the kitchen.

"Jesus," Delilah exhales, her eyes fixed on his receding figure. I hear the unmistakable creak of the cabinet where my parents keep their liquor, the freezer door opening and closing, the clink of ice hitting a glass. My father has never been a big drinker—a few beers while watching baseball, a glass of wine with dinner. For a few years when Luke and I were kids, I'm pretty sure my parents still smoked the occasional joint, the weedy stench permeating their bedroom on warm summer nights, that feral, skunky odor of burning herb, my mother's high-pitched giggle floating out from behind their locked door. But in recent years, that's all stopped. I picture him standing at the kitchen counter swallowing heavily, his lips wet with the sting of scotch, face slack, his eyes closed in something like relief.

"I know," I say. "It's pretty bad."

"Where's your mom?" Her brown eyes dart around, searching.

"In her room, I think. C'mon."

I hear the liquor cabinet open again as we climb the stairs, and I walk past Luke's room quickly, too freaked out to even look and see if I left the door ajar or if the desk lamp is still on. I feel Delilah staring as we move past, her hand in mine, her body tensing the way it does when you know, absolutely, that pain is imminent.

Luke, are you in there?

In my room, door closed, I start to feel a little better. This is an old story—Delilah and me sitting on my bed, knees close. Delilah looks around my room as if she's never seen it before, her eyes skittish. Is this what shock looks like, because I don't know what we're all supposed to be feeling, what I should do or say, and everything that comes out of my mouth feels wrong.

"I've been calling you *forever*," Delilah says, picking at a loose thread on her pants. "I tried texting too."

"I've had my phone off for most of the day." I take my

iPhone out of my pocket, the display a black mirror. "I turned it on for a few minutes this morning, but freaked out and turned it back off. Reporters have been camped out here all day, and I had to go with my mom to buy a stupid dress for the funeral tomorrow."

"So you've been offline *all day*?" Delilah scrunches her forehead up, incredulous.

I nod, walking over to my desk and powering up my laptop, while turning my phone on too. If Delilah is here with me, I can face whatever is waiting for me out there.

"I talked to Ben," Delilah says carefully. She stops for a moment. "You heard about Katie?"

"Yeah." I turn away and fiddle with my laptop so I don't have to look at her. "I heard."

"I can't believe it," Delilah says, shoving me over so she can sit next to me on the chair. Just the warmth of her tightly coiled body makes me feel better. Saner. Not like I'm going to fly off into space at any given moment. "I can't believe . . . any of it," she says, her voice seizing up in her throat. "I mean, Katie . . ." She stops speaking, her words evaporating in the quiet of the room. She doesn't have to finish her sentence. I know exactly how she feels, what she means to say.

"I know," I say, opening my e-mail and scanning it quickly. The first message that comes up is from an address I don't recognize, and in large, black letters proclaims:

I HOPE YOUR BROTHER DIED IN AGONY!!!!!!!!!!!!!!!!!

"Oh my God." Delilah rears back from the screen as if she's been hit in the face with hot coals. Her hand reaches for mine, cradling it in her lap, her nails painted the sheerest shade of pink. I am shaking, my heart pounding furiously. The next message reads:

FUCK YOU, ASSHOLE MURDERER!!!!!!!!!!!! HAVE FUN WITH SATAN.

"Don't read them, Alys. Don't. Just close it." Delilah shoves my hand aside. I feel like I'm dying. I bend over at the waist, pulling away from Delilah, and wrap my arms around my stomach. She turns to look at me, her eyes narrowing with concern. "Alys? Are you breathing? Alys, you have to *breathe!*"

(LukeKatieLukeKatieLukeKatieLukeKatieLukeKatie)

Delilah rubs my back the way she did when we drank too much of her dad's Jim Beam last year and I puked all over her bedroom floor. The feeling now is similar, the room tilting, stomach heaving, brain revolving in circles. Everyone used to just ignore me mostly, and now they hate me. How can we still live here? How can I go back to school, the same place where Luke walked in with a gun and shot down our classmates like a vigilante in some video game? How can I go on at all when he's not here anymore to do everything first, to teach me what to do, where to go next?

When my heart finally slows, I sit up, leaning heavily against her, my chest rising and falling in time with her breath.

"You should shut down that e-mail address completely and open a new one," she says. "If you give me your password, I'll do it for you if you want. Facebook too."

I hadn't even thought about Facebook since I barely use it anymore, but now a wave of dread crashes over me as I imagine the posts, what's waiting for me in my inbox, the obscenities written on my brother's wall. Oh God, his page is still up . . . Strangers rifling through his public photos, his thoughts and dreams, judging him.

And why shouldn't they judge him? Doesn't he deserve it after what he did?

The answer to this is undoubtedly yes. But Luke isn't here anymore to face the music, so judging him is, in effect, judging me. Judging my whole family. I sit up and open Safari again, hit the bookmark for Facebook, and watch as the page loads instantly with its familiar blue-and-white graphics. I have fifty-six wall posts and sixteen messages in my inbox. I ignore all of them and type my brother's name into the search function. When I pull up his page, I am stunned. His wall is an atrocity, a massacre. Expletives everywhere. I can barely read it or take in what I'm seeing; the words all blend together in an endless diatribe of hate and anguish.

"Holy shit," Delilah breathes as I scroll through the litany of posts. "Do you know Luke's password? If you do, we can shut down the page."

I shake my head no, my eyes hypnotized by the words scrolling across the page. "I don't."

"I think that you can write to Facebook and tell them Luke is . . ." I turn to look at her, willing her to finish the goddamn sentence.

Just fucking say it—he's dead.

I don't know why I'm suddenly so angry, but I am. With Delilah, with Luke, with Ben, with myself for letting all of this happen in the first place, for not noticing something was wrong before it was way, way too late. "Anyway, they'll take the page down then."

The thought of having to write such an e-mail makes me even more tired than I already am. How would I even begin to explain what has happened to my brother, a person I am connected to by blood. What's in him is also in me. The thought is terrifying.

I shut the laptop, unable to deal any longer with what I see there. My head hurts like the worst hangover ever, my stomach rumbling insistently. That piece of toast this morning was the only bit of food I had all day. At the same time, I can't imagine going downstairs, opening the fridge, and shoving food into my mouth. Opening containers. Chewing and swallowing.

"Do you think . . ." Delilah takes a deep breath before continuing on. "Do you think that Katie . . ." She looks at me, her eyes pleading with me to finish her sentence, but I stay silent, waiting, digging the nails of my right hand into my leg. "Do you think that maybe it wasn't . . . an accident?"

"What are you saying? That he did it on purpose?"

She doesn't answer, just sits there looking away from me, her eyes fixed on the wall behind my head, and everything she's not saying sits between us like a time bomb. An accusation. She pushes her hair back from her face, her cheeks white as ivory. "Alys, Luke . . . hurt a lot of people yesterday. I'm just asking what you think, that's all. You know I loved Luke."

Loved.

"You think he shot her on purpose. You really think that." I stand up, pacing the confines of my room, which is growing smaller by the minute.

Finally she looks at me, her eyes angry, but hurt too, welling up with tears. "I don't know *what* to think, Alys. I practically grew up with him! You, me, Ben, Luke, Katie! I don't know what to think about any of this; I hope it was an accident. I *pray* that it was."

"Well, I *did* grow up with him, D! He was *my* asshole brother, and I don't know any more than you do! Is this what your parents think too? That Luke was some kind of psychopath? Is that why you had to sneak over here tonight in your *pajamas*?"

She drops her head, rubbing one wrist. "They're just worried, Alys. And you know how close they are with Ben's family."

How close we all are.

Were.

I stop. "Worried about *what*? Luke's gone, D. He's gone."

She looks up at me, and what I see there in her gaze is unmistakable. A kaleidoscope of fear and regret and sadness and the absolute truth as everyone else will see it, which is that I am someone now who can't be trusted, who could fly off the rails at any given moment, who might, if she's anything like her brother—

Hurt people.

My brain feels like it's pulsing inside my skull, and I raise my hands up to my temples, pressing hard with my fingers.

"So they think I'm a monster too. Is that it?" I drop my hands and notice that her cheeks are reddening the way they always do when she's embarrassed. It feels good to say it out loud, what I already sensed the minute Delilah showed up in her pajamas, the chilly night air clinging to her clothes. But in spite of this one moment of release, shame falls over me in a suffocating weight. I know that from now on, I will be tainted to all who meet me. Soiled. I may as well be wrapped in yellow tape, or wearing a giant sign that reads CAUTION.

She doesn't answer me, just looks away, biting her bottom

67

lip like she always does when she's trying not to cry. I look at the floor beneath my desk, suddenly exhausted, the closed laptop before me a silent accusation.

"Maybe you should just go."

The last time Delilah and I had a fight, we were thirteen, and she thought I liked Brian Ackroyd, this guy with stringy blond hair whom she had a monster crush on. We didn't talk for two days, then made up in the cafeteria in the space of five minutes, wrapping our arms around each other and splitting a cookie precisely in half, chatting excitedly as if nothing, nothing at all had happened. Something tells me that this time things are going to be different. Maybe it's the resigned look on her face or the tension moving through the room, infecting us like a virus. She walks to the door, closing it carefully behind her with a small, metallic sound. I close my eyes, willing the world to stand still, to stop turning so rapidly on its axis, making me sick.

When I open them again, Luke is sitting on my bed, turning the pages of a slick magazine: *Guns & Ammo*. He looks up, the wall behind his head clearly visible through his skull, his sandy hair.

"God," he says with a smirk. "I thought she'd *never* leave."

And, with those words, I feel myself pitching forward, sliding down as the room, Luke's face, the night, fall away and I hit the floor.

SEVEN

In the car, on the way to the funeral the next morning, my head still throbs. I rub the sore spot on my forehead, the skin underneath tender and smarting. When I woke up, the room was empty, but for the same strange floral smell mixed with burning leaves, and a wisp of sulfur, the remnants of a struck match.

I'm wearing the shapeless black dress I got at the mall, my hair held away from my face by a long silver barrette. Dressing this morning, I stood in front of the mirror, unable to move, overcome with anxiety. Would people be outside the church? The cemetery? Because my hair was combed neatly, my clothes pressed and wrinkle-free, would they think, *Oh. She's not really grieving. Look how carefully she's combed her hair, how neatly she's dressed.* Or would it be worse if I turned up disheveled, a run climbing up the leg of my stocking like a ladder going nowhere? *I can't believe she's dressed so sloppily at her brother's funeral. They must not have been very close* . . . I held on to my dresser and tried to breathe, my eyes burning and gritty.

"It's a closed service," my mother says from the front seat, reaching over and pulling the visor down to smooth her hair, touch up the lipstick at the corner of her mouth. Seeing her wearing lipstick looks strange, like eye shadow on a small child. Usually when she's working at the gallery, she's bare-faced, her artfulness reserved for her hair, pulled back in a French twist. *A closed service.* The words spin in my brain. We're not religious, but my mother usually makes us go to church for the holidays—Christmas, Easter, all the big ones. Personally, I don't see the point. "Just immediate family."

Immediate family. Which I guess means us. My grand-parents are too old and sick to make the trip from Iowa on such short notice. My grandfather had a stroke last year, and now he pretty much lives in la-la land. Must be nice.

In front of Saint Anne's, reporters are parked at the curb, and they rush at our car the minute we exit, clutching their microphones, their notepads. The sun is shining brightly, but the day is cold and bitter, as it usually is in mid-March, the wind cutting through my dress and long wool coat. We push through the crowd, each individual voice blending to-gether like the incessant chirping of birds. I try to pretend I'm at the zoo, that we're passing through an aviary, rustling feathers in shades of turquoise and coral, somewhere lush and beautiful, but I can't. I just can't. My father stops at the stone steps. He's wearing a black suit and his shoes are scuffed, in sharp contrast to their usual mirrored shine. He brings one hand to his chest as if he's in pain, his wedding ring glinting in the sunlight in a flash of gold.

"Paul?" My mother's voice sounds frightened. "Paul? What is it?" She grabs his arm, pulls off her dark glasses. Beneath them her face is white, her eyes puffy.

"I don't think I can," my father whispers. "I don't think I can go in there."

He bends at the waist, still clutching his chest. The reporters swarm around us, hungry, wanting to be fed, and my mother turns to look at them, her face full of rage.

"We are *burying our son* today. *Please* let us have some privacy," she shouts, her voice echoing in the cold air. The reporters take a step back, though reluctantly. My shoulders shake violently, and all I want is to go inside, to be warm again. Even if it means seeing Luke for the last time. My mother takes my father by the hand and pulls him close to her. "You can do this," I hear her whisper. "We have to do it together." She looks over at me, tears streaking her cheeks, and puts the glasses back on as we begin to move forward, me trailing behind like a lost puppy, my heels clicking on stone.

One female reporter stares at me as I pass. She's young, maybe around twenty-five, tops, nervously twirling a pearl stud in one ear. As we pass, the look of sadness on her face almost stops me in my tracks, makes me want to sit right down on the stone steps of the church and never get up. At the same time, I'm furious at Luke for putting us in this situation, turning us into people who need to be pitied in the first place.

The service is mostly a blur. I stare up at the long stained-glass windows or down at my hands folded neatly in my lap, looking anywhere but at the polished wooden box at the front of the altar, the crate holding what is left of my brother. His remains. Which is a strange expression because when you die, nothing really *remains*. Isn't that the point? You lose it all. The altar is covered in white flowers, the blossoms cool and damp, and I wonder if my parents have paid for them. It's hard to imagine that anyone else would've sent them, considering what Luke's done. The minister drones on about love and forgiveness, and my ears close entirely. His mouth moves, but I hear nothing. The altar and pulpit are a glittering gold in the sun streaming through the windows, but I don't feel the presence of God. I don't feel anything at all. A numbness has set in, weighing down my limbs. I want to cry, to tear at my hair, my clothes, but I am strangely spent. Detached, almost. As if I'm watching these events unfold from somewhere far away. The choir box is empty this morning, and I long for some kind of melody, the crash of the organ, the flight of angelic voices. My fingers twitch against the fabric of my dress and I close my eyes, remembering the Debussy, the Brahms lullaby I played each night before bed, my face pressed to the pad beneath my chin, arms cutting the air around me. The fact that Luke doesn't deserve music, the blissful lilt and salvation of it, makes me, for some reason, saddest of all.

Outside, in the cemetery across from the parking lot, the reporters stand at a distance, their cameras snapping, my heels sticking into the soil. There is a terrible grinding sound as the coffin is lowered, and my mother turns away, a white handkerchief pressed to her nose, half of her face obscured. My father picks up a shovel and digs it into the hard ground, filling it with loamy earth as the day grows colder, the temperature dropping. He tosses dirt atop the coffin, and my nose runs wetly. I don't want him in the ground. "We should've cremated him," I mumble, my lips barely moving, but my parents just stare at the hole, their bodies tense. The sound of dirt hitting wood is louder than rain, rhythmic and unrelenting, and I close my eyes, unable to watch as the earth pelts the mahogany box, dulling its shine and covering him forever.

After the burial, we head back toward the car, fighting our way through the reporters, our bodies moving on autopilot. I keep my head down, trying not to make eye contact, trying to ignore the clicking cameras, the words hurled through the air at our back. Usually after a funeral, there's some kind of gathering. I haven't been to any funerals before, but I've heard about them, seen them on TV, in the movies. People come dressed in black, bearing huge trays of food and soft words of comfort. But not for Luke. His actions don't warrant this. Instead we will go home with our grief, alone. Maybe we will eat something late at night, scrounging around in the refrigerator like thieves, bellies aching and sore. But maybe not.

There is a figure waiting by our car, slightly stooped with age, her oxfords sensible and brown against the pavement, her legs thin beneath her navy woolen coat, arms crossed at her chest, her wrinkled face tilted toward the sun. Grace. At the sight of her, the silvery-gray hair cut in a blunt bob at her chin, the way she, always cold, is rubbing her upper arms to stay warm, I want to hurl myself into her arms, the scent of *L'air du Temps,* wood shavings, Jergens hand cream, and rosin blocking out the outside world. Grace was a concert violinist when she was young, a soloist, touring the world by the time she was eighteen, playing the opera houses of Vienna, Prague, Paris, Berlin—where she grew up—but gave it all up for love, getting pregnant at twenty-one and marrying an American soldier. They eventually moved from Berlin, where they'd sit on her days off, flirting with one another over the porcelain rims of their cups, to Madison, Wisconsin, far from the gilded chambers she once played in, crystal chandeliers dripping from frescoed ceilings. Her husband is long dead now, but photographs of them at the height of their youth and beauty sit on top of her piano, dusted and shined each day so that when the light pours in through the bay windows, the snapshots come alive, winking at me in black and white, the paper silvered with age.

"Alys." She steps forward and opens her arms, and I fall into them, closing my eyes, feeling her small bones, but despite how delicately she is made, no one would ever call Grace breakable. She speaks into my hair, nonsensical words, sounds, really, and the lilt of her voice, the hint of an accent, even after all the years she's spent in America, helps me let go of all the unshed tears in the church, of all the sorrow camping out in every corner of my body. I know that I am soaking the shoulder of her coat, the wool wet beneath my cheek, but I don't care. After a few minutes she releases me, and I pull away and try to get it together, rubbing my dampened face with my gloves.

Grace glances over at my parents, who are hanging back, not wanting to intrude right away, my father jangling his car keys against his leg, a nervous tic, and in his jerky movements I see my brother's face, his impatience as he waited for me to get ready for school each morning, turning the car keys over in his hands restlessly. My father's eyes sweep the perimeter of the lot, searching for advancing reporters, his body tensed, ready for battle. Grace steps forward, her eyes locked on my mother and father, her expression solemn. "Dani," she says. "Paul. I'm so very sorry."

My mother nods, still spent, her face drained of emotion. My father looks down at the pavement, then thanks her in a voice as empty and perfunctory as the expression on my mother's face. His face is white as new snow, and when he glances up again, it is through a veil of tiredness so profound that it almost hurts to look at him.

"I wanted to come to the service"—she points at the church—"but those men wouldn't let me in." The ushers, the people my parents paid to keep strangers away from us. Grace pulls her black patent leather purse more firmly over her shoulder, a gesture that lets me know that she is nervous, that she wonders if she should have come at all, made that hour drive on the highway, dodging traffic, moving swiftly toward us through the thin, reedy air.

"We thought it best to keep it a closed service," my mother says. "Considering what things have been like since . . ." Her words evaporate, and my father walks over to the driver's side, unlocking the doors with a loud click.

Grace takes a step closer, tentatively reaching out and putting one gloved hand on my mother's arm. "I cannot imagine how hard it has been—for *all* of you," she says, and my mother's face tightens, her body going rigid. My father opens the car door and climbs inside, the engine roaring to life, startling me.

"It's not easy for anyone," my mother answers, pulling away from Grace's arms and opening the passenger door.

Grace nods, her eyes settling on me. She hovers near the car, her watery blue eyes darting back and forth between my mother and me. We've driven the long highway once a week to see Grace for five years now, had her over for dinner countless times. I've even stayed at her house the night before an audition or a competition, slept in her guestroom, my feet dangling off the end of the narrow twin bed, eaten toast and bacon she's cooked me in the mornings, her pretty china plates glowing like mother-of-pearl. But now it's as if she's a stranger, like we've already gotten into the car and stepped on the gas. It feels like I'm not only leaving her but music itself in the past, a place that no longer has any meaning. My chest hurts at the thought, and I concentrate on breathing deeply, moving air in and out of my lungs.

"Alys won't be coming this week for her lesson." My mother climbs into the car, pulling her long coat in after her, smoothing it over her knees. She stares straight ahead and through the windshield, her features sharpened in profile.

"Of course not." Grace says, matter-of-factly. "But do not forget—there is the audition coming up for the summer program, Alys."

(—I'd like to forget. I'd like to forget everything. But I can't. It's all there every time I close my eyes—)

"I can't." I'm mumbling now, on the verge of disintegration. "I can't think about that right now."

Even as I say them, I wonder if the words are really true. They float dubiously between us. My hands are empty and purposeless without the weight of the violin in my arms, my ears stuffed with cotton. But I can't imagine surrendering myself to that beauty again, the hope that music keeps in its own secret heart, how it speaks for me, uttering the words I can't say out loud.

Grace nods. I can tell she wants to reach out to me, drawing me into her embrace once more, but that she's holding back.

"I am here when you're ready," she says, her eyes speaking more than the words themselves.

I nod, afraid to say anything more, that I will start crying again if I do. Instead, I watch as she dips her head, breaking eye contact, and with that release, I get in the car, close the door and busy myself with the seat belt, pulling my dress down over cold knees. As we drive away, she's still standing there, watching our car as it pulls out of the lot, her purse clutched tightly to the side of her body, her figure fading to a silhouette, then a dark pinpoint as we move out of range.

EIGHT

——

Once we get back to the house, I fall into a deep, dreamless sleep, fully clothed, shoes on, on top of the covers. When I wake, the sun has dropped from the sky, and night is pressing down upon us. I feel closed in, my head still foggy from sleeping too hard, too long. I pull off the dress, kicking it into a corner of my room, and change into a pair of jeans and a long black sweater, rubbing my cheek against the soft knit before pulling it over my head. In the corner, there is a rustling, Miranda's face glowing out of the shadows, her pale blond waves shining in the moonlight. Blood runs blackly down her cheek, and I can see that on the top of her head there is a round hole the size of a bird's egg, distorting the bland prettiness of her features. "I'm still under the table," she says in a gravelly whisper. "You're supposed to be here too."

A sound escapes my throat, part moan, part jagged cry. If I don't get out of this house, I will go insane. "Play 'Death and the Maiden,'" she whispers, in a voice that rakes cold fingers down the knobs of my spine. "Play it for me, Alys."

I run past her to the door, one, two, three leaps, and out into the hall, slamming my bedroom door behind me. I see a sliver of light, a lurid glow, Luke's door pushed open a crack, and my blood thuds at my temples. I don't want to look inside, but I have to. Have to.

My mother sits at Luke's desk, piles of papers spread out in front of her, immersed in a round circle of light. She's wearing her reading glasses, small rectangular frames that always seem to slip down her nose whenever she bends her head too far forward. She's still wearing the black sheath she wore to the funeral, a pearl choker looped around her neck. In profile, she looks regal, elegant, miles away from the woman I'm more familiar with, the one with dirt under her nails and tangles in her blond hair, a dollop of icy blue glaze dotting one cheek as she bends over her potter's wheel, carefully sculpting the delicate neck of a bottle with her long fingers.

"Mom?" I don't want to scare her, so I speak softly, but she jumps anyway, holding the stack of loose leaf to her heart as if it offers some kind of protection.

"Jesus, Alys, you scared me to death!" She puts the papers down on the desk, takes off her glasses, and rubs her eyes vigorously. I can see that she's been crying again. Maybe she's never really stopped.

"I'm sorry," I say. "What are you doing in here?"

She lets out a sigh, her shoulders slumping. "I have no idea." She gestures toward the paper littering the desk. "Old chemistry tests, honor roll notifications . . . I don't know what I'm *looking* for. The police didn't leave much." She lapses back into thought, staring down at the papers as if they might hold the answers to everything, if she could just make sense of them.

I don't know what to say to this. The obvious answer is that maybe there's nothing to find. There's no way Luke could've fooled us all for so long if he weren't an expert at keeping the deepest, ugliest parts of himself a total secret. Sure, there were the dark moods that crept over him, sticky and thick, but I never thought him capable of such violence and rage, this

(murder)

I wonder if he laughed to himself every night at how stupid we all were. How blind. Funny, if you had asked me last week, I would've said that my brother was one of the most honest people I'd ever met—pathologically so. And not just because he was my brother, but because I believed it to be true. Luke always said what he thought. If anything, it was kind of his downfall. Brutal honesty, my father called it.

"I'm going out for a little bit," I say nonchalantly, as if

going out for a walk on a cold night at nine thirty is par for the course for me, who would usually be watching episodes of *The Real Housewives* with Delilah or practicing for my audition, fingers plucking the taut strings. But most likely I'd be holed up somewhere with Ben, the two of us correcting each other's Spanish homework in between kisses. The thought of kissing Ben, feeling his warm, smooth mouth against mine, fills my head with a searing pain that makes me worry that I'm having an aneurysm. But it passes just as quickly as it arrived, and I'm still here, still standing, but why, I don't know. It feels like I died with Luke, alongside all of those kids who looked up from gossiping in the quad, from the useless pages of their books in the library, to meet the barrel of my brother's gun, his face filled with hate. In a way, I died the moment Luke walked into that library, the moment we came face-to-face. Now I'm trapped in the land of the dead, a barren landscape, shards of bone cutting my feet, their voices a soft chatter, telling me to follow.

"Now?" My mother wrinkles her forehead.

"I won't be gone long," I say in my most persuasive voice, shifting my weight impatiently. "Can I take the car?"

I can tell that she wants to protest—refusal is written all over her face—but the desire to sift through the detritus is too strong, and so she relents with a sigh, turning back to Luke's papers and her own unanswered questions. "But have your dad walk you out to the garage, just in case the reporters are still there when you leave."

In the kitchen, I grab the car keys from a hook over the phone, my fingers closing around the sharp metal. As I pass the den, I can see my father sitting in the huge leather chair he loves, his feet up on the ottoman. He has a drink resting on the arm of the chair, the whiskey mostly melted into amber-colored water, the glass sweating onto the worn leather the color of an old saddle. He's wearing jeans and a sweatshirt, the blue one with the letters *MIT* emblazoned across the chest. My dad went with Luke for a campus visit last October, and when they came home, Luke was as animated as I'd ever seen him, waving his hands excitedly at the dinner table as he described the campus, the town of Cambridge, with its picturesque squares and efficient train system—the blue line, he called it—how you could hear bells ring out in the mornings, and students sat in cafés drinking tiny cups of espresso. Not like high school, he said, where either you were a dumb jock or a loser. He described the colors of the falling leaves—redder, more vibrant than Wisconsin's, he said—how the air smelled of smoke. Intoxicating. He actually used that word, rolling it around in his mouth as if even the syllables themselves were luxurious.

I stand in the doorway, waiting for my father to notice me. Bob Dylan is playing softly on the stereo, his nasal twang reverberating off the walls. The CD case sits discarded on the floor beside my father's chair: *Blood on the Tracks.* His eyes are trained on the ceiling, so I clear my throat, which I notice is slightly sore, and he blinks twice, then looks up at me, his face impassive. "I'm going out for a little while," I say, holding up the car keys as what? Evidence?

She always wanted evidence that we were some happy family . . . (Weren't we, Luke?)

"No, no," he says, struggling to his feet and weaving there for a minute. "You need to stay here." He's trying to sound dad-like, authoritative, but he's so blitzed, it would make me laugh if it weren't so sad. If you'd asked me a few days ago, I would have told you that my father was not the kind of guy to dive for solace at the bottom of a whiskey bottle. But here we are, and this, like everything else that's happened the past two days, makes me feel like my life has been hijacked, like everything I knew about the world has been an utter lie. Including my parents. Maybe *especially* my parents.

"It's okay, Dad," I say softly. "Mom said it was okay. I'll just be gone for a little bit."

He still looks unsure, so unsteady on his feet that I wonder if he'll fall over without me there to prop him up.

"Why don't you just walk me to the garage so we can make sure the reporters aren't there when I pull out?"

"Reporters," he mutters. "Yes, yes, let's get you taken care of," he says in a falsely jovial tone of voice. He reaches out and musses my hair, the way he's always done since I was a kid, his palm lingering on the top of my head. His eyes are rimmed with purple, and his clothes smell stale, as if he's been wearing them for days. His hand moves down to cup my cheek, and I feel the calluses on his palm from afternoons playing b-ball with Luke in the driveway, back when Luke would still play with him. Back when Luke still cared about things like sports.

When I get into the car and open the garage door, clicking the remote, the driveway is blessedly empty, and I sigh in relief, watching my father in the doorway, his hands shoved in the pockets of his jeans, his eyes vague and unfocused. Miranda stands in the shadows, behind my old red bike with the sparkly blue banana seat, her eyes glittering. *Be careful,* she mouths, the sound of blood dripping on the concrete floor masking her words.

We wouldn't want anything to happen to you . . .

My father raises one hand in a wave as I pull out of the driveway, dipping his head slightly as he retreats back into the house. I step on the gas hard, too hard, moving backward into the night.

NINE

I drive through the winding roads. Every block I pass a land mine of memories, the tree-lined streets at once so familiar and alien. The parking lot near the dry cleaner's where Luke first learned to skateboard when he was twelve, the hill we all sledded down whenever there was a snow day, cheeks flushed from the cold winter air stabbing our lungs. Everyone always says that Plainewood resembles a postcard of what a small, Midwestern town is supposed to look like—the tall, leafy oaks, their branches curving protectively over the streets, the stately pastel Victorians, the town square—it's right out of a Norman Rockwell painting. You almost expect to see an old-fashioned soda fountain at the back of Ray's Drugs, its blue neon sign and fifties façade still intact, the wrought-iron, old-fashioned streetlights peering down from every corner. This is a town where kids play outside well past dark in the summertime, their sweet, thin voices echoing in the air. Where you can walk your dog late at night without fear, where people sit out on porch swings in the early evening in the warmer months as dusk begins to fall, suffusing the day in muted blue light. A place where kids still make their own lemonade stands, charging fifty cents a cup, loudly proclaiming that they squeezed the lemons THEMSELVES, and where not contributing a dish to the local bake sale or potluck is considered not only downright un-neighborly but borderline treasonous. Basically, we're a total cliché, but I can't imagine living anywhere else. All of the things that my mom seems to find abhorrent about Plainewood are what lull me to sleep at night, make me glad to wake up each morning and walk out into the calm streets, pavement still wet from sprinkler overspray.

Tonight, the streets are mostly deserted, everyone inside after dinner. My hands are cold against the wheel, and it feels strange to have nowhere to go, no one to talk to, the feeling lonely but liberating all at the same time. I think about getting on the interstate and just driving, the miles ticking by on the odometer, wind whipping by the windows as the scenery gradually alters before my eyes, brown bare branches giving way to flat rocks and endless warm desert skies as I drive farther west. The urge to flee is so tempting that I have to force myself to point the car away from the interstate entrance and back toward town.

After driving around in circles for a while, I find myself drifting in the direction of school, yellow caution tape wound around the fence that surrounds the school like a birthday present gone wrong, the redbrick façade looming just beyond. Letters and posters are tacked to the fence, rows of candles in glass jars, religious and otherwise, burning at the foot of the makeshift memorial. Flowers are stuck at random angles into the holes of the chain link, blossoms of red, purple, and white, cool green leaves decorating the sharp metal. WE WILL NEVER FORGET YOU, one hand-drawn placard proclaims in shaky blue marker, and I feel my eyes begin to mist over. A group of teddy bears have been arranged on the sidewalk, heaps of stuffed toys. A baby lamb catches my eye, its white, woolly fur matted and stained. I pull over to the curb, my fingers scrabbling on the seat belt, yanking it from across my body. There are a few adults milling around, their faces drawn with sadness. One woman I don't recognize gets down on her knees next to the fence, her lips moving in soundless prayer, eyes closed.

I touch the flowers, fingertips lingering against the cool, silky petals, and try to avoid looking directly at the notes, the anguish and desperation contained in them searing my eyes.

There are pictures hanging from the gate, yearbook photos and casual snapshots, baby pictures—tiny, fat feet and chubby hands waving at the lens. I scan them, my eyes glazing over as I begin to recognize faces, a sinking feeling in the pit of my stomach. Mila Germain. Alexis Peterson. Randall Perry. Camille Montrose. Jared Liebowitz. My brother is responsible for these deaths—all of them. The knowledge hits me squarely in the chest, and I almost sink to my knees, the joints buckling, cold air whipping through my hair. Camille Montrose once let me borrow her calculator during an AP Bio exam. Randall Perry would have been homecoming king this year. Alexis Peterson wanted to go to Michigan State, but she worried, Delilah told me conspiratorially, that she wasn't smart enough to get in.

Katie Horton.

Oh, Katie.

I reach out and trace the contours of Katie's cheeks, dark hair tumbling around her face, still plump with baby fat. She looks straight at me, so much like Ben, her smile clawing a new hole at my core. *It's your fault,* she seems to be saying, her eyes wide, accusatory.

The school is quiet and dark, and the candle flames flicker, but don't go out. One of the candles has a picture of the Virgin Mary embossed on the glass jar. She stares at me benevolently from beneath her sky-blue hooded robe, her gaze full of sorrow and compassion, one hand stretched out in front of her, reaching endlessly. I lean my head against the fence, the metal pressing into my skin. *I'm sorry,* I think, though I don't know whom I'm talking to anymore—Katie, Luke, Ben, or maybe just myself. *I'm so fucking sorry.*

"Are you okay?" A voice directly behind me makes me jump, spinning around so quickly that I almost lose my balance.

It's dark, and he is half in shadow, but when he moves forward, reaching one arm out to steady me, a sliver of light illuminates his face.

"Alys?" His grip on my arm tightens. "Is that you?"

"Riley." The word leaving my lips is a sigh, relief coursing through me.

"What are you doing here?" He releases my arm and takes a step back, shoving his hands deep into the pockets of his worn leather jacket, the one he got in the tenth grade and has been wearing religiously ever since. I can't look at Riley without thinking of Luke. I can't remember a time when they weren't locking themselves away for hours to play video games, set off stink bombs, and do God only knows what else, though all Riley had to do was flash that wide smile of his and everything was usually forgiven. And later on, Riley just hung in there through Luke's moods, patiently waiting for them to pass, never trying to force him out of them.

Riley's tall, like me—except he's well over six feet—
something I think he was kind of self-conscious about before he became the school's basketball and cross-country
star, which I can totally relate to given that I feel like a lum-
bering giant most of the time. Everything about him is long
and lean—he's what my mother calls a tall drink of water.
I'm not sure exactly what that means, but I always thought
it sounded kind of gross. His dirty-blond hair hangs a bit
past his ears, and his eyes are the color of the water in Fiji:
blue, then green, then blue again, their depths bottomless
and crystalline. People are always asking him if he's a surfer,
which amuses him to no end. "Does this look like California
to you?" he'll snap, pointing out the window. This is especially funny when there are two feet of snow on the ground.

"What are *you* doing here?" I ask defensively, crossing my
arms over my chest. My hair falls across my face, sandy and
streaked as Luke's, and I shake my head briefly to clear it.

Riley looks out at the school in the distance, scraping
his feet against the rough pavement. "I don't know. I just
couldn't stay in the house anymore, you know? Couldn't
deal with my folks having such a tight rein. Ever since the
shooting, it's like they're afraid to let me out of their sight. It
makes me feel like I can't breathe. So I went out for a walk."

I like that he says "shooting" like it's just another word;
he doesn't try to sugarcoat it. Still, when I hear it spoken

aloud, released into the air where it can't be taken back, my right eye begins to twitch inexplicably.

"I guess I just ended up here. I've never had insomnia in my life, but now, even though I'm so tired I can barely see straight, I just stare at the walls." He pauses for a moment. "It doesn't help that the fucking reporters won't leave us alone. They've been in front of my house ever since it happened, wanting to talk to me, my parents, whoever they can get ahold of." Riley stops, clearly frustrated, kicks at the fence with one foot and knocks a candle over, red wax spilling on the concrete. I watch, transfixed, as it spreads across the pavement, cooling rapidly, a large, crimson stain. I reach down and right the glass jar, thankful it didn't shatter. "Nobody gave a rat's ass about this town before last week, and now . . ."

"We're news," I say quietly, finishing his sentence. "Did you talk to them?" I ask, not really wanting to know the answer, but compelled to ask anyway.

Riley shoots me a look of astonishment.

"The reporters? Hell no. But a lot of people have. Celine Carruthers has been on every network blubbering about how well she knew your family, and how grateful she is to have made it out alive." Riley snorts in disgust. "It's getting to the point that every time I turn on the TV, I see her brainless face."

Celine Carruthers is the captain of the cheerleading squad. Hair the color of autumn leaves and skin like a fresh pail of milk, a smattering of freckles dotting her cheeks. I think the last time I hung out with her was in fifth grade, when my mother forced me to invite her to my birthday party because Celine had cried when I'd sent out invitations and she didn't get one. At the party, Celine noisily opened my presents before I did, then threw a temper tantrum, eating most of my cake with her hands before her parents dragged her out kicking and screaming. Good times.

"She didn't know me—or Luke."

"Well, no shit," Riley says with another snort. "But people are opportunists. And this is a big story."

A big story. My brother, who went out of his way to fly under the radar.

(Until now.)

"I had to talk to the cops, though. Then after they left, I couldn't sleep at all. I just sat up, staring into space like a zombie."

I look at him more closely. There are pouches under each eye, valleys of discoloration, and his skin is white and papery.

"I slept for five hours this afternoon," I say. "Maybe six."

"Just rub it in, why don't you," he says with a smile. It feels good to bullshit with him, to talk normally with someone, even if it's only for a moment.

"After the funeral, I was so exhausted that I just crashed." I stop, the word "funeral" catching in my throat.

(—the sound of the earth falling on his coffin like the lash of a

whip, the wind searing my cheeks to raw red apples. Luke trapped in darkness, his lips sewn shut—)

"I really wanted to go," Riley says, looking away. "Even went down to the church wearing the suit I wore to prom last year, but the ushers wouldn't let me in. I looked like an asshole." He runs his fingers hesitantly over a photo of a girl, maybe two or three years old, holding a teddy bear in her lap, smiling brightly for the camera.

"Yeah, my mom made it a closed service—just immediate family."

A hurt look crosses his face. Judging from how much time he spent at our house, Riley always struck me as looking for any excuse to put off that moment where he'd have to walk home in the night, alone at last with his thoughts. He was kind of a mooch too, if you want to know the truth, used to getting a free ride. You know, the kind of guy who somehow always knows to show up five minutes before dinner lands on the table? *I'm sorry . . . Did I come at a bad time? Hey, are those pork chops, by the way?*

"Oh," he answers, his voice wavering a little. "I guess . . . I guess after all this time, I kind of thought I *was* family or something." He won't make eye contact, so I turn around and stare at the school. I imagine a dark stain on the sidewalk just shy of the entrance, even though I know there's not enough light to make out much of anything at all. I shiver, holding on to the fence, and he turns so that we are now standing shoulder to shoulder. The candles are burning down lower, the flames shifting in the wind.

"Don't take it personally," I say lightly. "We've been hounded by reporters too, so I think she just wanted to make sure they couldn't get in."

He snorts, leaning on the fence, his fingers scratching against the metal links.

"By the way, I really hate when people say, *Don't take it personally*." He mimics my voice, but not meanly or out of spite, his tone a gentle chiding. "It's such a bunch of bullshit. It's like when people say, *It's not you, it's me*." He lets out a dry laugh. "That's when you know it's *really* you."

I laugh, turning to look at him, his profile sharp against the night sky, clouds hiding the stars above. Usually I'm anxious when I talk to anyone, especially guys, but I don't feel nervous around Riley. Maybe it's because he's always been there, standing in the background of my life. Strangely enough, in all the years I've known him, this is the longest conversation we've ever had. Riley is kind of like furniture—it's nice and comfortable and everything, but after a while you stop noticing it's there.

"You still getting ready for that competition?"

I must look as confused as I feel, because Riley stares at me helplessly.

"Competition? You mean my *audition*? Did Luke tell you about that?"

"Yeah, the audition. Madison, right?"

I nod, wordlessly, my neck stiff and wooden.

"When is it?"

"The end of May. Not that it matters now."

Doesn't it? I can almost hear Luke's whisper cutting through the rustling of the trees. *Isn't that what's always mattered to you most?*

I twine my fingers around the metal links of the fence, half hoping that one of them will come loose, the sharp spikes cutting into my hands so that I never have to play again. Right now I can't imagine making something so beautiful and timeless as music flow from my fingers, releasing it into a world so full of sorrow, regret, and pain—a world my brother helped create. It feels wrong, dirty somehow, to contemplate that kind of happiness, the notes leaping over the walls of my bedroom in a swollen cascade, floating out my window and mixing with the smell of spring rain and early lilacs, purple and dripping, coming from our neighbor's yard. I don't know if I deserve that kind of salvation, that kind of release.

"Why doesn't it matter? You're really good, Alys. I mean *really* good."

"How would *you* know?"

"Oh, so I'm just a dumb jock, right?" He stares straight

ahead. "Some stupid athlete who can't tell Prokofiev from punting. Is that what you think?"

I raise an eyebrow, unable to hide the fact that I'm momentarily stunned, not to mention slightly impressed, that he knows who Prokofiev is.

"I didn't say that!"

I hate when people put words into my mouth. It never fails to unnerve me.

"Look," he begins again, taking a deep breath, "I've heard you play for years. I may not know much about music, Alys, but I know talent when I hear it. I'm not a moron, you know."

With those last few words, his voice cracks, and we stare at one another until I smile tentatively.

"It's true—you're not a moron," I say, my face stiff, unused to smiling. "But you *are* a pain in the ass."

He cracks a grin—that same one that makes it possible for him to get away with doing so very little, at school and in life so far—then effectively changes the subject.

"So how was it? The funeral, I mean."

I look at him in amazement, my expression broadcasting my thoughts—*Seriously? What kind of question is that?*

"Sorry." He laughs, sounding a bit like he's choking. "I guess you're right—I really *am* a pain in the ass."

"No, it's okay," I say, surrendering to the pull of social graces, even though the funeral is the last thing I want to talk about right now. "It was surreal. The minister was going on and on about forgiveness, that sometimes good people do bad things, and that everyone's a mystery, blah, blah, blah—as if he really cared."

I look down at the Virgin Mary again, her face as serene and blissful as ever, her blue robe flickering with light.

"He didn't know Luke—we barely ever went to church. He doesn't know anything about us. And I couldn't stop thinking about Luke inside that stupid box, just lying there forever." Tears well up in my eyes, and I blink them away angrily, drops of salt water falling to the pavement. I imagine them hissing as they fall, boring holes in the rough cement and extinguishing the candles once and for all.

Riley nods in agreement, shoving his hands more deeply into his pockets.

"I just can't believe I'll never see him again," I say.

Except for those, well, let's just call them hallucinations you've been having, a nasty little voice inside me pipes up. *And while we're on the subject, don't forget to mention the fact that you're currently in the process of losing what's left of your fucking mind . . . That's pertinent information, right?*

I drop my head, the tears falling fast now. For some reason I'm embarrassed, cringing inside as if I've just been caught naked. I don't want anyone, not even Riley, to see me like this.

"Hey," he says, but I don't look at him, just keep focusing

on my ankle boots, how worn and scuffed they are at the toes. If I just stare at my feet long enough, if I think about how I should've replaced these boots six months ago, maybe I won't break down completely. Images of Riley and Luke flash before my eyes: all those nights Riley stayed over our house, plaid sleeping bags nestled in the tree house, the endless games of Grand Theft Auto and Doom they played late into the night. If anyone knows what happened to Luke, it would be Riley.

"Did you know?" I ask. "Did he say anything to you?"

The woman who was on her knees, praying in front of the fence, walks by us, her shoulders hunched and heaving. As she passes us, she glances up, and in her face I see so much sadness and heartache that I want to reach out to her, place a hand on her shoulder, but I don't know what to say. What could I say? There are no words.

Riley looks straight at me, and I can see that his eyes are wet too, and for some reason, this makes me want to put my arms around him and hold on tight, rest my head on his shoulder and let the tears flow until we're both spent and exhausted. But if I put my arms around him right now, it might decimate whatever remains of my composure. It's like the crying I've done since all this began—when it starts, it feels like I will never be able to stop, the hysteria rising in me like a car alarm that won't shut off, growing louder and shriller with each passing second.

"I didn't know anything. He was my best friend, Alys, and I didn't know anything at all. He never said a word. About any of it." He shrugs his shoulders, defeated. "Did you . . . notice anything?" he asks as we start walking down the sidewalk along the fence. "I mean, before."

I kick a rock out of the way. It hits the trunk of a tree with a hard, satisfying thwack.

"He was, you know, depressed," I answer, shuffling my feet against the pavement. "But you know Luke—he was always in some sort of a mood. One day he'd be locked away in his room surfing the Web for hours, and the next he'd be throwing peas at me across the dinner table, trying to make me laugh, you know?"

Riley dips his head in agreement. "Up until the past few months, he talked a lot about college, going to Boston. Said he couldn't wait to get out of here and start over someplace else, where no one knew him, which I thought was a little weird, if you want to know the fucking truth, but I didn't say anything about it to him, really. Then, all of a sudden, it seemed like he never mentioned school much anymore. Just stopped talking about it, like it wasn't really happening. Even when I'd bring it up, he'd just change the subject. I think that was around December." Riley sighs, his face contorted in pain. "Even in the last few months—hell, the last few *days,* he still seemed like . . . himself. Well—mostly.

I mean, he didn't act like someone who was going to—" Riley breaks off. "If he was planning something, Alys, I didn't know. I didn't see it. Maybe I should have."

I didn't see it.

"And I just can't believe he could . . . pull off something like this with us all so close." He pauses, taking a deep breath as if he's starved for air. "I keep feeling like it's my fault. Like I should've known somehow. He was my best friend."

"That's stupid," I say softly. "I mean, if *I* didn't know, then how were *you* supposed to? I lived with him every day for the past seventeen years, Riley, and I didn't know anything was wrong either.

(Did I?)

"I never thought he'd do something like this in a million years. The Luke I thought I knew wasn't

(a killer)

"Crazy. Or violent. He couldn't have killed all those people. People he knew. People he . . . loved." I shake my head in disbelief.

"I read about Katie in the paper," Riley says as we turn the corner and begin walking toward the park across the street, a set of swings and a red-and-blue jungle gym standing out in the blackness of the night. I want to go back to the time when everything was so carefree, when all we had to worry about was making it home from the playground before dinner, before the streetlights turned on one by one. "I hear Ben's pretty broken up."

In this town, news travels fast, and gossip even more quickly. Ben and Riley aren't really friendly, so I know that Riley must have heard this bit of information second- or thirdhand, at least. The weird thing about Riley is that as popular as he is, he mostly keeps to himself, something Luke loves

(loved)

about him. A shiver runs through me, and I rub my hands together for warmth. Even though he's in the ground now, I'm not ready to consign Luke to the past tense. Not yet.

(—in the dark where he can't get out, can't see or hear, can't feel—)

We walk over to the swings and, as if by mutual agreement, sit down, our feet dragging on the ground as we sway aimlessly back and forth.

"They're tearing out the library—the carpet, the floors, everything. They say we may have to finish the year at Holbrook. But I doubt it."

Holbrook is a high school in the next town over.

Riley pauses for a minute, choosing his words. "You were in there when it happened, right?" He holds on to the metal chains of the swing with each hand, gripping them tightly.

Suddenly I am on red alert. The library. Luke. Miranda.

I cannot talk about it. I can't. My eyes narrow. "Are you asking because you really want to know? Or so you can tell the papers?"

I am nasty, full of bitterness. My words surprise even me. I picture myself in a bubble, separated from the rest of humanity with no one to trust. He stops moving and his face cracks wide-open, fractured, and something inside me stops entirely, like the hands of a clock halting midsweep.

"I told you that I didn't talk to them!" His voice rises in pitch, and he looks away from me. All at once I'm ashamed—ashamed of myself, ashamed of Luke, the feeling spreading over me like hot sauce, searing my skin. "Jesus, Alys—you really think I'd *do* that?" For the first time since the conversation began, his voice is cold, removed.

"I'm sorry," I whisper, and even as soft as it is, my voice sounds deafening in the square, the enormity of the words filling the park, the town—the whole world with a sense of impermanence. The instability of everything I thought was solid and immovable. "I don't know what to think about anything anymore," I say. "Or any*one*. I'm not even sure who I'm supposed to be—now that he's gone." It feels weird saying this out loud, and to Riley, but I can't deny the truth of it, and something about being with Riley makes lying impossible. He's known me for too long.

Riley nods in assent, and we sit there in silence, swinging

sometimes but mostly just hanging there, the bottoms of our shoes trampling the green shoots springing from the earth despite the rough cold that still wraps its tentacles around the town, despite there being no sign, no evidence at all, that things will eventually thaw.

TEN

When I get home, the downstairs lights are blazing, illuminating it like a jack-o'-lantern. The minute I walk in the front door, I hear yelling, muffled shouts coming from the basement, a room that functions as both my mom's potting studio and my dad's makeshift office, though he's constantly complaining that she leaves it too messy to actually work in. I creep down the carpeted stairs slowly, soundless, greedy for their secrets. They haven't had any kind of a substantial conversation for days, as far as I can tell, and the sound of their raised voices strangely fills me with comfort. At least they're still fighting. At least one thing in my life is exactly the same as it was before.

"You should've let him go to that space camp when he was twelve!" my father shouts. "But it was always about Alys, wasn't it?" I sink down on the stairs, one hand in my mouth, biting at what's left of my nails. I feel dizzy, almost like I'm dreaming. "If it wasn't 'creative,' then you just weren't interested."

"Well, at least I was *here*." My mother's voice is raw, hoarse. "You were always at the office, on the phone, more worried about your *clients* than your own son!"

I've never heard my mother criticize my father's job this pointedly, out for blood, her words digging in with iron claws. Usually her complaints come off as a joke, dark humor, a needling under the skin. But until this moment, I've never taken her jabs seriously. And from his reaction, neither has my dad.

"Somebody had to grow up and pay the bills around here!" my father yells back. I watch their shadows moving back and forth as they pace around the basement, their arms thrown up at each other in long black arcs. I put my head in my hands, leaning my face against my knees. "Because you sure as hell weren't going to sacrifice your ridiculous principles!"

My mother is silenced. I raise my head. Even I can see that was a low blow.

"I thought they were *our* principles," she finally says, her voice laden with hurt and disappointment. My father has always supported my mother's artistic aspirations, attending all of her gallery shows, bragging to friends about how talented, how creative she was, until she'd bury her face in his shoulder, laughing in embarrassment and begging him to stop.

"I have a good job at the gallery," she says, her voice shaking with newfound anger. "*You* were the one who told me I should go part-time so I'd be able to focus on my own work more. I may not make much money, but at least I was *here* all of these years. With our children. Raising them the best I could." I hear her sigh through the exasperation, the anger, and I can tell from the frustration in her voice that right now she's more exasperated than angry. "Jesus, Paul, how the hell could you let this *happen* to him?"

"Goddammit, I didn't *let* this happen to him! I calculate damage for a living, Dani—*that's* what I *do*." My father's voice is tight and resigned. "But I couldn't have calculated this. That *thing* that walked into that school and—" I hear heaving sobs, a sound like choking. "That thing was *not* my son. He couldn't have . . . hurt all of those people, using them for some kind of sick target practice. He couldn't have done that. Not Luke."

The house shudders in the wind. I hear the sound of my father sitting down in a chair, the wood groaning beneath him.

"Yes. Yes, he could," my mother says quietly. "Yes, he could, Paul, and he *did*. He did it."

My father cries, and his sobbing, the particular cadence of it, triggers an automatic response; my face screws up, but my eyes remain dry, as if I've somehow used up my yearly allotment of tears. I imagine that my mother puts her arms around him, their bodies fitting together in the kind of familiarity that many years foster between two people. Two people who are still in love, despite all the pain they have inflicted on each other. The fighting. The disappointments. The compromises neither side wanted to make.

"What about Alys?" my mother says after a long moment. I can hear my father sniffling, trying to compose himself, then the loud foghorn blast of him blowing his nose, and the loudness of the gesture almost makes me pitch forward and fall down the stairs, clattering to the bottom in a noisy heap. I grip on to the wall, my fingernails scraping against the plaster.

"What about her?"

"Do you think we should . . . get her some help? Send her to another school? Maybe she could stay with my parents for a little while."

My grandparents live in Iowa, on a farm out in the middle of nowhere. If I had to stay there, I'd go completely nuts.

"Alys doesn't *need* help. She's not the problem here. She's not responsible for any of this."

I want so badly for that last sentence to be even just a little true, so badly I would give my life to make it so.

"That's what you said about Luke." My mother almost

whispers, as if she's afraid to say the words aloud. "That he didn't need help."

I hear the slight shuffling sound of feet against the hard floor, and a long silence spreads thickly through the room.

"You're right," my father says, almost inaudibly, and I lean slightly forward. "I should've known. *We* should've known. Shouldn't we have?"

"I don't know." My mother sighs again, and I hear a creak as she sits down. "How could we have? All I know is that something changed in these last few years—all those nights he spent in his room, locking himself away from us . . ." She stops for a moment, and I picture her hands in her hair, wrapping it around her fingers, pulling at it. "I thought it was a phase—that it would pass."

"Some phase," my father says bitterly, his voice etched with acid.

"The lawyer says we need to write a statement. We should have released something to the press already."

I picture Bob Lane, my parents' lawyer, his tie in an expert knot. Of course they would've spoken to their lawyer. All those

(*victims*)

wanting something from us. Some kind of compensation. Retribution, even. I wrap my arms around my knees, hugging them to my chest.

"Fuck the press."

"I feel the same way." My mother shifts in her seat, and I imagine her crossing her long legs over each other, one elbow on her knee. The way she always sits when she's worried, or lost in thought. "But Bob says we have to do it. He said it will look worse if we keep quiet—people might start thinking we're complicit, that we condone Luke's . . . actions. All of those children, just . . . *gone* . . ." Her voice trails off. "For God's sake, Paul, Jesse Davis is in the hospital in intensive care. They don't know if he's going to wake up or, if he does, what kind of brain damage he'll have. His poor parents. I can't imagine."

Jesse Davis was a senior, like Luke. Class president this year and scheduled to be valedictorian. Harvard bound in the fall. Always had a smile for everyone, even freshmen. The idea that Luke shot him is inconceivable. Monstrous.

Maybe it was an accident, like Katie—just like Katie . . .

My heart sinks in my chest, and I shut my eyes. I feel Luke's presence moving over me, through me even, something barbecued, all smoke and cinders, petals on fire. When I open my eyes, Luke is there beside me. I can feel the heat from his body on my legs, my arms.

His gaze is focused on my parents at the bottom of the stairs, and he cranes his neck a bit in order to hear them better, maybe catch a glimpse. His whole body gleams, a shimmering mass of light and shadow. I can hear him breathing, the sound the air makes moving through his chest, his face fractured by the light.

"What are they bitching about?" Luke asks without turning to look at me, his tone vaguely amused, the curve and contour of his cheek still smooth, radiant, as if pinpricks of light flicker softly beneath his skin.

"You," I say, putting my hand on his leg and leaving it there. But, to my surprise, he doesn't fade. I can feel the heat from his skin passing through my fingers, the temperature growing hotter by the second. "They're bitching about *you*," I manage to stammer. I feel sick, dizzy, the stairwell narrowing like the walls of a fun house.

He's warm. And he's really here. At least for now . . .

"Huh," he says, nonplussed. "Typical."

I move closer, lean my head on his shoulder though the stink of fire is almost overwhelming. Hot coals and lilies. *My brother,* I think, closing my eyes, listening to the sound of Luke's breathing, the impossibility of it, his unwashed maple-syrup scent rising up through the ashes.

My brother did this.

WISCONSIN
FRIDAY, MARCH 13, 2015

DAILY RECORD

Parents of shooter Lucas Aronson ask for "compassion and prayers"

In a statement released today the parents of Plainewood High School gunman Lucas Aronson, who shot and killed fifteen students, called the shooting an "appalling act of violence."

Addressing the families of the victims directly, Paul and Dani Aronson stated that they had "no explanation" for their son's actions, and that their grief for the families affected by the tragedy was "simply overwhelming."

In closing, they expressed gratitude to the community of Plainewood for their "support, compassion, and prayers in this very dark time."

The family asked for the media and the public at large to respect their privacy, as "we too

have also suffered a loss, the loss of our only son, Luke."

In an interview on *Good Morning America*, Phyllis Germain, the mother of 15-year-old Mila Germain, who was killed in the attack, expressed disbelief in a lack of clear motive for the fatal shooting that left fifteen dead and four injured.

"Well, it's about morals, isn't it? And it all comes down to the parents," Ms. Germain stated. "Things like this don't happen if you're raising your kids with decent values."

Officials report that a Facebook page appearing to belong to Aronson contained "disturbing messages," including what is believed to be a short story detailing a mass murder at a local shopping mall.

Four days before the shooting, Aronson posted a rant in the "notes" section of his Facebook page, describing a man who takes revenge on the "arrogant fools" who once ignored him. The note ends with these words: "You're all going to die."

Victims Alyssa Jones, 16, and Regina Parks, 17, are reportedly in stable condition at Plainewood Memorial Hospital. Plainewood High School Principal David Clarke was treated for minor injuries and released. Jesse Davis, 18, who sustained a gunshot wound to the head during the attack, remains in critical condition.

Aronson was buried yesterday in Saint Anne's Memorial Cemetery.

ELEVEN

The morning after the statement is released, I'm sore and achy, like I've slept on a pile of rocks. I tossed and turned all night, finally giving up around four, and just stared at the ceiling for two hours, willing the daylight to come, my eyes puffy and dry. It's early, and the house is quiet, the clocks ticking off the minutes. I slip on a pair of dark skinny jeans and the same black sweater I wore yesterday, pulling at the tangles in my hair with my fingers. What's the point of brushing it? Good grooming won't change anything.

My phone buzzes with a text, and I look down to see Riley's name, along with, **You awake?** Sleepless, the both of us: a matching pair. Except we're not—I'm in this alone, despite how badly Riley may feel about what has happened, what he did or didn't do. I shut off the phone and move downstairs, ignoring the half-open door that beckons, tempting me as I pass Luke's room.

Our den is worn and comfortable, with yellow walls the color of weak winter sunlight, my dad's heavy leather chair, matching couch, and a rug in graduated shades of beige and bronze covering the scuffed wood floors. When the set springs to life, I stand back as if it might burn me with its incandescent glow. I switch on CNN, and my brother's face appears almost instantly. He stares right at me, a close-up, his eyes flat and lifeless. I slowly sink to the floor, the remote slipping from my hands and dropping with a soft thudding sound onto the carpet. I want to think that I'm still dreaming, tossing and turning restlessly in my bed. But as much as I want to believe it, I know this is really happening. I watch helplessly as Luke holds up a rifle, the same one I saw in the library, and waves it menacingly at the camera. He's in his room—I recognize the dark green walls, the globe perched on top of his wooden dresser. He loads the gun, cocking it, his face set in concentration, and I watch transfixed for a minute or two before I realize that the TV is on mute. I scramble to pick up the remote and turn the volume up just as my brother disappears, replaced by a newscaster's sharp silent gaze, hair combed straight back from his overly tanned face, his red tie an affront to my senses.

"Once again, that is leaked footage from the computer of Wisconsin shooter Lucas Aronson. The file was released anonymously to the press this morning and Plainewood police have not yet issued a statement explaining how this kind of breach could have occurred in the midst of a sealed investigation."

The camera pulls back, and I see a blond anchorwoman sitting next to him, wearing a crisp white blouse, her makeup so heavy and caked on that my own pores feel on the verge of asphyxiation just from looking at her.

"You really hope that at a time like this, Bob, the families of the victims aren't watching," she says, shaking her head.

The camera dissolves and there is Luke's face again. He's yelling into the camera—Luke, who I have heard angry, *really* furious, maybe twice in my entire life. My brother is not a screamer, someone who rants and raves uncontrollably. Luke is a bottler, as my mother would say. He must have stifled his feelings for years, sitting on them, holding everything inside, stone-faced until

(he exploded)

He holds the gun up defiantly and waves it over his head before pointing it at the screen, cocking it, and everything stops. He looks straight into the camera, his eyes squinting slightly. I can see him breathing heavily, panting almost. If this person is my brother, I don't know him.

"What's going on here?"

My father in the doorway, frozen, my mother standing behind him, still in her nightgown. My cheeks burn hot with shame, as if somehow I am responsible.

"I just turned on the TV and—"

My mother pushes past my father, shoving his body aside, and rushes toward the screen, drawn to Luke's flickering image.

"How did they . . ." She points at the TV, then turns to me, unable to finish, her eyes wide and frantic. I can see by the dark patches below them that she hasn't been sleeping any better than I have, that maybe she hasn't been sleeping at all. "Where did this . . ."

"Turn it off," my father orders.

No one moves. My mother and I, both prisoners to the images flickering across the screen, Luke's harsh voice, screaming about punishment and retribution, chilling my blood until it slows in my veins, sluggish and icy.

"This is your fault. All of you. Now you're going to die."

"I SAID TURN IT THE FUCK OFF!"

My father strides over, grabbing the remote from my hand with such force that I wobble and almost capsize. He hits the power button, and Luke's face vanishes.

"Nooooooooooooooo," my mother screams, grabbing at my father's arms, her hands reaching violently for the remote. "Give him back! Give him back to meeeeeeeeeeeeeeeeeee!" Her screams rise higher, the sound somehow worse than my brother's ranting.

(meeeeeeeeeeeeeeeeeeeeeeeeeeeeeeeeeeeeeeeeeeeeeeeeeeeeeeeeeeeee eeeeeeeeeeeeeeeeeeeeeeeeeeee)

My father throws the remote across the room. It hits the wall above the couch and shatters, breaking into pieces. I back away, my heart beating frantically. I can't catch my breath, and I don't recognize these people who raised me, held me in their arms when I was cold or sick. I don't recognize myself. He grabs my mother's shoulders and shakes her, her head flopping forward and back. She's wailing now. The couch is suddenly against my legs, and I sit down abruptly, as if pushed from a great distance.

"I can't give him back!" my father yells in her face. "Dani, look at me." My mother ignores him, lost in her own hysteria, eyes wild and unseeing, twisting her torso away from my father's grip. "He's gone. He's gone now." My mother's body deflates in his arms all at once, as if the air has suddenly been let out of her, the anger vanishing, replaced by something so much worse, I don't dare contemplate it.

Shame.

I have never seen my mother ashamed of either me or Luke. She's always gone out of her way to praise us, to tell the both of us how proud she is to be our mother. But there's no mistaking the look on her face. My father rocks her in his arms like an infant, a bizarre reversal of their argument last night—now my father is the strong one, the one offering comfort, holding her up. My mother's sobs wrench at my gut, twisting it, and as I begin to cry, watching her, I wonder how much longer we can go on like this, how much more we can take.

The doorbell rings. My father looks up, startled, and in his weary gaze I can see that no matter what waits behind our front door, he is already expecting the worst. This tears at me more than almost anything else. What has always defined my dad is his openness toward the world, his generosity toward strangers, his unflagging belief that with a positive attitude, Luke and I could accomplish just about anything. From the slump of his shoulders, the set of his jaw, his wary expression, I know that, once and for all, those days are over. My father is someone else now. Someone who will never let his guard down or approach the world with open arms. He'll forever be looking around the corner, ever watchful, afraid of what lurks just out of sight.

He gets up, leaving my mother, who is on her knees, sobbing helplessly, her shoulders shaking beneath her white nightgown. I go to her, kneel down, and she latches on to me, her body hot with grief. "Mom," I whisper. "It's okay, Mom, it's okay." I say this over and over again, and she is heavy in my arms, her eyes closed, tears running rivers down her smooth cheeks. I hear voices in the front hall, the tone officious and impersonal. When I look up, it is at the sound of approaching feet, my heart scattering in my chest like a scared rabbit.

"Detective Marino is here," my father says, his face drained of all color. "He has some new information about Luke." He looks at my mother, her white flannel nightgown billowing around her slight frame. "I'll get your robe, Dani." My mother gets to her feet, wiping her eyes and nodding at nothing at all. "Alys," my father says distractedly, as if he's just realized that I'm still in the room, "you should go upstairs now."

I look at my father, incredulous.

"No way."

My father's stance is defiant, robe pulled around his body like a tourniquet, rough patches of stubble covering his cheeks. "You don't need to hear this, Alys," my father says, irritated now, out of patience, the way he always is when I argue with him. "Just go to your room."

"He was my *brother*," I yell, and time seems to stand still. "He belonged to me too," I say, the words coming out with a surprising amount of force. "Did you ever think of *that*? Besides, everything is all over the TV, the newspapers, the Web! Do you really think you'll be able to keep it from me? It's out there—where *everyone* can see it!"

We stand there for a long moment until he turns away from me, dropping his eyes, defeated.

"All right," he says, more to my mother than to me. My mother nods almost imperceptibly, her hair matted and disheveled.

"All right, then."

. . .

In the kitchen, I sit between my mother and father at the table, my mother's hand wrapped around mine. Detective Marino sits across from us, a manila folder in front of him. His suit looks rumpled, like he's slept in it for a few nights, on a couch somewhere. My mother gets up, turns on the coffeemaker, and the machine comes to life with a slow hiss as the dark, rich scent drifts slowly through the room. She sits back down, bracing herself, her face drawn with fatigue.

"What the hell is going on?" My father speaks through gritted teeth, his face hardened.

Detective Marino's hair is steel gray, and reminds me of a scouring pad. His blue eyes look as tired and watery as they did on his last visit, as if at any moment they might spill over with tears. "I want to apologize on the behalf of the entire police department for the leak this morning. We're looking into it, and, rest assured, we'll have some answers in due time." Marino leans his elbows on the table, still wearing his coat, even though the heat's on and the temperature in the kitchen borders on stifling. "But obviously the video raises some new questions. And then there's this." Marino opens the folder and removes the top sheet of paper, pushing it across the table.

"Were you aware that Luke had posted a note on Facebook four days before the shooting?" I pull the paper toward me, unable to stop my hand from reaching out and grabbing it, anger and disgust rising off of the page like steam.

(—and the arrogant fools who walk these halls will face my wrath. It is I who decides your fate, not God. I will hunt you down, split your skulls like walnut shells, grind you to powder, destroy everything you hold dear. You've taken so much from me—all of you. Now you're going to die—)

My mouth goes dry, the coffeemaker emitting a strangled sound, a gurgling. I look up, helpless. Maybe someone hacked Luke's page; maybe he posted it as a prank, a joke. Maybe it was an assignment for that creative writing elective he was taking.

It was him, something whispers inside me. *It was him, he meant every word—and you know it. It's right there in front of you in black and white. His words, so full of rage and hate and the disappointment we never knew he felt at all. Look at them.*

My mother takes the paper, her lips moving as she reads, forehead creased in concentration.

"Alys, did you see this post before the incident?" Marino's voice is soft, as if he's afraid of scaring me, jarring me into action. "Did any of you?"

My mother pushes the paper at my father, who hands it to Marino without looking at it.

"No?" Detective Marino addresses my father, his eyebrows slightly raised.

"I saw it in the newspaper, but that's not the way I want to remember my son."

"Did any of you see this post before the incident?" the

detective repeats, his eyes flitting between the three of us, not sure of where to land.

"I don't use Facebook that much anymore," I say. There is a long pause, and Marino's chair creaks loudly as he shifts his weight. "But even if I had logged on, I probably wouldn't have looked at his page, anyway." I stare at the wooden table-top, digging my nail into a gouge in the wood, feeling along its deep ridge. "Luke liked his privacy. I mean, he friended me, but said he didn't want me commenting on his posts all the time. He said it was bad enough that we went to the same high school. I guess I kind of saw his point."

"You did." Marino's voice is without inflection. "What point was that?"

"Our rooms were down the hall from each other." My words are deliberate, the careful building of a wall, one brick placed against the next. "We went to school together—drove there in the morning and home at night together. It's not like we never saw each other."

(—but I didn't see; I didn't. He was right there in front of me the whole time and I didn't see him, the real him, who he really was. Someone who wanted to hurt people, people we loved, who plotted it, fantasized about it, wrote stupid notes on—)

"What Alys is trying to say," my father interjects, "is that she and her brother considered their relationship to be close enough without monitoring each other's actions online. They simply didn't feel it was necessary."

I squirm uncomfortably on my chair. My father is wrong. I wish, more than anything, that his words were true. But they're not. Luke and I weren't close—not anymore. The Luke I remember is trapped behind glass, suspended in time and made up of fragments from my past. That Luke is twelve, ten, fourteen, and gone forever, living on only in my brain as a series of faded memories. Luke tickling me after my bath when I was six until I peed my pants and he had to help me into dry pajamas. Luke guiding my fingers around a fat yellow pencil, his touch impossibly light. Luke's arms wrapped firmly around my waist as I set off on my first bike, moving carefully down the driveway, the turquoise paint sparkling. *Don't worry,* he said authoritatively, leaning over my shoulder. *I won't let you fall.*

"You mean *Luke* didn't think it was necessary," Detective Marino says, correcting my father, who glowers at him, a slow seething.

"I will not have my daughter cross-examined, goddammit." My father bangs his fist on the table, and I jump visibly in my chair. "You said you had new information to share with us, so either hurry up and share it or get out."

There is silence. My mother gets up and pours my father a cup of coffee, gently placing it in front of him before pouring herself a mug, the wedding ring on her hand spinning loosely on her finger.

My temples throb, and I press my fingers into the sides of

my head, pushing in against pain. I want things to go back to the way they were, the way *we* were: Luke refusing to eat his cereal, my mother flying around the kitchen searching for her car keys. A family. Not these broken puzzle pieces, the picture gaping and unfinished.

Luke.

"Yes, there is," Marino says after a pause. He places the paper back in the folder and closes it. "We found plans for a bomb on your son's computer."

The light in the kitchen is bright, too bright, burning through everything. An X-ray exposing every lie, every secret. A bomb. Luke *was* the bomb, armed and waiting. Biding his time. Tick, tick, ticking.

"We don't think he ever built it, but we're going to do a thorough sweep of your home, and the school, just to be safe."

My mother knocks over her cup, letting out a sharp cry, coffee spreading across the table. She rubs her hand where some of the hot liquid has splashed, and goes to the sink, sticking her hand underneath the cold water, biting her lower lip. I sit there in the house I grew up in, the kitchen growing warmer by the minute, and I can faintly remember being an average seventeen-year-old girl, studying for SATs, my pencil bitten down to a nub, the taste of wood shavings sprinkled on my tongue. Thinking about prom, what I'd wear, worrying about Ben's horrifying penchant for pastel tuxedos. My audition. Summer unfolding like a humid fever dream, classrooms and theaters pulsing with Brahms, Debussy, and Chopin. But it seems like it was someone else's life, borrowed, nothing that belonged to me permanently. Just a few days ago, I was impatient for the future, wanting things to change, to hurry up, to be different—for my real life to begin.

I got what I wanted, didn't I, Luke?

But not in the way I expected.

TWO

"There is a crack in everything
That's how the light gets in."

—LEONARD COHEN, "ANTHEM"

ONE

The first day back at school dawns with a clap of thunder, an arc of rain pelting the sides of the house, a bright siege of lightning intermittently flashing across the sky.

(—*the gun going off, obliterating everything, the world gone deaf*—)

Yesterday was Easter, Luke's favorite holiday. Gray sky outside the windows, a light drizzle coating the glass. When we were small, there were egg hunts in the backyard, candy-colored dresses swishing against my legs. And always, the spring leg of lamb, new potatoes, shelled peas. "You just like it because you get to eat tons of lamb," I'd say, watching Luke pile it on, the meat perfectly pink at the center. Last night we ordered Chinese, and sat at the kitchen table without speaking, the intermittent whine of cutlery, the scrape of my father's fork, setting my teeth on edge. After almost a month off, you'd think I'd be rested, but I'm as tired as ever. Sluggish spring rain for days on end. Along the front walk, the crocus flowers my mother planted last year have begun to rise up, pushing through the soil in a profusion of white and violet petals, arms outstretched, the hedges that surround the house suddenly covered with green leaves, as if they've been waiting all this time to show their small, upturned faces. The clouds gathering damply overhead in the sky telegraph a warning.

Stay inside.

For the past few weeks I've watched as the police swept the house with metal detectors, as men in hazmat suits searched our garage for volatile chemicals, my thoughts floating up and resting on the ceiling so that I wouldn't care, so I could pretend it didn't hurt to see them rummaging through our things as though we weren't right in front of them. Pawing through Luke's room, another violation, where even the stupid porno magazines he kept at the bottom of his closet were taken away to be studied, categorized, analyzed. Luke's sexual preferences reduced to investigational fodder, reduced to . . . what? Volatile chemicals and a thing for big tits. "Rare to see a kid with actual magazines these days," one cop said, fingering Luke's copy of *Hustler*. "Usually they just download it."

Spring break has come and gone, and I should be tanned

right now, my cheeks pink, a stripe of sunburn running down the length of my nose. I should be on the phone with Delilah, planning what I'm going to wear in order to maximize my newly bronzed skin, lips rough and reddened from last night's make-out session with Ben, eyes glittering with lust and sleep deprivation. I look at the clothes I laid out on the chair last night—the plaid skirt from Anthropologie, the dark tights and black sweater—and now it looks all wrong. A stupid costume. If I wear black, every time they look at me they will see the loss, the devastation—a walking reminder. I might as well be carrying all of the dead on my back, my spine twisting under their weight.

"They'll be reminded anyway, stupid," Luke whispers. He sits on the edge of my bed, picking at his nails, furiously ripping at the cuticles as is the family way—we all do it. Worry-warts that we are. But Luke's fingers look disgusting, caked with dried blood around the nail beds. Raw meat.

When I think of walking through the front doors of the school, sliding into my familiar seat during first period, I am filled with a sense of dread, my mouth dry. But the thought of staying home another minute, walking through the mine-field separating my parents each day, time punctuated only by the arrival of the mail at three, the lights clicking on in the streets at dusk, is enough to make me crave the monotony of a rotating schedule, the banality of pep rallies and student council elections.

I grab a white cardigan from the closet, along with my favorite pair of black jeans, slide a pair of leopard ballet flats onto my feet, and stare at myself in the mirror. Everything is wrong. My skin is sallow from a lack of sleep, purple moons beneath my eyes that are so dark now, they almost look like they've been colored in. No matter how hungry I am lately, I can't seem to choke down more than a few mouthfuls. I look longer and thinner than ever, my hipbones protruding from my jeans, my chest almost concave beneath my sweater. The only thing that I can seem to manage is coffee with lots of cream and sugar, and dry salty crackers. Last night when I opened the refrigerator, the smell of rotting food wafted out in a blast of cold air—leftover pork chops lying in a sauce of their own pink juice, eggs rolling placidly in a bowl, hard-boiled, waiting on fingers to strip the shell away. The globs of mayonnaise in the glass jar with the bright yellow label, half-empty bottles of ketchup, a red that called to me with the sweet stink of violence. I clapped one hand against my mouth and ran for the bathroom, retching over the sink.

My violin waits in the corner, propped against the wall, abandoned. I haven't played at all over break, and I am drawn to it like a drug. I pull the instrument from its case, fitting its curved contours to mine, my cheek pressed to the cold wood. I wrap my arms around the mahogany frame, willing it to warm, and tentatively run my fingers over the strings at the neck. I pluck them once, hard, and a burst of sound fills the room, startling me into the moment. "Play something, Alys," Luke pleads, his breath hot on the back of my neck. "Play something for me."

"I can't." My mouth forms the words, but no sound comes out. I blink rapidly, surfacing from the deep, then shove the violin back into the soft velvet lining, out of sight, before I can be tempted, before my hands reach for the bow and I am lost in a lull of quiet and peace that I don't deserve. When I turn around, the room is empty but for the faint scent of flowers and the reek of burned paper.

I pull my hair back into a ponytail, lean into the glass, and peer at my face, think about popping the zit on my chin that looks like it's finally reaching its full potential, but manage to restrain myself. The truth is, it doesn't matter what I wear, what I look like, whether or not there's a bright red bump on my face drawing everyone's attention. I am the sister of a mass murderer, and that is what people see when they look at me. Luke's face superimposed over mine, our features melting into one another like chocolate and strawberry mingling inexorably at the bottom of a bowl.

"This was my prom dress," Miranda says from the half-open closet, a sea of unfamiliar fabric sticking out of the door, splashes of silver glitter woven into a black skirt. "But now I'll never get to wear it. Will I." Her voice, an icy whisper, goes right through me and I shiver, shutting the door tight so I can't see her face, the blood matting the ropes of her hair. "Why don't you come in here with me," she pleads through the wood, her voice waterlogged and thick, the sound of something dragging, belly down, along the bottom of the river.

Keep me company.

In the kitchen, my mother stands at the counter drinking a cup of coffee. She's wearing the beige skirt suit that she pulls out whenever she has to do something "official" like go down to the courthouse to pay her parking tickets. A gold link bracelet jangles noisily as she raises the cup to her lips. My father sits at the kitchen table, staring out the window and into the yard. I don't even need to go near him to know that the smell of stale scotch lingers in his wake, an invisible cloud partly covered up with cologne he slapped onto his cheeks and throat. I also know that he can't meet his own eyes in the mirror, that he stays up late at night and paces around the basement, a glass in one hand, while my mother lies in their bed, sleepless, waiting for some kind of release.

My father has gotten quieter and quieter over the past few weeks, while my mother has grown more animated, throwing herself into household projects with the zeal and focus of the newly converted. She's planted daffodil bulbs in a patch of soil at the far end of the yard, hauled years' worth of broken toys and junk out of the attic, cleaning the floorboards with Murphy's Oil Soap, her hair tied back with an old blue bandanna my father sometimes uses on the rare occasions he goes jogging. She bakes banana bread and chocolate chip cookies, flat and bland as communion wafers, stirs endless pots of chili, and bastes rump roasts. At dinner, I push my food around the circumference of my plate while a torrent falls from my mother's lips, the words rushing out to fill the empty spaces in the room where Luke hides. And the more she talks, the quieter my father and I become, the more distant.

"We have to leave in five minutes." My mother addresses this remark to my father, her tone vaguely annoyed. "You know we've got to be there by seven-thirty at the latest."

My father nods, his eyes clearing as he notices, maybe for the first time, that I've wandered into the room.

"I still don't understand why we have to do this." There's an edge to his voice. "Hasn't she been through enough?" He tilts his head in my direction, chin raised. She. I am a she now.

I have a name. My name is Alys Anne Aronson. My name is Alys. My name is AlysLukePsychoKillerAronson. This is my name.

"They want to make sure she's . . . integrated back into the school properly," my mother says, looking slightly frazzled as she shoves the milk back into the refrigerator, searching the countertop for her keys, moving stacks of newspapers and mail. Our housekeeper, Isobel, hasn't been here in almost a month, and the house is slowly groaning beneath the stacks of unruly papers, the thick layer of white dust coating the furniture. I heard somewhere that dust is composed of 99 percent skin, tiny flakes left in our wake. I wonder how much of Luke is left in these rooms, his skin abandoned in every corner. A sloughing.

"They just want to meet with us before she goes back to classes today. Under the circumstances," my mother says distractedly, "I think it's more than reasonable."

"Under the circumstances?" my father repeats slowly, swiveling to glare at her. "What the hell is that supposed to mean?"

My mother looks up, frozen.

He stands, pushing his chair back. The air in the kitchen is heavy as a lungful of smoke. Words are dangerous now.

"What *circumstances*?"

In a moment, anything might happen. And now I know that anything could.

Anything.

"We have to go," I say, stepping in between them, the air charged and electric. I pull my mother's car keys from the deep recesses of a plant on the edge of the counter, the tinkling sound of metal on metal breaking the spell, dirt lodging its way under my nails. My father blinks as if he doesn't quite know where he is, doesn't recognize his surroundings, the yellow kitchen, my mother's pottery lining the cabinets. "We're going to be late."

. . .

Driving into the parking lot, my body begins to shake, shutting down. Just the sight of that redbrick building in the daylight makes me feel like everything's sliding away, fast, my breathing shallow and forced. When we step out of the car, I hold on to the hood for a moment, trying to take slow, deep breaths. My mother's voice is insistent and meaningless, her hand on my arm. News vans are already parked just outside the gates, setting up, ready to document and exploit our reentry.

The show must go on . . .

As I move toward the building, I don't know if I'll be able to do it—walk in there again—and my footsteps trail off until I am barely moving, the ground warped and uneven. I imagine I can smell blood and powdery gunshots just outside the entrance, a residue. But the pavement is clean and unmarked, the red doors of the school shining with a fresh coat of paint, a cluster of raindrops clinging wetly to the metal.

Gunshots, Keith Rappaport said. Somebody has a gun out there. For real.

I heard later that Keith died in the hospital, shot in the chest right outside

(—did his glasses fall off, his head thrown back, body twisted on the floor, chest blown open in the blast?—)

the bio lab, where my brother had gone in order to kill himself, gun pressed against his forehead. The last stop.

Were you happy to go, Luke? To finally be rid of us all? Did you welcome that sharp blast, then nothingness, sinking into it like a dark pool, your head slowly slipping under?

I make it inside. I make it. The hallway is empty and reeks of an astringent mix of ammonia, floor wax, and new paint. The walls glisten ghostly white, the paint glossy and fresh. I reach out and touch it as I pass, slick beneath my hands, grounding me. Everything looks the same—the girls' bathroom at the end of the hall, the green linoleum underfoot—but there is a layer, a memory of what happened that rises up to the surface, distorting everything, a field of blurring images, the past and the present shifting before my eyes.

The principal, Mr. Clarke, ushers us into his office, and I sit down tentatively on an orange vinyl chair between my parents. He's wearing a pin-striped dress shirt and a black blazer, a tie knotted at his throat in a muted blue. Mr. Clarke has always had the build of a high school quarterback. But his face is drawn and thinner now, his cheekbones sharply etched above his ginger-colored beard. I picture the wound on his upper arm where fragments of bullets lodged, hiding beneath the crisp cotton, the bandage dotted with minute specks of blood. He takes a sip of coffee and smiles, his face tight. Uneasy. Because that's what we do now—we make people uncomfortable.

"How are you all doing?" He pushes the coffee cup to the

side and leans his elbows on his desk, the look in his eyes sympathetic if a bit removed.

My father glances away. The quiet in the room is overwhelming, and I don't know what to say. Somehow, "fine," the usual answer to stupid questions like these, seems ridiculous. We're not *fine*. Not even close.

Well, since you asked, Mr. Clarke, basically I stay up all night staring at the walls in my bedroom. I don't eat. I don't touch my violin, except to remove it then put it back in the case like a zombie. Sometimes I don't shower for days, because really, what's the point? Luke will still be dead even if I'm clean. And my father? He spends his nights emptying a liquor cabinet it took my parents twenty years to build. My mother copes by keeping herself as busy as possible, gardening, fussing, baking—basically pretending she's Martha Stewart. Oh, and did I mention that I've been seeing my dead brother everywhere? The bodies of the newly dead springing back to life? Yeah, I think that just about covers it . . .

"Things have been . . . difficult." My mother takes a deep breath, her voice wavering. "To say the least. But we're surviving."

I look down at my legs, play with a loose thread on one knee, wrapping it tightly around my index finger, cutting off the circulation entirely. The more I hurt, the better I feel.

"I'm so sorry for your loss," Mr. Clarke says, the prescribed response. You can almost set a watch by it. "I'm sure it's been an extremely difficult time for *all* of you." His tone is soothing, a vat of warm water or blood. I feel the heaviness of his gaze as it falls on me, a slow burn, but I don't, can't look up. What was barely tolerable before is now completely unbearable, the feeling of eyes on me. Judgment. *Don't look at me,* I think, the voice in my head a growl. *Just. Fucking. Don't.*

"I just want to make sure," he continues on, "that Alys is really ready to come back. Of course, we'll do everything in our power to support her—if that's what she wants."

There's more silence. I nod emphatically. I want. I cannot stand another minute in that house, waiting for Luke to appear again. Listening to my parents argue deep into the night, their eyes nailed to my face, watching me as if any moment I might disappear. And disappearing doesn't sound so bad those nights when I'm lying sleepless in my bed, the hours stretching out interminably.

"All right, then," he says, almost reluctantly. I feel like I've disappointed him in some way by coming back, that he was almost wishing I wouldn't.

It's easier that way, easier for everyone if you don't exist . . .

"But I'm not going to lie to you." Mr. Clarke looks over at my parents. "It's not going to be easy. People are going to judge her, blame her even, and though we'll do our best to head off any possible issues before they surface, we can't be with her twenty-four seven."

"Alys is not her brother," my father interjects. "She hasn't done anything wrong."

(—Haven't I? Isn't that what you were trying to tell me, Luke?—)

"Of course not," Mr. Clarke says quickly, in an attempt to mollify my father. "Of course she hasn't. But I'm afraid that won't make much difference to some people around here."

"What do you mean by that?" my mother asks nervously.

"Well, I mean that people are angry and looking for someone to blame, and some of them won't care that Alys had nothing to do with this . . . incident. Now, as I said, we will try to protect her as much as we can, but realistically, there's only so much we can do." Mr. Clarke sits back in his leather chair, one hand rubbing his left arm. I wonder if it still hurts, if the wound will ever really heal. Sure, it will scab over, the flesh knitting itself back together, but the scar will remain. Sometimes I wish that Luke had just gone ahead and pulled the trigger so my pain would be on the outside, visible, where everyone could see it. Not hidden away and imperceptible. A muted agony.

"Is Alys . . . seeing anyone? In order to help her . . . process what's happened?" Mr. Clarke treads lightly, his words stilted.

"Seeing . . . anyone?" my father repeats slowly, method-ically. "What do you mean by 'seeing anyone'?" His voice is short, clipped, and Mr. Clarke looks immediately apologetic, his face falling.

"I just meant a counselor or a therapist. Someone to help her come to terms with . . . what's happened recently."

"I don't want to see anyone," I blurt out before my father can speak again.

The thought of having to sit in some horrible beige room trying to explain what Luke did is enough to make me shudder once, hard. How can I explain Luke's actions to anyone else when I don't even understand why he did it, why he

(killed)

those people. I was his sister. If I don't know why he did it, no shrink with an annoyingly calm voice and a bunch of degrees hanging on the wall is going to be able to explain it to me.

Mr. Clarke's eyes are full of kindness, wrinkled at the corners. "We have people here, Alys, at school, that you can talk to, if you want—but only if you want. All you have to do is ask."

I nod briskly, my cheeks red and inflamed. It's bad enough that everyone thinks Luke was a psychopath. Now I'm the one they'll be watching, waiting to see if I slip over the edge.

"Now, then," Mr. Clarke says, getting down to business. "We'll have an assembly this morning, right when school reopens, and then classes will resume as usual, but with forty-five minute tracks instead of the usual fifty. At the assembly, I will make it clear in my remarks just where I stand on bullying and scapegoating—there will be a zero-tolerance policy in place."

Luke is standing at the back on the room, leaning against the door, arms crossed over his chest. Mr. Clarke just keeps on talking, my parents nodding in response. "Zero tolerance." He snorts. "He was always so full of shit." The scorn in his voice is enough to make my mouth fall open, though no one seems to notice. Luke points at Mr. Clarke's arm and smirks. "I should've aimed higher."

The blood drains out of my face. I can feel my cheeks go numb.

When I finally tune back in, Mr. Clarke is wrapping up his speech. He shoots me a broad smile that seems a bit forced and says, "We're so glad to have you back." He pushes his chair away from the desk and stands up, walking over to me and holding his arms out. I know he is only trying to be kind, but I am stiff in his embrace, my limbs unyielding, afraid to exhale, my heart beating fast beneath my ribs. His shirt smells of laundry detergent, coffee, and the cigarette he snuck in preparation for this meeting. My mother is crying again, tears cracking her carefully applied mask. I close my eyes and think about graduation. If things had been different, Mr. Clarke would be standing in front of a podium, shaking my brother's hand as Luke crossed the stage, black gown sweeping the floor, his diploma held up in triumph.

You should have aimed higher, Luke. You should have.

But not with that gun.

TWO

As the gym starts to fill for assembly, I watch the crowd stream in. Some people are wearing spirit shirts—T-shirts with our school's name emblazoned across the front and a picture of a cougar, our mascot, stamped on the back. I sit at the top of the bleachers, trying to be as inconspicuous as possible, my heart ka-thumping every time a pair of eyes lands on me, looking me over. I crane my neck, searching for Ben, wanting to see him, my hands trembling at the thought of it, and at the same time, wishing that I didn't have to. There is nothing I could do or say that will take away the loss, Katie snatched away to the underworld, pulled to the ocean floor, her eyes wrapped in seaweed.

The air smells of floor polish, paint, and the heat of bodies filling the space, the sweet, fruity reek of gum and mingling perfumes creating a toxic funk. I stare at the floor mostly, at the red and blue lines embossed on the shiny wooden surface, and try to pretend that none of it matters. Their glances burn, and the whispering begins, mouths hidden behind hands, voices dipping toward me then flitting away. The bleachers begin to fill up, and I'm given a wide berth. The bench I'm sitting on remains empty.

A freshman I know vaguely gives me a tentative smile, her braces shining metallic in the harsh overhead lighting, but when she moves to sit down, her friend grabs her arm, pulling her back. "Don't sit next to *her*," she says, tossing her auburn curls. "C'mon." She grabs the girl by the hand, leading her away. The freshman looks over her shoulder, and I try to smile, but my lips are stuck in cement. I knew that if I came back to school, I wouldn't exactly be welcomed with open arms. But now that it's happened, I'm shaken. I wanted the everyday sameness of a daily schedule: lunch at noon, the alarm clock ringing at seven a.m. But there's nothing normal about any of this. I don't belong here any more than I belong in my house, in the wide world, on this strange, tilting planet.

You should've just killed me, Luke. Why didn't you?

Why didn't you just finish the job?

Delilah walks in wearing jeans and a loose violet hoodie. My heart expands in a shower of sparks and silver light at the sight of her waxen face, her eyes ringed with darkness. She looks up, and I raise one hand in a wave, but she just stands there, blank-faced and silent, before turning to Alana Jenkins (blond, cheer squad, plastic), grabbing her by the hand, and sitting down in the front row as if I'm invisible, as if I don't exist at all. My hand lowers slowly, my arm numb. I bite my bottom lip, happy for the pain, the blood that is suddenly dotting my mouth. Everything in me sinks all at once, deflating rapidly. I hate Alana Jenkins. Even though Delilah and I haven't talked since that night she came over, I still held out hope that once we were back to school, somehow, things would be the same as they've always been. Arm in arm walking through the halls, the scratch of her voice in my ear each night as we went over the day's events. What am I without her? The thought panics me, the walls closing in like a trash compactor, the room getting tighter and tighter.

You will not cry, I tell myself, turning my attention to Mr. Clarke, who has taken his place behind the podium and taps the microphone with an index finger. *You will not even think about crying.* There is a loud shriek that reverberates through the room—feedback from the mike, I know, but, like most people here, I recoil a bit, wincing. I wonder if Luke is smiling wherever he is, happy that even just weeks after, probably for years, his actions will have the ability to terrify us.

Maybe forever.

"Welcome back," Mr. Clarke says. "I can't tell you how glad I am to see all of your faces sitting here today, back home at Plainewood High. And make no mistake—Plainewood IS home. And despite the tragedy we've experienced, no one can take that away from us."

The crowd begins to cheer, along with a few whoops, and I see hands raised in the air, fists clenched.

"We've been through a terrible, senseless tragedy," Mr. Clarke continues, his voice low and somber, "and no one's trying to make light of that—least of all me." His face blanches a little, as if in sudden, sharp pain, and for the first time I think about how hard it must be for him, like all of us, to be back in this place, the center of so much suffering. "But now we need to turn our attention to the present and knit our community back together again—and the only way that's going to happen is with love. With forgiveness."

The word rings out, echoing through the room, and I flinch slightly, shifting on the wooden bench.

"Forgiveness is the only way we can move forward and begin to heal—as a school, as a community, as human beings."

I can hear the soft wind of our collective breathing, the rasp of limbs rubbing against one other, the rustle of legs nervously crossed and uncrossed. The word "forgiveness," said just like that. As if it could be that easy. As if we could all just snap our fingers and return to business as usual, turn our attention to prom, SATs, the all-important question of who to sit with in the cafeteria at lunch. *"Yeah right,"* I hear a girl a row in front of me whisper, the venom in her voice unmistakable. She turns around and glares at me, her dark eyes boring holes into my forehead, and I stare straight ahead, concentrating on breathing in and out, the hot air leaving my lungs before I suck it back inside me.

"This isn't about assigning blame." Mr. Clarke pauses, his eyes sweeping the crowd. His expression is grave, and I can see that he's starting to sweat, beads standing out on his forehead. "In fact, such actions would only impede our progress as a school and a community, and let me be quite clear: that kind of behavior will not be tolerated." He seems to look straight at me, and I drop my head, cheeks burning. "This is about moving on. Not forgetting what has happened, but not allowing it to define us as a school either. Because we are MORE than this senseless tragedy."

A slow clap breaks out, hands smacking together in the sickening sound of flesh against flesh. It sounds halfhearted. What does he expect? That he would stand in front of us, say a few words, and then things would magically snap back to the way they were? But it's too late for that—we've crossed some sort of line and now, no matter where we go, what we do, who we eventually become, we will take the shooting with us, dragging it behind us like an overfilled suitcase, dirty underwear and socks spilling out in a tangle of filthy colors.

Mr. Clarke says a few more words, tells us he loves us (*"Bullshit,"* Luke whispers, his breath tickling my ear), mentions that there will be counselors on campus until the end of the school year, and steps back from the mike with the magic words, "Assembly dismissed." I notice that after he utters the word "counseling," there are a few snickers, the sound of coughing, and when I find the courage to look around, I see that some people are crying, faces wet, their arms draped around one another. Some are steely-eyed, bracing themselves against pain, but in the dazed, vacant expressions I see my own. All around me there is sudden motion, people getting up, the sound of feet on the wood louder than my own thoughts, louder than the voices in my head telling me that no one wants me here. I make my way down the bleachers, keeping my eyes trained on the floor, and behind me I hear the sound of noses being blown messily into tissues. *The guy was a fucking freak,* one voice whispers at my back, the words branding my skin like a hot iron. *Asshole murderer.*

(—they don't know how he helped me with my math homework, the funny faces he drew for me in the margins, the carved wooden box he made for my mom's birthday last fall, the lines graceful and intricate. They see only the gun, the pull of the trigger, the newspaper, his senior yearbook picture on the news. But it's not all black and white; it's not, it's not, it's NOT—)

I keep moving, knowing that if I stop I will cry. I will not cry in front of them. I will not. I think of ice, great sheets of it, frozen in opaqueness, of large doors of iron twisted with spikes, keeping out what's unwanted, of a blizzard that swirls around the fractured chambers of my heart.

THREE

After the assembly, we have a break before first period begins, and I wander out the front door of the school, oblivious to the buzz and chatter surrounding me. The rain has stopped its punishing assent, but the sky is streaked with charcoal-gray and violet clouds that tell me more waterworks are on the way. *If I just stay locked inside myself, I'll be all right.* I say this over and over, repeating the words in my head until they blur together and become as meaningless as the cacophony of voices surrounding me.

Out in the parking lot, I notice a red car draped in flowers, stuffed toys, balloons, cards dotting the windshield, and I float toward it, as if in a trance. A makeshift shrine. I would know that car anywhere—it's Kitty Ellison's, the license plate spelling out KITTY E in large black letters. Kitty is

(was)

a senior. Early acceptance to Princeton, long blond hair, and a body that made boys stop speaking when she swished past. But the thing about Kitty that separated her from a life of complete and total banality was that she was nice. She wasn't cliquey, didn't put others down to make herself feel better. She was just . . . sweet. Tutored kids after school not just to pad her college applications, but because she thought *it was the right thing to do.* Didn't suck up for college recs. She didn't have to. Everyone—and I mean everyone—in Plainewood practically worshipped the ground she walked on. And now she's gone.

(—will I find her under my bed tonight when I turn back the covers, her bloodless face rising out of the darkness—)

There are people milling around near the car, and I walk through them, drawn to the shiny red finish, enticing as a poison apple. I want to walk up to my pain and impale myself on it, drag a knife across my skin until it splits under a serrated blade. I imagine the relief it would bring, the blood streaming out of my body until my brain fills with whiteness.

Melissa Anderson, Kitty's best friend, is standing next to the car, tracing designs on the hood with one finger. Her black hair hangs past her shoulders, held away from her face with a thick band, and a gray peacoat swallows her thin frame, toned and athletic from afternoons spent in the pool with the rest of the swim team. Her face is set in concentration, tears falling from her eyes although her expression is still. If you didn't see the water streaking her cheeks in slow, silent rivulets, you wouldn't know she was upset at all. Watching her, I feel like I'm eavesdropping on something horribly private, and I start to move away, my feet scraping against the pavement. Melissa wipes her face with one hand and sniffs loudly, turning to face me, her green eyes oblivious at first but then widening in gradual recognition. She looks like she's seen a ghost, and maybe that's what I am now. A phantom. Something to be feared and avoided.

"You," she breathes, her lips barely moving. "You're . . ." Her lip curls in a grimace, as if saying the next word is revolting or even painful. "His sister." The word is like a lead weight falling from a great height. "Aren't you?"

I am caught in the headlights, unsure if I should answer at all. Is there a right answer? I don't know anymore. Panicked. I nod once, a quick jerk, shame flooding my cheeks in a rush of blood, the capillaries beneath the skin expanding.

I drop my eyes to the ground, and she looks over at the car. Once she glances away, I feel better, the air returning to my lungs.

"She was my best friend."

Her voice is low and raspy from tears and a lack of sleep. I can feel her voice in my own mouth, the cadence of it. She stares at the car, the raindrops glinting on the finish as if it holds all the answers, an oracle. A mirage that might fade into oblivion if she tears her gaze away, even for a second. People have gathered around and are watching us closely. I hear the hiss of whispers, judgment falling over me like a fur cloak, the rows of gleaming black pelts knitted together, weighing me down.

"She died right here, you know," Melissa says, her voice wooden. "She was trying to get to her car."

The car stands there patiently, waiting for me to answer, the red paint pulsing under the foreboding sky.

"I know," I say. "I'm sorry."

Because I am. Sorry. Sorry for her, sorry for me—sorry for us all. Not that it does anyone any good.

Her head whips around. Her long dark hair blows into her eyes and she brushes it away impatiently with her fingertips. "You're *sorry*? That's all you have to *say*?"

"I don't know," I mutter, looking away from her cold eyes. Something inside me wants to run, to turn abruptly and take off, feet sliding on the wet grass. But I stay. "What do you want me to say?"

She takes a step toward me, her expression distorted in anger, her face red and strained, the veins in her neck clearly visible beneath the skin.

"What do I *want* you to say?"

Everything is moving fast, too fast, and I take a step back, then another, my shoes hitting the curb, my arms reaching out into the air frantically before regaining my balance.

155

"What do I *want* you to say?" she repeats, grabbing my arm. Her touch burns like a naked flame. "I want to know why—*why* the fuck did he do it? *Why?*"

Whyyyyyyyyyyyyyyyyyyyyyyyyyyyyyyyyyyyyyyyyyyyyyyyyyyyyyyy yyyyyyyyyyyyyyyyyyyyyyyy?

She is shaking me, hands on my shoulders, my teeth banging together. I can't move. Her eyes stare into mine, full of hatred, her spittle hitting my cheeks. I go limp in her grasp, my limbs collapsing in on themselves. *Do it,* I think. *Tear me to pieces.*

"You're gonna let her get away with that?" Luke's hot breath, a tickling like tiny ants crawling over my skin. I close my eyes, gritting my teeth to block him out, the scent of rotting flowers filling my throat.

"I don't know," I hear myself finally whisper. "I don't know why."

She stops, her face still close to mine, so close that I can see the tiny dots of sweat on her upper lip, the smeared black eyeliner on the left corner of her eyelid. She is breathing hard, and all at once she lets me go, releasing her hands from my shoulders and backing away. She looks down at her hands, holding them out from her body as if they don't quite belong to her, as if she's never seen them before.

"What the hell is going on?"

It's Ben, even more beautiful than I remember. His dark hair is pushed back from his face, and his sudden, forceful intensity burns through the gloom in the sky above, vanquishing it. It is everything I can do not to sink to my knees at the very sight of him. I try to open my mouth but I cannot speak, can't move. "It's okay," I manage to say, even though what's going on at this moment is clearly pretty fucking far from anything that could even vaguely be considered okay.

"You're going to stick up for her? Is that it? After what he did? Her piece-of-shit brother?" She crosses her arms over her breasts, her bottom lip pushed out in a sullen pout. Even exhausted, even with her dark clothes and lack of sleep, she is still beautiful standing there beneath the falling sky, her eyes like green leaves coated in dew, and I wonder if Ben notices, if he sees her the way I do right now, at this very moment. Beautiful. Tragic. Defiant.

"What *he* did," Ben yells, stepping closer to her. "Not *her*!"

"Same difference," Melissa scoffs.

"It is *not*, and you know it. Or if you don't, you really *should*." Ben points a finger at her chest, his jaw so tense that I can see the muscles working under the skin.

"I can't believe that after what that murderer did to your family, you're going to take her side." Melissa shakes her head slowly, in disgust. "That's just really pathetic."

"I'm not taking sides," Ben says, breathing deep. The tone is the one he always uses when he's trying to get a grip on himself, rein in his emotions. "I'm just trying to move on. Just like you. Just like Alys—just like everyone else here."

He grabs me by the hand, and at the touch of his skin, I almost cry out. The feel of his hand in mine is like climbing into a warm bed on a cold night, like diving off the end of a pier on a hot summer day and knowing for certain that the water will rise up to meet you, the cool, soft liquid cushioning your fall.

"C'mon," he says, pulling me along with him. I follow him blindly as a child, one step behind.

We walk behind the school, Ben pulling me around the corner. No one follows us, for which I'm grateful. The back parking lot is full of cars, and for the first time I notice how cold I am, my cheeks frozen and numb from the wind that rakes across campus, the gale like millions of tiny needles hitting my skin. He leans against the brick wall, exhaling loudly, and drops my hand, our connection severed. He props one Converse sneaker up against the brick, shoving his hands in the pockets of his leather jacket. I want to touch him, but I'm unsure. I want to pull his jacket apart and push my hands beneath the soft blue shirt he wears until I reach bare skin, slide my palms over the heat of his chest, kiss him until we don't know where we are or what has happened, the world falling away.

But looking at the way he stares out over the parking lot, avoiding my face, I know that I can't. That he won't. That if I try, he will push me away, and it will hurt.

"Are you okay?" He doesn't wait for my answer before continuing. "She was totally out of line."

I am silent. Listening to my own heart beating under my clothes, the relentless thrum of it.

He turns his head to look at me sharply.

"You know she was, Alys."

Now it's my turn to look away. I am melting under the directness of his stare, those eyes so richly fringed with lashes that I'd often asked him jokingly if he was wearing mascara.

"I'm not so sure." My voice wavers, and I brace myself to keep from crying, tensing the muscles in my body one by one.

"Nothing that happened was your fault."

He says this forcefully, as if he really believes it, and I wonder how he can be so sure about me, about anything at all. Especially since Katie . . .

(Oh, Katie)

"I'm so sorry about . . ." I cannot finish. I cannot say her name aloud, in front of him. It seems obscene. "About everything."

Ben sighs, shuffling his feet. "You don't need to apologize, Alys. You didn't *do* anything wrong. I told you."

We watch as a car pulls into the parking lot, and the slamming of car doors echoes in the air. I watch as a flock of birds fly overhead, darting and dancing, their bodies aligned in a V.

"Then why can't we . . ." My voice falls off, and in the

quiet between us I'm aware of how silly my words sound, how shallow.

"Look, I'm just trying to get through the day, the next hour, the next five minutes. Every time I think about her, the way she . . ." He looks at me again, and this time I let him, even though it feels like a sword piercing my heart.

(died)

"I can't take it. I break down all over again. It's endless, you know? There's no bottom."

His eyes shimmer with tears, and I realize that in all the years I've known him, I've never seen Ben cry. Not even when he fell off his bike when he was eight, shattering his arm in two places, and Luke and I had to carry him home. Not even then.

I nod, my hand reaching out to touch his face, my fingers stopping inches from his skin and pulling back as if I've been burned. I cannot touch him. I know this. But the ache is there, taunting me like a phantom limb.

"We can't . . . be like we were." He says this slowly, the words precise. Exacting.

"Why not?"

Even though I know the answer, can predict what he will say, I have to ask, to hear him say it out loud. I close my eyes for a second before opening them again, waiting for the words that will lacerate what's left of my heart.

"We just can't." He shrugs his shoulders as if the question

is too ridiculous to contemplate seriously. "I don't blame you for anything—really, I don't. But I can't go back."

I bite my lip and look up at the sky, willing myself not to cry. My chest throbs so intensely that I wonder for a second if I'm having a heart attack.

"I don't want things to be like this," I whisper, sniffing loudly, my lips swollen, my nose beginning to run in the cold air.

"I don't either."

"Then let's not," I say, my hands working without my permission as I finally reach out and pull him to me, my lips finding his. All I want is him, and for just this once, the need overpowers my fear. For a split second, his mouth opens, his tongue touching mine with a groan that seems to come all the way from the deep recesses of his body before he shoves me away, wiping his mouth roughly on the sleeve of his jacket. And with that one action, something stops dead in me and hardens, crystallizing.

Just like that, he wipes me away.

"Goddammit, Alys, what did I just *say*? We can't do this anymore. *I* can't. It has to end. My sister is dead. She's dead and she's never coming back. And Luke . . ." He breaks off, unable to go on. Tears fall from the corners of his eyes onto his jacket, and he drops his head. I want to put my arms around him and hold on tight, but I can't. His body, so familiar, is now off-limits. Contraband.

"His loss," Luke whispers, a smug satisfaction coloring his voice. "I always thought you could do *a lot* better . . ."

I ignore him and force myself to stay in the moment, here with Ben.

"I'm sorry," I say for what feels like the millionth time. I know, even as my mouth forms the words, that I will say them for the rest of my life. Forever. That there will never be a time when I am not, in some small way, apologizing for the damage my brother has wrought. Luke is dead too, like Katie, I know, but this makes no difference. My grief will always be less important.

We stand there as the first bell rings, signaling that the day has officially begun, listening to the shuffling of feet as people make their way inside the building, the creaking of the front door of the school as it opens and shuts, my eyes focused on the clouds beginning to break up and dissipate on the horizon. Ben and I stand together, side by side, so close we could reach out and touch each other easily—so easily. An uncharted vista of barren tundra stands between us, patiently waiting, our hearts stranded miles apart.

FOUR

Somehow, I make it through the first two tracks of the day, ducking into the girls' bathroom between classes to hide in the stalls, leaning my forehead against the blessedly cool metal wall, Ben's anguished face filling my mind each time I shut my eyes, his hands pushing me away roughly. I can still feel his touch on my skin, and I rub my arms distractedly, pretending they are his hands, his fingers curled around my bones.

At lunch, I stand awkwardly in the cafeteria, balancing a Coke and a bag of pretzels on an orange tray, unsure of where to go or who to sit with. It feels strange not to be sitting with Delilah on the steps outside in the quad, tilting our faces up to the sunlight, talking so fast that we run out of air, inhaling in deep gasps between sentences. Practicing in the music room, deserted at lunchtime, the violin warm in my hands, almost alive, breathing in time with the notes that fall from my fingers. Sneaking off campus with Ben, popping French fries into his open mouth in between kisses. My stomach hurts, remembering these things, and the air in the cafeteria smells of the slightly rancid stink of hot dogs and baked beans. People stare at me as I stand there, and I try to act like I don't care, my face impassive. Finally, I ditch the stupid tray and just carry the soda and pretzels in my hands and walk out of the cafeteria, stopping at the stairwell next to the gym, sitting down on the cold steps. Even though I'm thirsty, I don't open the can. I just sit there in the quiet of the stairwell, listening to the clatter of the cafeteria just beyond, my stomach gnawing and churning in a way that is anything but gentle. I know I need to eat, but I cannot bring myself to tear open the bag, imagining the pretzels turning to dust on my tongue, sticking to my molars like a strange, bready adhesive.

"Hey."

A voice reverberates from somewhere behind me, and I twist around, craning my neck. A boy stands at the top of the stairs, looming over me, his hair outlined in a golden glow from the light coming through the window behind him, a backpack slung over one shoulder. He makes his way down, his long legs moving quickly.

"What's up?" Riley sits next to me, folding his lanky body like an accordion.

"Oh, you know," I say, reaching over and finally opening my Coke. "The usual: math and history—followed by lunch and total social annihilation."

Riley laughs, reaching into his backpack and pulling out a sandwich. I picture his mother in the kitchen early this morning, carefully mitigating the thick spread with rivers of deep grape jelly, the sky still shimmering with the last flicker of stars.

"Yeah," he says, pulling the plastic wrap aside and taking a huge bite. "Things haven't been that great on my end either."

"Like how?" I pick up the bag of pretzels and think for a minute about opening it, then put it down again.

"Either people won't talk to me at all, or if they do—"

"They just want to know if you knew anything, right?" I finish the thought before the words can leave his lips. "If you saw it coming."

Riley nods, his mouth full and sticky. He reaches over and grabs my Coke, swigging a mouthful of fizzy liquid. He wipes his lips on the back of his hand, and I can see that his sandwich is already almost a memory. Guess all the drama isn't hurting *his* appetite any.

"And Janelle broke up with me last night, in a fucking *text*, so there's that."

Janelle and Riley have been dating since the middle of their junior year. All I know about Janelle is that she's some kind of insanely talented gymnast. Whenever I see her, the word *severe* comes to mind—she walks through the halls with extreme concentration, as if she's perched high up on a balance beam competing for the gold. I want to ask what happened, but something in his face tells me not to. He crumples up the plastic wrap and shoves it into his bag, removing a small package of cookies.

"Whatever," he says, shrugging and pulling the cookies open. "We're graduating soon anyway."

Whatever that means. In boy-speak it probably works out to a combination of *I'm hungry* and *I'm going to pretend I don't give a crap.*

"What about college?" I ask, changing the subject.

"What about it?" he answers with a snort, slightly defensive. He reaches in and grabs a cookie, looking at it for a minute, turning it over in his hand before taking a bite.

"Are you excited?" Riley doesn't answer, just chews as if he wants to pulverize the cookie completely, the muscles in his jaw tensed beneath his skin.

Riley won a basketball scholarship to Penn State in November, full ride all four years. I remember the day he found out, how I'd opened the front door to find him standing there, waving the acceptance e-mail he'd printed out like a flag. I can still hear the whoop Luke let out as he bounded down the stairs, pushing me out of the way, the hard slapping sounds of their hands against each other's backs.

"It all just seems like such bullshit now—after everything that's happened. I mean, what's the point?" Riley swallows the cookie, having inhaled it in two bites. "So I go to college, play ball, get a good job when I get out so I can move up in the world?" His tone is full of mocking condescension. "Marry some chick I can't stand the sight of after a few years, and watch as she pops out a couple of kids I never see 'cause I'm working all the time—just like my dad. Then, after about twenty years, they'll give me a gold watch and I'll retire, drop dead of a heart attack as I'm dragging the trash to the curb one morning." He stops, looking me in the face. "What's the fucking point of it all, anyway?"

I've never seen Riley this angry. Riley is always, if nothing else, easygoing. If I had to use one phrase to describe him, it would probably be *laid-back*.

"I mean, Luke got into MIT," he continues, the plastic bag crinkling in his hands loudly, echoing in the stairwell, "and where did it get him?" He looks at me almost accusingly, waiting for some kind of answer.

"You're not Luke, Riley," I say quietly, dropping my eyes to the floor.

There is silence as I try to think of what to say next, coming up as empty as the white wall behind me.

"You doing okay?" He keeps his eyes forward as he asks the question, his tone nonchalant—deliberately so. "You never texted me back."

"I guess," I say as he holds out the bag of cookies to me. I reach in and take one. "Not really. Not at all, actually. Melissa Anderson cornered me in the parking lot earlier, demanding some kind of answer. Like I have one."

The cookie is chocolate chip. It lies, small, dry, and crunchy, in the palm of my hand. Its brownness is reassuring somehow, the chips studding the surface like tiny moles. It smells of comfort, of family, of Luke and I fighting over cookie dough on late Sunday afternoons when we were little, a yellow ceramic bowl between us, sugar crystals spilled over the counter.

"Seriously?" Riley shoots me a look of incredulity laced with irritation.

I nod, biting into the cookie, which breaks apart like sawdust on my tongue.

"Well, that was pretty screwed up," he muses, licking the crumbs from his lips.

"I don't know," I say slowly. "I'm not so sure."

(—*Kitty Ellison sprawled on the asphalt, the back of her blond head a star shot out—*)

Riley swallows hard, his Adam's apple moving fluidly.

"I'm not even gonna dignify that with a response," he says finally, pushing the bag over to me, the plastic rustling like fire. "You should eat something." I ignore it and we sit there mutely for a while, his body so close to mine that I can smell soap mixed with the sharp tang of sweat.

"I miss him," he says quietly, staring straight ahead, unblinking.

"I do too," I say. And I do. I miss Luke's presence in the house, the sound of him moving around in his room, just one wall away. I miss his smile, on the rare occasions it made an appearance, the way it would light up his whole face so that you could see, just for a moment, how good-looking he was, how alive. "But I feel like I'm not allowed to. After what he's done."

"Yeah," Riley answers, his voice husky with emotion. He turns to face me, searching for a connection, some kind of understanding. "That's it. That's exactly how it is."

I hold very still, trying not to breathe.

The bell rings once, shrilly, breaking the moment. Riley gathers up his backpack and the cookies, tossing the bag at me before I can protest. I catch it one-handed, and he grins, his face opening up like sudden sunlight after a hard rain. "So you have something for later," he says. "All you girls are getting too damn skinny."

I blush, stuffing them in my bag, where I know they'll remain for the rest of the day, my chemistry book grinding them to fine powder. I think of Luke nestled in the sanctuary of his coffin, his dried bones separating from the husk of his body, disintegrating further with each day the sun rises in the sky, each passing hour that ticks away, how we will never be able to put him back together again.

FIVE

When I get home, the house is quiet, and I am greeted by the aroma of pot roast, the one dish of my mother's that I love unreservedly. A mix of onions, tomatoes, and the caramelized smell of browning meat rise from the stockpot on the stove, and a plate of brownies dusted in powdered sugar waits patiently on the kitchen counter. I pick one up and hold the fudgy heft of it in my palm before setting it back down again. More baked goods. All the carbs in the world won't fix what's happened, and I wonder why my mother, who before now engaged in this activity maybe twice a year—if we were lucky—is suddenly so compelled toward the kitchen, buying butter in bulk at Costco, hoisting economy-sized bags of flour and brown sugar into a metal cart. If she's trying for mother of the year, it's too late. Luke's gone, and I'm the only one left. All the pastries in the world won't change what he's done, or make me forget.

I hear noise coming from the basement, the sound of something dropped on the cement floor, a trail of music, and I follow it downstairs, the steps creaking as I descend, a piano melody growing louder, a minor key gaining momentum, clawing at my chest. My mother sits at her potter's wheel, which spins frantically, molding a lump of clay with her fingers, the long, vertical shape rising triumphantly out of the muck. She is deep in concentration, her head bent over her work. She's wearing what I like to think of as her artist uniform—clay-stained jeans and a white dress shirt that used to belong to my father a million years ago, the sleeves rolled up and splattered with red clay and the various shades of glaze she's experimented with over the years. Slate gray. China blue. Bloodred. Pale gold. Joni Mitchell plays on the stereo in the corner, her reedy voice needling my skin.

Oh, I wish I had a river I could skate away on . . .

My mother takes her foot off the pedal, and the wheel stops, her hand coming down to smash the tower of clay, ruining it, a long sigh escaping her throat. She stares at the mess she's created, reaching out to stroke the flattened clay with one finger.

I made my baby say good-bye . . .

"Mom?"

She looks up, startled, her eyes blinking steadily behind

the black-framed glasses she always wears when she's work-ing. She needs bifocals but, vain to the core, struggles along with the same glasses she's had for four years. "Bifocals," she tells me often, "are for grandmas, which, in case you haven't noticed, I most certainly am *not*."

"Alys! Did you just get home?" She looks worried, as if by not waiting by the door with a glass of milk she's some-how failed some complicated maternal test. She wipes her hands on a white towel, and stands up, wavering, uncertain if she should hug me or let me be. She points one finger at the ceiling. "I made you some brownies—they're upstairs on the kitchen counter." The piano sprinkles its notes through the room, the vocals fading out as the track ends, the quiet suddenly oppressive. I haven't heard my mother listen to Joni Mitchell in years. Luke made fun of her so mercilessly over the last few years for her "hippie music" that she mostly rel-egated the CDs to a drawer—at least whenever he was home.

"I saw them," I say, and walk over to the bookshelf lin-ing the back of the room before she can hug me, the shelves crammed with pots and vases. "I'm not really hungry right now."

"Well, maybe later." I hear the soft slapping sound of her moccasins on the floor, and then her hand is on my back, the scent of flour and sugar rising from her skin. I move away from her touch, picking up a small shallow bowl, the glaze green as the moss at the bottom of a swamp, swirling into blackness. "Where's Dad?" The house feels eerily quiet. I listen hard but hear nothing overhead. For the last week or so he's insisted each night at dinner that he'll go back to work soon, but each morning I find him at the kitchen table, an empty glass at his elbow, ice melting at the bottom.

She avoids my eyes. "I don't know. He must've left while I was cooking. I'm sure he'll be back soon." Her words wobble unsteadily on her tongue, and she doesn't sound sure of anything, much less my father's eventual return.

"When are you going back to the gallery?" I ask, watching her expression shift to slight annoyance at my question.

"I don't know, Alys." Her hands are in her hair now, pulling the bulk of it over one shoulder, her fingers twisting the strands tightly together until they resemble a length of coarse rope. "I'm not sure if I'll ever go back, to tell you the truth."

"Why?" I ask, although I already know the answer.

"Elena feels my presence might be a bit . . . distracting right now, and I tend to agree with her."

Elena is my mom's boss. They bicker incessantly, but only because they are so totally similar—opinionated, artistic, driven. They even dress kind of alike, favoring the same long strands of colored beads wound round their wrists and necks. "You do?" I raise one eyebrow, broadcasting my skepticism.

"I do," she says without hesitation, and I wonder if she really believes what she's saying, or if she's trying to convince not only me, but herself too. "Besides," she continues wryly,

"I think we all know that selling paintings of sunsets and constipated-looking dogs wasn't exactly my life's work."

She turns away so that only her profile is visible. But I don't have to see her face to know that she's lying. Even though she grumbles about her job nearly all of the time, I know, despite her frustrations, she loves going to work every day. It was in the way she strode around the house in the mornings, her heels clicking purposefully against the floors, the look of vindication in her eyes when she sold a painting or acquired a piece she actually admired. And when she was feeling especially gracious, she admitted that just to have a job around art was a respite in a town she always considered too small, too quaint. Not edgy enough. Now edgy is *all* we are.

"So, how was school?" She seems almost chipper as she changes the subject, and I wonder if it is as exhausting to her as it is to me, this endless playacting.

"How do you *think* it was?" I turn the bowl over in my hands, one finger tracing my mother's signature etched into the bottom, the hardened clay rough against my skin.

I hear her sigh, and I close my eyes briefly, her footsteps reverberating against the cement floor as she walks to her desk, tucked into the corner. I hear the chair creak as she sits down and the sound of a match being struck, the smell of sulfur. When I turn around, she's sitting with her knees drawn up to her chest, smoking a cigarette. In that pose, she looks younger somehow, like a girl again, her limbs folded neatly as paper.

"You're *smoking* now?" I ask, incredulous. My mother has been lecturing us on the perils of smoking for years, and has even said on occasion that she'd rather that we grew up to become Republicans than smokers, which probably tells you everything you need to know about her.

I watch as she tilts her head, blowing smoke at the ceiling. "I smoked before you were born. I have one every once in a while, when I feel like it. So get that look off your face."

I have never, even once, come home and smelled cigarette smoke in our house, or on my mother's clothes. I feel dizzy, the world suddenly unfamiliar again. There is a strange woman smoking in my basement who claims to be my mother, though at this moment I'm pretty sure all bets are off.

"Besides," she says, taking a drag and blowing the smoke toward the ceiling in a perfect ring, "I'm an adult."

"Oh, so that will make it okay when you keel over from cancer?"

She shoots me an annoyed look through all the smoke, and promptly changes the subject.

"Did you see Ben today at school? Or Delilah?"

At the mention of Ben's name, something shuts down inside me, some vital mechanism, and all of a sudden I'm exhausted. I flop down into the chair behind her potter's wheel, one foot toying with the pedal.

"Yeah," I whisper, clearing my throat to make room for the words. "D just acted like I didn't exist, and Ben . . ." My voice trails off, and I step forcefully on the pedal, making the wheel spin in circles for a few seconds with a loud hum. "Well, he doesn't want anything to do with me either. Not really. And who could blame him?" I look at the ruined lump of clay so I don't have to meet my mother's eyes, fully aware that if I see any sympathy or emotion reflected there, I will start to cry.

"That . . . is very disappointing," my mother says, her breath coming out in a long hiss, the smoke circling her slender frame.

"Tell me about it."

"Alys," she begins gingerly, as if walking into enemy territory, "are you sure you want to finish up at Plainewood after everything that's happened? You could go stay with Grandma for a while, and finish the school year there if you want. I could call her tonight."

I have thought of this myself many times since the night I heard my parents arguing down here, turning the idea over in my mind like a shiny silver coin.

"I don't want to go anywhere.

(I don't?)

"I'd have to come back here sooner or later, and then what? Besides, my audition is at the end of May. And if I went to Grandma's, I wouldn't be able to rehearse with Grace beforehand. It doesn't make any sense."

As soon as the words leave my mouth, I regret them almost immediately. I would never admit it to my mother, but it would be a relief to start over someplace fresh, no history, no one staring when I walk down the street, no insults lashing my back in the locker room. And despite the fact that I haven't played since the

(shooting)

I don't want to give up hope entirely that I might be able to stand on the stage in a month's time and play, face the row of judges seated out in the darkness. But it's not just the audition—I'm not ready to relegate everything to the past—Ben, Delilah, Luke—my whole stupid, pointless life up until now. It's small and broken, but it's what I have left.

"Maybe the audition can wait, Alys," my mother says in a voice that's soft, reasonable, the tone she uses when she's trying to cajole, to pull me in. "There's always next year. And even if you came back a few months from now, after the summer's over, maybe that would be enough time to . . . let things die down."

My forehead wrinkles as the words leave her lips. Enough time. As if the passing of time itself would be enough to negate what has happened, the damage Luke has left in his wake. My mother has always been the one to push me when it comes to my playing, applying for programs, competitions. This is the first time I've ever heard her insinuate that music might not be the most important thing in my life, some kind of ticket out.

"Die down?" My own blatant disbelief bounces off the

walls of the basement, reverberating in a way that strikes me as harsh, unkind even. "Do you really think this will *ever* die down? After what he did?"

My mother crushes out her cigarette in the top of a jar of glaze with a series of sharp jagged movements, her expression both steely and far away. She won't look at me.

I wish I had a river I could skate away on . . .

My phone buzzes with a text, and when I pull it from my pocket, my heart jumps at the sight of Delilah's name and the words that follow it: *Meet me at First Presbyterian. 8 p.m.* A smile pulses at the corners of my mouth. The image of Delilah stepping foot in a church is just about as incongruous as that of a six-year-old dressed as a prostitute. Delilah's only concession to religion is basically Christmas, where the only thing she worships are the presents piled under the tree. As I reread her message, a blanket of confusion falls over me. Why a *church*? Suddenly, I'm nervous, my senses on high alert. When I raise my head, I'm almost surprised to see my mother still there, the acrid smell of tobacco permeating the room. The remnants of a white veil drift between us, and I cannot see my mother's face clearly, her angular features softened by the smoke.

Luke, what have you done to us?

I say the words in my head, but Luke refuses to appear, stays quiet, as stubborn and willful as ever.

Isn't that just like him.

SIX

The night has suddenly turned warmer, almost balmy, and as I lock the car door and cross the church parking lot I look up, craning my neck to search for a hint of stars, but they're hidden behind the darkened, impenetrable sky. I am sweating inside the sweatshirt I'm wearing, the hood pulled up in an attempt to hide my face. The silky air smells of damp earth, the cloying haze of white flowers touched by rain. It reminds me of Luke's funeral, the pulpit thick with candles and lilies, their petals framing the long wooden box, the smell of melting wax and incense clinging to my clothes. I think of him in the cemetery, fresh black dirt smoothed over his grave, and my knees buckle momentarily beneath my weight.

The front door is propped open, yellow light shining

from within, and there are people huddled on the stone steps, drawn together in groups, some crying, arms tightly wound around one another, some smoking cigarettes, staring off into the night. My blood crawls to a stop in my veins as I realize that this is a vigil. Nobody mentioned anything about it at school, but then again, no one really talks to me. The scent of incense drifting through the open wooden door mixes with clove cigarettes, the sharp slap of cologne that hovers, cloud-like, over the boys' heads. Alex Simmons, a senior, looks up as I approach, but his face registers nothing. He could be gazing at a wall, a shoe left lying inexplicably in the middle of the road. My heart turns somersaults in my chest. I shouldn't be here.

Delilah sits on the steps off to the side, almost entirely out of sight, arms wrapped around her knees as if she's giving herself a much-needed hug. As I approach, I'm aware of the nerves jumping beneath my skin. Her face is so familiar, so much a part of my life that I can't imagine going on without her. Her black hair is pulled back, her brows framing hollowed eyes. When she sees me coming toward her, she exhales deeply, offering up a weak smile. Her heart, I can tell, is not really in it, though. It's in the way she glances quickly away. I sit down on the steps beside her, the coldness of the stone radiating through my jeans.

"Hey," she says without turning to look at me. "I'm glad you came."

There is a beat, a moment of quiet where she pulls absent-mindedly on the end of her ponytail the way she always does when she's nervous, and that one gesture pierces the core of me. Delilah and I have been many things around each other, but nervous has not been one of them.

"Are you?"

She finally looks at me, hurt written all over her face.

"Of course I am, Alys. Of course I am."

"You didn't seem too glad to see me today at assembly," I say, watching as a group of freshmen climb the steps to the front door, the heels of their shoes clicking against the stone. Their eyes flit over me, widening, and I hold their gaze defiantly. *Say it,* I think as they pass in a wave of flowers and fruit, gum and hairspray. *Just go ahead and say something.* My fingers curl into fists, and all of a sudden I'm vibrating as if I've become some kind of conduit, a mess of copper wires, exposed and fraying. I will myself to unclench my hands, and play with the string of my hoodie instead, wrapping the cord tightly around one finger before releasing it.

Delilah looks out into the park that faces the church. I remember playing on the jungle gym there when we were small, hanging from the yellow bars like a pair of wiry monkeys. Burying Luke in the sandbox, the grit and scour of sand up to his chin, his arms and legs gradually disappearing as we dumped another red pail full over him.

"I didn't know what to do. I mean, everyone was *looking.*"

She takes a deep breath and lets it out slowly, pulling on the end of her ponytail again, her teeth worrying her bottom lip. She says this as though it matters. She says this as though it's important. That people were looking at her and, by extension, looking at me. As if the last hundred years of our friendship won't hold up under scrutiny. And maybe it won't. The thought is like an icy hand on my neck, a pair of dead fingers reaching out and squeezing. Hard.

"Since when do you care what people think?" I say, and in my tone I hear Luke, his voice in the note he left on Facebook, rage inflecting every syllable.

Now you're all going to die . . .

"Don't act like this is so easy," she snaps, out of patience now. "Okay?"

"Oh, you mean easy for *you*?" This comes out louder than I wanted it to, with a force that surprises even me. People stop talking and turn to look at us, so I drop my voice, willing myself to stay calm. "What about me, Delilah? Do you have any idea how hard this has been for me? No, you wouldn't, would you? Because you haven't *been here*. Because your brother didn't walk into our school a month ago and gun down our teachers, our *friends*. But mine did. So every time you stop and think about just how hard it's been for you, why don't you think about *that*?"

I am steaming, my sweatshirt a sweaty, musky prison. Delilah looks at me uncomprehendingly, as if she doesn't know me, her face perfectly white. She drops her eyes to the ground, wincing as if my very presence causes her pain.

"I do," she says quietly. "I do think about . . . how hard it must be for you."

She says this like we're discussing my terrible track record in geometry, calmly, over a soy latte at Starbucks, notebooks open, pages ruffling in the air-conditioning. Like my world as I know it isn't pretty much over, as if a bomb didn't go off in my life, decimating everything in its path. My heart feels askew in my chest, dislodged, and I swallow hard to keep from crying.

"You can't even look at me, can you?" I cannot keep the accusatory tone from my words, and when she looks up, the hurt I see in her face almost makes me cry out.

"I'm right *here*," she says, her voice so low I have to lean forward to hear her over the chatter and laughter surrounding us, the sound of the church organ as a melody tinkles out the front door and into the night air. "And I *am* looking at you, Alys. But I just don't see things the way I used to." She shrugs as if she doesn't know what else to say, giving up on me, on everything that stands between us. *Stay,* I think as she stares at me, wordless. *Please stay with me.*

"I didn't *do* anything," I say, my voice getting smaller and smaller. "I'm not the one who's responsible, D."

I wish I really believed this. I say it, but it doesn't ring true. The words echoing between us.

"I know that," she says quickly. Almost a little too quickly, as if she's not really sure. "I know you aren't. But Luke is." She grimaces, as if the taste of his name in her mouth is both bitter and painful. "And you—you remind me so much of him, of us, of *everything*. Just the way you look, your expression right now, you look so much like him that—"

Her voice breaks and she looks out over the park, and I wonder if she's remembering how small we were, hanging from those brightly colored bars, if she can still see us the way I can, running through the long grass of our backyards for one more game of tag before the sun went down, our mother's voices calling us in for hot baths and warm meals. "It just hurts," she finishes finally, digging down deep enough to find the words. "It hurts to be around you, Alys. It hurts to remember what happened. I can't help it."

It hurts to be around you. The words Ben couldn't say. Falling from Delilah's chapped red lips, they sting like the sudden prick of a needle.

"So I guess that's it, then," I say, my words as hollow as a dead tree, the roots ripped out of the ground.

Delilah nods slowly, her eyes glistening, the whites radiating out of her pale face like bits of the broken moon. "For now," she says in a whisper. "I'm sorry. I wish . . ." Her voice breaks off, and she reaches up, wiping away a tear, her face slick. "I wish things could be different. I wish everything could go back to the way it was."

"I know," I whisper, my throat constricting. First Ben, now Delilah. My chest hurts, and I wonder how many more of these conversations I can take.

This is the first moment I really know this to be true—I can't go back to who I was before, that girl whose biggest problem was whether or not she'd get into some stupid music program, whether or not she'd be able to afford a better violin someday, whether she was really good enough to earn a chair in an orchestra or play concert halls in Vienna, London, Paris, Prague, Grace watching proudly from the confines of her red velvet seat, chandeliers draped in crystal sparkling above her head like an elaborate mobile, a fallen meteor. The girl who wandered through the halls of school mostly invisible, head down, music streaming through her brain like a river.

Luke, you took their lives, and your own. Do you have to take ours too? Is there nothing you will let me keep? Nothing at all?

We sit, me and Delilah, her name as fresh and beautiful as petals in my mouth, our legs barely touching, so close to each other that I can smell her sweet, clean baby scent that makes the water falling from my eyes run faster.

No more tears.

We stare straight ahead, breathing in unison with nothing left to say, no words to fill up the space my brother left behind when he aimed the gun at his first target and pulled the trigger.

SEVEN

—

When I pull up to the house an hour later, tears are still drying on my face from the drive home, my face frozen, masklike. My father stands on the porch, his back to me, a bucket at his feet. He holds a large yellow sponge that drips onto the stone floor as he scrubs, the sleeves on his wrinkled blue dress shirt rolled above the elbow. He turns around briefly at the sound of the garage door opening, and his face is caught in the glare of headlights, weary and expressionless.

When I get out of the car and walk outside, I can see red paint streaked across the front door as my father moves the sponge determinedly in a circular motion. Although he's clearly been at it for a while, smudged as the letters are, I can still make out the word written in block print, marring the white surface like a raw, gaping wound.

KILLER

My hand goes to my mouth, clapping over it reflexively, as if I've said the word myself. At the sound of approaching footsteps, my father turns around and the sponge drops wetly to the floor. He's pale, like me, corpse pallor, and in his face I see my own—the thick, straight brows I am forever plucking, the rounded cheeks. If he's been drinking again, I can't tell.

"Where the hell have you been?" he barks, bending over to pick up the sponge, dipping it into the bucket. He wrings it out as if he wants to strangle it, his hands working furiously.

"I went to meet Delilah. I was only gone for a little while."

He turns back around and begins scrubbing at the door again. If he's cold out here, he doesn't show it.

"You *need* to tell us when you're going out, Alys Anne. You know that."

My father only uses my full name when he's extra pissed. Immediately I go on the defensive.

"I *did* tell someone—I told Mom. Didn't she tell *you*?"

He keeps scrubbing. The only sounds are the exhalations of breath, the metallic buzzing of the streetlight outside our house, the low drone of the TV playing somewhere beyond the front door. I wonder if my mother is in front of it, stretched out on the couch in our den, trailing a series of flickering images across the screen. I wonder when the last time they talked might have been, if they've had anything resembling a normal conversation since the funeral, or if arguing is the only way they can relate to each other anymore.

"Guess not," I mumble, pushing past him, one hand on the front door, opening it wider so that it creaks loudly.

"Alys." My father grabs my arm with his one free hand, stopping me before I slip through. This close-up, I can see that he's not drunk this time, just exhausted. "I'm sorry. I didn't mean to snap at you." His voice is softer now, almost gentle.

I blink at him, my eyes tired and sore from crying, from the shitty amount of sleep I've been getting—or not getting—from looking at things that make me want to turn away and close my eyes indefinitely. Like my father's face right now, so full of pain and regret and confusion that I long to collapse right here on the front doorstep.

"It's okay, Dad." He releases me, and I tentatively reach out and pat his arm, my fingertips moving lightly over the material of his shirt as if he might bolt. My father hasn't seemed himself, that cheerful, jovial presence I'd always counted on, since Luke

(killed everyone)

died, but in the past few weeks he's become more and more of a cipher, slipping through the rooms of our house unnoticed, so far away from the dad who helped Luke and me orchestrate water balloon fights on the hottest days of summer, who made popcorn on Sunday nights, letting me carefully pour on the melted butter so that every piece was coated in a slick, oily sheen. Lately it feels as if he could slip out of our lives so easily, get into the car one night and just keep driving far away from me, from my mother, from all the memories that rush in every night like an avalanche, keeping us from the warm cradle of sleep.

"It's not," he says, his voice tight in his throat, and begins scrubbing again, the word still clearly discernable on the white paint, no matter how hard he tries to erase it. "It's not okay, Alys."

We are not, I know, talking about the fact that he snapped at me anymore, or that he was worried, or the fact that he thinks I left and went out without telling anyone. It's in the set of his jaw, the way he is fixated on that tainted door, as if he wants to destroy it entirely, chop it into pieces, burn it as kindling.

"Why can't they just leave us alone?" he asks, gesturing at the soiled door, the white paint streaked with a cornucopia of pink smears.

I feel Luke's presence hovering somewhere nearby, feel the sudden agitation of his spirit. The sharp scent of rotting flowers, a struck match. But he stays hidden in the blackness, refusing to show his face.

"You know why," I say softly, staring at my hand on the door, the long fingers that are so much like my mother's, so much like Luke's

(dead)

hands, hands that once held me up. Hands I thought I knew.

"Don't we have the right," my father says, the words coming thick and forced from his lips, "to get on with our lives? Don't we, Alys?"

I turn to him, and the naked bewilderment I see on his face stops my heart. How can I help make sense of what I don't understand myself? Of what has happened to my father. To Luke. To all of us.

"I don't know," I whisper, dropping my eyes away. "I don't know if we have the right to do anything anymore."

Without saying another word, I shuffle inside, leaving him on the porch with the bucket. The sound of the TV echoing through the foyer is reassuring, calming my thudding pulse. Even though I know my mother has heard me, that she's probably sitting up on the couch, rearranging her face into a pleasant mask, I don't go to her. Instead, I walk up to my room, thinking of bed, of white sheets and the cool pillowcase that will lie beneath my cheek. How I will stare up at the ceiling, waiting for oblivion, sleep that I will chase around the room all night long and never quite catch. My feet move soundlessly on the stairs, the banister cold and smooth beneath my palm, the leaden weight of Luke's presence following in my wake. My whole body aches for something, anything, that will make me feel that things haven't changed, that I have one thing left in my life that is recognizable to me, that is familiar—besides my dead brother walking so close behind that I can feel his hot breath on the back of my neck, smell the stench of a burned-out campfire sticking to his clothes.

In my room, I stare at the case of my violin for a long moment before finally unlocking it, wondering, even as the metal locks click under my fingers, if what I said to my father downstairs was true, if I have any right to get lost in the tilt and sway of music. I hold the instrument in my hands, turning it over. Luke is sitting at my desk, his face expectant, quieter than usual. I put the violin down on the bed and grab my block of rosin, adding more to the tip of the bow than to the midsection, the way I always do, my hands moving confidently, without thinking about it. His eyes lock on to me as I attach the shoulder rest, tuck the violin beneath my chin, and pick up the bow, bringing it down on the strings so that they trill out into the room in a sudden burst of brilliance. After weeks of neglect, my violin is hopelessly out of tune, so I have to spend a few minutes working with my digital tuner until I get a perfect tone. As always, I start by playing a few scales, some arpeggios, thirds, sixths, fingered octaves. If Grace is in a particularly bad mood, she'll sometimes have me play scales in D flat major as punishment, a key that I hate with a passion. After a few minutes, my fingertips are smarting and sore, which tells me that the weeks I've spent not practicing have taken their toll, that I've started to lose my calluses ever so slightly, those hard pads that make it possible to subject them to the tyranny of strings for hours on end. Luke's eyes follow my movements, the corded muscles in my forearms, my jaw set in concentration. If he speaks, I will stop, throw the violin to the floor, and never pick it up again. I will run from the room, my feet thumping against the carpeted hall, race down the stairs, out the front door, and into the night.

But he stays quiet, and so I weave the bow over the strings, beginning the Brahms in D minor, my hands moving in intricate patterns through the warm air, the heat from Luke's body spreading out over the room, filling it, the haunting melody soothing as a slow slide into warm water. My arms move through the air, their surety mocking the chaos that surrounds me, the world of rage and death that Luke has left behind, pain that not even music as beautiful as this can ever assuage. Miranda pushes open the closet door with one hand. Her eyes blink out at me, slowly as a kitten's, the irises glowing out of the darkness, a green not found anywhere in nature. Her head lolls to one side, the dried blood on her face the color of the inky sky outside the window.

I watch as Luke slips down to the floor, breathing deeply, his back against my desk, his face half hidden in the shadow thrown by the desk lamp, its gooseneck as graceful and curved as the bow in my hands, the musical notes that dance and flow beneath the lids of my eyes as they flutter closed. Even if tomorrow comes, as it will, and the thought of picking up the violin at my lesson with Grace, or even in the morning light, is laughable, right now I'm grateful for this respite, this one waking moment that finally feels something like oblivion—a quiet that settles over the room and moves through the walls of the house, bringing with it a kind of peace.

EIGHT

——

I'm sitting in history class the next morning, stats on WWII filling the dusty chalkboard, when my phone buzzes from the depths of my backpack. I reach down and pull it out when Mrs. Williams turns to write a long list of treaties on the board, my eyes glancing fearfully at the screen, not sure what to expect. Sometimes my phone stays quiet for days, a small, sleeping child lying prostrate on the desk, buried under piles of papers and books, abandoned and forgotten. Riley's name pops up on the screen the minute I unlock it, and I feel my body relax.

Joe's. 12:15. Eat something.

I smile at the screen, my face stretching in a way that feels so awkward and foreign to me now that I almost immediately stop and look around to make sure no one's noticed.

Mrs. Williams is still scribbling on the board in her strange, loopy handwriting, and everyone else is bored, staring out the window or surreptitiously checking their phones beneath their desks. Joe's is a diner a few blocks from school where seniors with off-campus privileges eat most days in order to escape the dreaded cafeteria fare, a place juniors like me sneak out to at least once a week, hoping they won't get caught. The food's not exactly gourmet, strictly grilled-cheese-and-burger territory, but if you're really hungry, it's not half bad.

When I walk through the door, the small, tinkling bell overhead signaling my arrival, he's already there, ensconced in a red leather booth at the back, the seat cracked and fading. The strong, meaty reek of burgers and onions sticks to me in an oily film I'll need a shower to erase. The linoleum underfoot is an ivory-and-lettuce-green checkerboard, the walls a yellow that might have been a cheery yellow at one time but now resembles the dirty haze chain smokers leave behind. There are a few seniors I don't really know huddled at tables near the front door, and I walk past them, head down, hoping they don't notice me. At the counter, I stop dead in my tracks for a moment, mesmerized by the zinc surface, the stools lined up neatly as soldiers.

When I was still in grade school, Luke would take me Joe's for a milk shake sometimes, my feet h the shiny chrome, my legs barely able to touc

It made me feel grown-up to sit at the counter, important. I loved to spin around until Luke reached out one hand to steady me, the room whirling crazily before my eyes. There was something comforting about those milk shakes, the sweet blandness, the red, syrupy cherry perched on top of a cloud of whipped cream. Sometimes, as a joke, Luke would drink all of mine when I went to the bathroom, and when I returned, he'd just order me another, his smile a crooked half grin.

(—don't think about the sound of his laugh, deep, guttural, but still somehow musical—)

"Alys. Over here."

I blink at the sound of my name, forcing myself to look away from the counter and at the booth where Riley is waiting for me, hunched over the remains of a cheeseburger and fries. The sight of the ketchup smeared across the white plate undoes me entirely, and I have to look away.

"How long have you been here?" I ask, slipping into the booth, which creaks companionably beneath my weight. "Lunch just started."

"I had a free track before lunch," he says, swallowing hard, then wiping his mouth with a paper napkin, "so I just walked over. I was fucking starving."

"So I see." I raise one eyebrow at his almost-empty plate.

"You should try it." Riley smirks, glancing at my pitiful frame wrapped in a navy sweater now a size too big. Riley takes a long drink of water, and before I can answer back or

196

protest, he summons the waitress with the raise of his hand. "She'll have a cheeseburger and fries." He jabs his thumb in my direction as he speaks, but she barely looks up from her pad, her black pen scribbling across the paper with mind-numbing efficiency. When I glance over at him, Riley is busily opening packets of sugar, emptying them into his soda. It reminds me so much of Luke that I am rendered speechless. Luke was forever dumping sugar into just about everything—but especially Cokes—a habit most people found disgusting. "How can you stand things to be so sweet?" I repeatedly asked my brother, shuddering as he added yet another packet to the fizzy drink. "Maybe I'm just that bitter," he'd say, grimly stirring the dark liquid with a straw. Watching Riley add one packet after another into his glass, I am overcome.

"What is it? Alys?" Riley looks worried, leaning forward, and I am trying to find the words to tell him, but they seem to be stuck somewhere in my solar plexus, images of Riley and Luke swimming before my eyes, clouding everything. I look down at my lap and breathe for a minute before raising my head again to meet his gaze.

"It's just . . ." I begin, knowing how stupid it will sound. "The sugar . . ." Riley's face is still, waiting for me to finish. I wish a hole would open up in the ground and swallow me entirely—which would be totally preferable to having to complete this sentence. "It just reminds me of . . . him. Luke, I mean."

Riley pushes his plate to the side and leans back in the booth, watching me thoughtfully.

"Huh," he says after a minute or so. "I mean, we were around each other enough—we were bound to pick up each other's habits and all." He stares into the muddy surface of his drink, his cheeks flushing a deep crimson. I have never seen Riley flustered or embarrassed.

"I keep remembering the most random things about him," I say, amazed that the words are actually leaving my mouth. It feels strange to talk about Luke aloud, not just in my head, where no one can judge him. But here with Riley, I feel protected. "Like when he used to take me here after school when I was in fifth grade. Or that time out at the lake when he taught me to swim."

"I keep remembering how obsessed he was with that damn tree house. That piece of crap took us all summer to build." Riley laughs, picking up his glass. "And we never did get it right. The thing was always lopsided. Of course," Riley goes on, shrugging almost apologetically, "that was before we discovered girls."

He says this without any sense of flirtation, like it's just a random fact, but I blush anyway. I'm grateful for the sudden arrival of the waitress bearing a tray crammed with burgers and fries. She slides a white plate before me, the cheeseburger topped with lettuce, pickles, and red onion. I immediately shove the onion to one side of my plate and busy myself with the saltshaker, dumping it liberally over my fries. I cut the burger into neat halves, figuring that the more manageable I make things the better, and pick up a fry, bringing it to my lips. I know Riley is watching, so I force myself to put it in my mouth and chew slowly.

"I guess you're still having a hard time with that." Riley gestures at my plate with one hand. "Eating, I mean."

"Sometimes," I say, swallowing the untruth along with the fry. It stays lodged in my throat, and I wash it down with water, but it won't budge. "It just feels so . . . pointless." I push the plate away, crossing my arms over my chest.

Riley reaches over, picking up half of my burger and bringing it to his lips.

"See?" he says, chewing, then swallowing hard. "That's how it's done." He wipes his hands on a paper napkin and shoves the plate back across the table. "Now you." He looks expectantly at me, and I hesitate before picking up the other half of the burger and taking a small bite, the flavors of grease, fat, and salt exploding on my tongue. I take another, bigger this time, suddenly ravenous.

Riley watches in silence as I finish my burger, my cheeks bulging like a squirrel's. I still can't deal with the fries, though, so I push the plate to the center of the table and watch Riley pick at them.

"Have you been dreaming at all?"

There are the same dark moons beneath each eye, and in

spite of his seemingly unending hunger, he looks worn-out, as if he still hasn't slept since the shooting.

"I try not to," I say, wiping my hands on a napkin, then balling it up. "I don't sleep much, but when I finally do drift off, I'm out."

(—*don't mention Miranda, the blood running in rivulets down her shattered face, the way your dead brother keeps showing up in your room, the garage, on the stairs, at school. That stink of rotting lilies mixed with ashes—*)

"I wish I were so lucky," he mutters, his face darkening. "It's getting to the point where I'm actually afraid to go to sleep."

"Do you see Luke?" My heart is beating fast, and all at once I'm sweating. *Maybe they're not dreams, Riley*, a small part of me wonders. *Did you ever think of that?*

He nods, his face growing paler still. "It's always the same dream. I'm in the library, back in the stacks, when I hear people start to scream. When I look up, Luke's right there, a gun pointed at my face."

(—*the darkness, the barrel elongating forever—*)

"I want to run, but I can't." Riley hesitates for a minute before starting again. "'Luke,' I say, 'what the fuck are you doing?' He just looks at me and winks—you know that look he used to give when he was up to something?"

I nod slowly, mesmerized into a stupor.

"He winks, and then the gun goes off and everything goes

dark. Then I wake up. It's the same every night." Riley sighs heavily, as if merely telling me has lifted some kind of enormous weight. "Always the same. Every time I close my eyes and drift off, he's there with that fucking gun."

There is a pause in which we say nothing. In this moment, there is no need for words, no need to say a thing.

"I don't get it—I mean, I wasn't even in the library that day." He runs his hand reflexively through his hair, frustrated. "But you were there." Riley looks straight at me. "Weren't you?"

I nod, not sure if I can find the strength to talk about it, the gun raised up to eye level, Luke's face peering out from behind. I feel him hovering nearby, that burning heat and restless agitation, a murderous spirit, and then all at once, he appears, sliding into the booth next to me, reaching across the table and popping a French fry into his mouth while chewing menacingly. There is a sound like fire, the smell of charred leaves in the air.

"Don't tell him," Luke warns, and although he is talking to me, his eyes are locked on Riley's face. "Don't," Luke repeats again, and I am silenced, the words stunted in my throat before they can be released. He smiles, showing rows of perfectly even teeth, before fading, his body dissipating like smoke, his last word ringing in my ears.

Don't.

"Prom's coming up," Riley says casually, changing the subject.

"Yeah . . . in *May*," I say, unable to keep the sarcasm from my voice, wondering how I'm going to fill the days of the month that remain on the calendar. "April is the cruelest month," my mother used to quip when I'd complain about the unpredictable spring weather, how many weeks there were before school let out in June. Now all I do is tick off the days one by one as they stretch on interminably, waiting for them to pass.

Riley grabs another fry and chews on it thoughtfully. "You going?" he asks when he finally swallows. Prom is mostly for juniors and seniors, although the odd freshmen and sophomores sometimes get asked by upperclassmen.

I fight the urge to bust out laughing. Riley is ridiculous.

"Uh, yeah—I'm just fighting off prospective suitors. Or haven't you heard?"

He laughs, happy to have a joke to distract him, to play off of. "Oh, that's right," he says, snapping his fingers for emphasis. "I forgot about your—how did you put it again—total social annihilation?"

"Sure, just rub it in," I mutter grudgingly.

"Hey, it's not like it's been all that much different for me, you know," he says, his tone almost chiding. "I was think-ing," he goes on, taking a deep breath, "I know we haven't hung out a lot in the past, but I thought that maybe we could go together. If you want," he adds quickly. An emotion fills Riley's face, something I've never seen before—certainly not where girls are concerned: uncertainty. Maybe a little fear. "Or not." He looks out the plate-glass window of the diner, watching people pass by. "It was just an idea. I mean"—he turns back to face me—"I always thought you'd go with Ben."

Ben. Most of the time I try not to think about him at all, push him from my memory, arrange my day into an elaborate maze to effectively avoid his presence. But at moments like these, where the breath is knocked out of me, suddenly, I'm aware of how much I miss him, how much I've lost.

"Don't you think it would be weird?" I say slowly, playing with my fork to have something to occupy my hands.

"For them or for us?"

"For everyone, I guess."

I cannot imagine it. Me stuffed into some slinky, silly dress, Riley's hair slicked back into submission, the both of us picking at the terrible food that will undoubtedly be served, the eyes that will circle us intently. And Ben. In the same room. Close enough to touch, but miles out of my reach.

"I don't know," Riley says, exhaling again. "I mean, I feel like I'm on some deserted fucking island most of the time. I don't want to be home, alone and sad, thinking about yet another thing I'm missing, another thing that's been taken away." He's angry again, agitated, and I want to reach across the table and take his hand in mine. But I don't.

"We don't have to go to prom to hang out, you know.

We can probably do that without subjecting ourselves to bad music and social judgment." I try to smile, to lighten the moment, but Riley only stares out the window as if I haven't said a word.

"I just want one night that's normal," he says with conviction. "Where I feel like everyone else on the fucking planet graduating from high school. Is that too much to ask?"

I shake my head no, even though I'm not sure of anything at all. When he finally looks into my eyes, I'm surprised at the feeling behind his words, the raw emotion. I can't argue with it—as much as I might want to.

"All right," I say slowly, when I can find my voice again. "I guess I'm in."

Riley's lips slowly crack into a smile, and it feels good to make someone, anyone, happy, even just for a moment. The room is warm, lunch rush mostly over, the sound of plates and cups being cleared from tables tinkling in the distance. I don't want to go back to school or to Grace's for my lesson, don't want to get in the car and drive the long straight road to Madison or face the fact that I haven't really played in weeks, my fingers clumsy and thick. I want to stay here, drinking one free refill of Coke after another, until the room disappears in a deep blue twilit haze as shadows lengthen and inevitably fall.

NINE

I've been to Grace's house so many times over the past five years that I've officially lost count. As I walk up the rickety front steps of her porch on Sunday morning, I can feel the tightness in my chest beginning to loosen. The porch is as cool and dark as ever, the floorboards spotted with patches of weak sunlight. A rocking chair sits at the far end, the seat cushioned with a deep blue pad, and beyond that, an empty birdcage swings in the breeze, curved and intricate as a locked gate in a fairy tale. Herbs in ceramic pots rest on the porch railings: dill, thyme, and what looks like mint. I put my violin case down on the wood floor and touch their small fragrant leaves, damp and smooth under my hands and soft as rainwater. Luke sometimes used to help my father in the garden in the early spring, turning the earth with a long shovel, tossing tiny seeds into the holes and covering them with his bare hands, hands that were capable of such gentleness, patting down the earth.

The door opens, startling me, and I grab my violin with an apologetic smile. Grace pulls her black cardigan more tightly around her, smiling broadly, her silver hair shimmering. She beckons me inside. "You made it," she says, as if she was afraid that somehow I wouldn't, and she draws me into her arms, hugging me against her. "My darling girl," she says into my hair, and I close my eyes, trying not to cry. After a few minutes, I pull back, and she brushes the hair from my face, cupping my chin in her hand, her blue eyes examining my face for a long moment before letting go.

I follow her into the living room, the place I've spent the most time in over the past few years, the baby grand piano sitting in the corner. The air smells of lemon furniture polish, fresh flowers, and old toast. What I loved most about Grace's house was that everywhere you turned, there was something beautiful that caught your eye and held it. Built-in bookshelves running along one wall of the living room, crammed with books, birds' nests abandoned and plucked from trees, one holding a lone white egg. Seashells in soft colors—gray or peach—jagged bits of rose quartz, and stones that felt smooth and polished when I ran my hands over them. And plants hanging like a lush, green curtain in front of the long windows. Being there made me feel that if I could just stay forever, sinking into the wide gray velvet couch and resting my head on the red needlepoint pillows hugging either end, that everything might eventually be okay.

"I'm not going to be so trite as to ask how you are, Alys." Grace walks over to the piano bench and hovers next to it for a moment. "I think we know it would be a stupid question, yes?" I nod gratefully, relieved to not have to lie. "You know that I am here for you. And if you want to talk—about anything—I hope you know that you can." I nod again, afraid to speak. My emotions are so close to the surface these days that the slightest misstep can send me catapulting into sobs. In a way, though, it's a relief. This is the one place where I don't have to talk about Luke or what he's done, the fact that my parents' marriage is falling apart, the wreck that's become my life. Here things can be as they were—Grace seated at the piano, the pictures of her on her honeymoon in Vienna perched on top, her smiling, shining face so open and youthful. "Now"—Grace shuffles the sheet music on top of the piano, looking through it—"have you been practicing?" I blink, Luke's voice echoing through the chambers of my brain, magnified and distorted.

Shouldn't you be practicing, anyway? The great virtuoso?

I place the violin case on the couch, unsnapping the locks. When I turn around, Grace is seated behind the piano, hands poised over the keys, watching me expectantly.

"Not much," I say. "Not really." And immediately I am guilt ridden. But Grace just slowly nods, then picks up the glasses hanging from a thin silver chain around her neck and places them on her nose, a gesture which tells me that she's ready to work.

"No matter." She runs her hands over the keys, her fingers nimble, moving with a fluidity that belies the crippling arthritis she's struggled against for years—not that I ever hear her complain about it. Grace isn't the complaining type. "Let's start with a few scales to warm up."

As my hands move, I concentrate on the music, the piano beneath all of the notes that stream from my fingers. My hands feel swift and sure on the neck, the bow. I let my mind drift away, lost in the music that fills the room, the regimen of one note following the next, my fingers warm and loosening.

When I lower the violin, I am sweating, the T-shirt beneath my gray cardigan dampened under the arms. "Good," Grace says, nodding authoritatively, and with that slight dip of her chin I can tell that I wasn't too bad, that maybe I haven't slid into a territory that could be called hopeless just yet. "Shall we work on the Brahms?" Without waiting for an answer, she pulls the sheet music for the sonata in D minor from the huge pile in front of her and pushes it over to me. I take a deep breath, placing the music on the metal stand next to the piano, trying to remain calm. Before Luke

(murdered everyone)

I'd been struggling with learning this piece, particularly the middle movement, which made everything I'd done up to that point in my training look easy. Every time I'd come

up against that bit, my hands would fumble, notes dropping like letters at the end of a sentence, making the music
choppy and unintelligible, the lilt and flow of the piece slipping away from me, sliding just out of reach.

I raise the violin again, watching Grace for the signal to
begin. Once it starts, the music rushes over me, breaking me
open. I lean into the notes, holding them, my fingers burning
against the strings. When I get to the middle movement, I hold
my breath, watching Grace for reassurance. She nods gravely,
never taking her hands from the keys, never stopping or hesi-
tating, flying right into the heart of the sonata, fearless. I begin
to smile as I realize that, for once, I'm doing it: I've passed that
tricky vortex and come out on the other side. Just then, as my
smile grows wider, my fingers slip on the neck, the bow moves
awkwardly in my hand, my wrist cramping as a shrillness fills
the room, making me wince. I lower the violin, breathing hard,
furious with myself, shaking with frustration and anger.

"Alys." Grace's voice jolts me out of my thoughts, which
mostly consist of berating myself for being a horrible excuse
for a violinist, a terrible person in general, and I look at her,
fearing I will see the worst on her face, the thing I've never
wanted to see when I look at Grace—disappointment. She
reaches up, removing her glasses so that they hang once
more against her sweater. "You know," she says slowly, "that
wasn't half bad for a girl who has barely touched her instrument for well over a month. Not bad at all."

With those words, I relax a little, unable to keep a grin from my lips. But the thoughtful expression on her face is replaced almost immediately by the steely, determined look I know so well as she bends over the piano again, lowering her head. "Again," she orders, and I pick up the violin, raising it to eye level once more, fingers poised and ready.

An hour or so later, I'm spent, my hair plastered to the back of my neck. I feel like I've run six miles, my body hot and my hands burning with effort, my neck sore and aching. When I look at the tips of my fingers, they are raw. I know that tonight they will sting so badly I will need to wrap them in Band-Aids in order to cut the pain.

After I wipe down my violin and put it away, Grace and I sit drinking tea, as is our custom at the end of every lesson, the fragrant steam curling from the delicate china cups, gilt edging around the rims. Today it is chamomile, which always smells, inexplicably, like hay to me. I pull my hair back more securely with a hair band, hating the feel of the sweaty strands against my skin.

"The audition is a little over a month away." Grace returns her cup to the saucer, sitting back in her big puffy chair and resting her feet on the ottoman.

May 30. One week after prom. As if I could forget.

"I'm not ready," I say quickly, a feeling of panic rushing over me. Because I'm nowhere near ready—I'm not even in the same zip code as ready. The realization makes me feel like just giving up completely, going home and crawling into bed, never getting out.

"You will just have to do your best," Grace says with a shrug, like it's no big deal.

"What if it isn't good enough?" I ask, staring at the gold liquid in my cup, tiny flecks of leaves swirling to the bottom.

"Then you will do what you can." Grace leans forward, resting her hands on her knees, peering at me intently. I can feel the gravity of her gaze, of her words, even though I don't look up. The way she examines my face, taking in everything I'm feeling, everything I cannot say. "That is all you can do, Alys. That is all *any* of us can do."

"It just seems so . . . unimportant now. Like it doesn't matter."

Grace is quiet for a minute, carefully weighing her words, then speaks slowly, deliberately.

"It will matter as much as you want it to, Alys. As much as you are willing to let it."

I think about what she's said for a moment before responding, placing the cup down on the table.

"I just feel like I don't have the . . . right to want anything anymore. For myself."

When the words leave my mouth, I hear how tentative they sound, how unsure. I think of Jesse Davis, a senior Luke shot, lying in a hospital bed, unconscious. What did he want in his future? What did *he* dream about? I think of his parents waiting at his bedside for him to wake up and rejoin the living, to climb out of the tangle of white sheets and sit up, walk back into the world. Valedictorian. Scholarship. He must've thought it was all a sure thing.

Grace nods, picking up her cup with deft fingers. She settles in her chair and drains her tea, staring at me pensively, her blue eyes softening at the edges. When she speaks, her voice is low, urgent.

"You have the right to *live*, Alys. You *always* have the right to do that." She places the cup in its saucer with a clink of finality. "But only you can decide, no?"

"Yes," I manage to say, my voice barely audible. It is hard to believe that I have the power to decide anything about my life anymore. But even so, Grace's words stick to me, lodging themselves in the dark corners of my brain.

When I leave, she stops me at the door, squeezing my hand in hers, kissing me once on each cheek, as is her way. She hesitates for a moment, placing a hand on my shoulder, her grip tight and sure. "You will be all right, Alys," she says quietly. "Even if you do not think so now. Even if it feels very far away."

I can smell the flowery perfume she always wears, the one that smells like lily of the valley, bourbon, and dark tilled earth, her touch lingering on my skin long after I walk down the porch steps, creaking slightly beneath the pulse and heft of my body, and drive away.

TEN

On Monday, after school, I drive distractedly toward the center of town, cutting a trail through the rain that pelts the windshield. Soon lawns will be an endless carpet of green, the air alive with the sinuous hiss of sprinklers. This used to be my time to practice or, on rare afternoons where I'd slack off, hang out with D, popping peanut M&M's into each other's mouths, feet entangled on the couch. She loved those waxy, long, red ropes of licorice, would wind them around my wrists like jewelry. Now, even after I finish my homework, I'm aware of how much time there is left to fill before I can crawl into bed and try to sleep, the stars like handfuls of glitter hurled at the sky.

You have the right to live, Alys . . .

Grace's face swims up in front of my eyes, and I blink it away, my lashes beating rapidly. Every time I think about the audition, my stomach churns with guilt and apprehension. Because of what it means. The future. That, in spite of everything, I might have one. I don't know if I deserve it after what Luke has done, all of that spilled blood staining my hands. Even though I know I should go home and practice, I turn onto Main Street and, before I know what I'm doing, pull into the hospital parking lot, winding through the garage until I find a space next to a bright yellow Datsun. I turn off the engine and listen to the car shut down, the hushed rattling noises as it quiets. The hospital is a giant white brick building outside my window, and I watch it warily, as if it might get up and come after me. I think of the people trapped inside, covered by sheets and blankets, hooked up to beeping machines. Jesse Davis is one of them.

I get out of the car, trying to act like I know where I'm going, even though I don't really have a clue. My hands are trembling, and I look down and glare at them fiercely, willing them to quiet. In the main lobby, the elderly woman sitting behind the information desk has a long, sharp face and bright red hair that borders on magenta. But her face is kind, and her eyes, when she looks up at me, are welcoming, heavily creased along the edges.

"Can I help you?" she asks tentatively, as if she's scared she'll frighten me away by speaking too much, or too loudly.

"I don't know," I begin, my eyes darting from side to side. I feel hunted. Like a criminal. "I'm looking for a friend?"

Jesse Davis was not my friend. Not even close. Nor would he be now if he knew what Luke did to him. But even though I never really knew Jesse, he always smiled at me in the halls, no matter how in a rush he was. He was that type of guy.

"What's your friend's name, honey?" She types a few strokes on her computer and looks up at me expectantly.

"Jesse Davis," I say, my cheeks burning. She punches a few more keys, her fingers hitting the keys firmly, authoritatively.

"He's upstairs in room two twenty-one. They just moved him out of the ICU a few days ago. Take elevator A at the end of the hall to the second floor and turn right. His room is the third door on the left."

"Is he . . ." I don't know how to find the words, how to ask what I need to know. "Has he woken up yet?"

She punches the keys again, her hands moving like a hummingbird.

"You'll have to ask one of the nurses when you get upstairs, honey. I can't tell from here." She points at the screen apologetically, as if she wishes she could do more. For all she knows, I'm his girlfriend, or maybe even his debate partner. A classmate. Not the sister of the boy who put him here.

I nod, thanking her, and make my way to the elevator before I lose what's left of my nerve.

Outside his room, I hesitate, watching as nurses walk past in a sea of light blue scrubs, the scent of antiseptic wash mingling with the smell of food from the impending dinner service. What am I doing here? What can I possibly say that will make up for what my brother has done? I lean against the wall, trying to take deep breaths, to compose myself when all I want is to hightail it back to the parking lot and lock myself in my car, where I'll be safe again.

"Are you all right?"

A nurse stops in front of me, holding a stack of charts, his dark hair receding on top.

"I'm fine," I say quickly, straightening up and clearing my throat. "I was just looking for my friend's room. Jesse Davis," I say, panic flooding my body, my pulse racing.

"Well, this must be your lucky day." He smiles at me, taking me loosely by the arm and turning me around. "You're right in front of his room."

"Oh!" I exclaim, feigning surprise and enthusiasm. "Great!"

"He can have visitors, but just don't stay for too long, okay?"

"Is he still . . ." I stop and look at the nurse, hoping the look on my face can fill in the missing words, tell him what he needs to know.

"He's still in a coma, yes." He says this gently, as if this information hurts him more than it may hurt me.

"Will he . . . wake up?"

"We don't know. We certainly hope so." He tucks the charts under his arm and looks at me intently now, his eyes searching my face. "Talk to him," he says urgently. "Coma

216

patients can hear everything we say, even if they don't always remember it when they regain consciousness again. Some even say it helps to bring them back." He walks off down the hall, his shoes squeaking noisily against the linoleum. Over the loudspeaker, a Dr. Singh is being paged incessantly, and from inside Jesse's room, I can hear the beep and rattle of machines, the synchronized hiss of breathing.

He's lying in bed, the sheets drawn up to his chest, which rises and falls around the tubes taped to his mouth, snaking down the length of his torso. From the doorway, he could be sleeping, his body relaxed and drowsy. When I get closer, I see the bandage that wraps around one side of his head, the lacerations on his face where he must've fallen, bruises changing from purple to green and yellow along the edges. Before he was

(shot)

Jesse was kind of a gym rat, but now he looks small, almost invisible, swallowed by white sheets.

There's a chair next to the bed, and I sit down gingerly, as if it might break under my weight. Jesse's breathing is heavy and regular, and I watch him for a while, my eyes drawn to the bandage covering the bullet hole in his head. I try to imagine what it must've been like, the roar of the gun blocking out the sound of his own screams, a blinding pain, the world cracked open, then darkness. Or maybe not. I know from watching stupid medical shows on A&E that sometimes, in rare cases, people remain conscious after being shot in the head, stumbling around blindly, lucid and alive, but not exactly functioning at full capacity. I hope, for Jesse's sake, that he went out immediately, that he didn't have to endure what must've been unimaginable pain, or see my brother looming over his fallen body, triumph written all over his face.

Jesse's arms are arranged over the covers, and I stare at his fingers, the short-clipped nails, and, without thinking about it or second-guessing myself, I take his hand in mine. The warmth of his skin is shocking against my palm, and as I curl my fingers around his loose, pliant digits, I can't help thinking that any minute he might wake up, open his eyes, and blink uncomprehendingly at the stark white walls, the tubes running through his body, the kaleidoscope of my face, so familiar and so strange all at once.

"I don't know why I'm here," I whisper, and even though I'm careful to be quiet, my voice echoes a bit in the mostly empty room. The silence is soothing rather than unnerving, a hush, and I feel for some reason like I'm in church, the bed an altar, that it wouldn't be totally out of place for me to ask for forgiveness, even if none is coming any time soon. If I had my violin with me, I would play in the fractured light coming through the window, the shafts of sun warming my fingers. The music would fill the room with the force of a spell finally broken, waking Jesse from his slumber like a prince in a fairy tale. "Ever since Luke died, I feel like all I do is apologize to everyone, all the time." Jesse's eyes are still closed. If he's listening, there's no sign of it. "But I am sorry, so sorry my brother . . . did this to you."

I look around the room, at the blinds, at the vases of flowers wilting on their stems, sad-looking bouquets of daffodils, stalks of freesia, and baby-blue carnations. When I look back at Jesse, his left eyelid twitches, and I wonder if he can hear me or if it's just a reflex, an involuntary movement, no more meaningful than scratching extremities in your sleep. I kneel down by the side of the bed, the floor hurting my bones, and rest my forehead on the mattress, my face cooled by the thin white sheets, which smell of bleach and strong detergent, Jesse's hand still in mine. The tears flow from my eyes, hot and fast, soaking the sheet. I hold on to Jesse's hand more tightly, and my nose begins to run. I am making deep, guttural sounds that come from someplace inside me that's been sealed off from the light, a place I've been afraid to examine too closely, or even acknowledge at all.

"He wasn't all bad, Jesse." I am mumbling into the sheets, my lips thick and swollen. "He wasn't. No matter what people tell you when you wake up . . .

(if you wake up)

"I miss him sometimes." I swallow hard, lifting my head to wipe my eyes with the back of one hand. "And I feel like shit for missing him, like I shouldn't bother because of what he's done. Because he hurt so many people. But I can't help it. He was my brother."

My brother.

Jesse sleeps on, oblivious, his mouth open slightly. I let go of his hand and drop to the floor, scooting backward so that I'm sitting against the hard white wall. I wait for a feeling of lightness to overtake me, a sense of forgiveness that will lift me back up into the land of the living. I squeeze my eyes shut and wait to feel something, anything that will let me know I've been heard, that I'm not alone. I'm straining with every pore of my skin, reaching toward the white light of absolution. I can hear the carts rolling in the hallway outside, delivering dinner, my own heart pounding away in my chest. But as hard as I try, nothing comes, so after a few minutes, I open my eyes. The room is the same, the IV dripping some clear chemical potion into Jesse's left arm, the dusty venetian blinds covering the window, the TV with its blank, dead screen hanging from the ceiling.

I wait, my eyes locked on Jesse's motionless form inside the metal cage of the bed, the waning sun setting his hair alight. I watch as it makes its way down his chest and begins to slip farther across the floor, the room darkening as the sun fades in a haze of pink, tangerine, and violet, and night, with its stealthy black wings, spreads slowly, inevitably over the room, the universe, our still, waiting bodies.

ELEVEN

A few nights later, I'm startled awake by a loud thumping sound coming from downstairs. I sit up in bed, pulling the covers around me, my heart sick with fear. I throw on a bathrobe over the old T-shirt and shorts I'm wearing, pulling the sash tight, the cloth around my waist steadying me. When I open my bedroom door, there is a crack of light, a yellow slice beckoning from the first floor of the house. I creep downstairs like I'm trespassing, my feet almost soundless, but for the creak of the last step. A light is on in the kitchen, and standing in the hallway, I can hear the opening and closing of the refrigerator door, the sound of a zipper being pulled, a chair scraped back from the table. I sniff the air, searching for the rotted stink of dead blossoms, the electric heat of ozone, but find only the faint, lingering odor of last night's dinner, a gluey mix of mashed potatoes and broiled turkey meat loaf.

When I walk into the kitchen, my father is bent over the kitchen table, his shoulders bunched up around his ears. When he turns around, I see a duffel bag lying on top of the dark wood, stuffed to the seams with what I know, without even asking, are his clothes—the few he's taking with him. I stare at the bag as if it's to blame, my mouth open. He's dressed in jeans and a Windbreaker, running shoes on his feet, the jacket zipped as if he was, moments before I entered the room, just about to head out the door.

His eyes are wide with fear, his hair brushed neatly back, cheeks clean shaven, and I know that if he could flee, just open the back door and run out breathless into the endless night, he would. The intermittent hum of the refrigerator punctuates the silence, a buzzing sensation I can feel through the soles of my bare feet each time the compressor clicks on, then off.

"Alys. It's late. What are you doing up?"

I stare at him uncomprehendingly, crossing my arms over my chest.

"I could ask you the same question."

He drops his eyes, the same dark brown as Luke's, and lets out a long sigh. He can't look at me.

"It's three a.m., Dad. Where are you *going?*"

My voice cracks a bit on the last word. My mouth is dry, and I lick the corners, wetting them with my tongue.

He mumbles something unintelligible, still staring at his shoes, and I fight the urge to walk over and shake him until the fog clears from his eyes.

"What?" I ask, unable to keep the edge from my voice. Things are spinning too fast, the kitchen, the house, the room upstairs where I know Luke waits for me, his ear pressed to the floor, eyes glowing with an otherworldly beauty.

"I can't do this anymore," he says, as if it's been years since the shooting. His voice is so low, I have to strain to hear him.

"Do *what*?" I ask, fighting to keep my composure. "What can't you do anymore? Act like you care? *Talk* to us?" He reels back slightly, a pained look on his face.

"I can't be here anymore, Alys." He walks over to the window, looking out into the darkened yard. "I've tried—God knows I've tried. But everything here reminds me of Luke, of . . . what he did."

What he did. As if Luke forgot to wash the car, or return his books to the library on time. Not shot and killed fifteen people in cold blood, people he knew, people he grew up with and sat next to in class every day of his life, people he

(loved)

"Even Mom? Even *me*?"

I know, even as I ask, that the answer will be something

I don't want to hear, that the question, once it escapes my lips, is not only pointless, but something I should never have asked in the first place.

"Yes," he whispers. "Every time I look at you, I see his face."

I am shivering. I wish I had socks so that my toes, long and spindly as a spider's legs, weren't so exposed. I hold on to my robe like it's a life raft, like it will save me, pulling it around in order to warm myself, even though I'm cold down to the marrow of my bones, a place that robes and blankets can't possibly touch.

"And Mom?"

I am little more than a whisper now, stripped down and broken. This is my father. And he's leaving us. And I know that in some ways, even standing here still looking at me, as present as he's ever been, that he's already gone, that he disappeared the moment the gun first went off. I know that when he leaves, the back door will open, then close quietly behind him with no more than a small squeak of the hinges. My mother will turn over in her sleep, her mouth slightly open as she chases away her dreams, a stale glass of water at arm's length.

"Your mother and I . . ." He stops for a moment, searching for the words. "Your mother and I can't seem to talk anymore. Not without fighting. So we don't talk at all."

He sounds so resigned as he says this, so defeated that I have to resist the instinct to go to him, to throw my arms around his neck the way I did when I was little, when I would wait impatiently, every night, for the sound of his key in the lock.

"Where are you going?"

As much as I try, I can't keep the pleading note from my voice, the hurt ringing through my words.

He sighs. "I don't know, exactly. I'm just going to travel around for a while, Alys. I've taken a leave of absence from work. I have some vacation time saved up. I'm using it."

A leave of absence. A polite term for walking out on all of your responsibilities, on everyone you supposedly love.

"So you're leaving. Just like that?"

I concentrate on making myself hard, impenetrable as wood. As I stand there, my sadness and disappointment slowly begin to turn to something colder, something more removed, icy at the core. *He's not acting like a father,* a little voice inside of me says, *so you don't have to be a daughter now.*

"Alys." He takes a step toward me and reflexively I shy away, shielding myself against his touch. "I don't know if I can live with the guilt, the knowledge of what he . . ." He swallows hard, choking on the words. "Of what Luke did. To all those people. I can't bear the weight of it. I sit up every night wondering if I did something . . . to make him that way, if I caused it somehow. I turn things over and over in my brain, until I'm so tired that I've talked myself out of sleep. I try not to blame myself or your mother, but who else is there, really?" He says this with his palms open, beseeching me. His voice cracks, and I want to look away, but I'm stuck, hypnotized. *What about me?* I want to scream. *Don't I need a father too?*

"If you walk out that door . . . then you're really no better than Luke." He blanches at my choice of words, visibly startled. "He may have ruined our lives—and his own—but you're making things worse for *all* of us, just because it's easier for you, just because it's . . . *inconvenient* to feel bad all the time." I take a deep breath, my chest tight, and exhale before continuing, the butter-colored walls of the kitchen blurring around the edges, the paint suddenly neon bright.

"Nobody talks to me at school anymore. Ben and Delilah, my two oldest friends in the world, they walk by me in the halls like I'm invisible. But I'm still *here,* Dad. If you want to take the easy way out, fine. Luke sure as hell did—he bought a gun, he *hurt* people, he hurt *himself.*"

Except sometimes, in my darkest moments, I think it must have been the hardest way of all, putting that gun against his head, closing his eyes, and pulling the trigger, the world exploding in a burst of red and black. I want to stop, to rewind and take back everything I've said. But I've gone this far now. And since I have, I let go completely, falling all the way over the edge.

"I guess, at the end of the day, it's true what they say." I am daring him to react, to stop me, grab my arms and shake me until I fall to the floor, limp as dirty hair. "Like father, like son."

Anger ignites behind my father's eyes, and he turns abruptly around, grabbing the duffel bag off of the table and pushing past me. I hear the back door open, and there is a beat, a hesitation, a long moment where I hear an owl hooting mournfully in a tree, a lone car passing on the road, *swish swish,* the click and whir of the night itself, drunk on its own routine mechanism. My father walks out the door, the moment of his departure stretching out unbearably, minute by minute, until I think I will scream or cry out. But I don't.

When the door closes, I sink to the floor, wrapping my bathrobe around my knees and hugging them to my chest. All at once, Luke is behind me, and even though I don't turn around to face him, I can feel that his energy tonight is quiet, almost pensive, not his usual frenetic heat, his stench of rotten nectar and hot coals. I feel his arms slip around my shoulders, his breath on the back of my neck, his hair brushing against my ear as he hugs me close, rocking me back and forth, the way he used to when I'd fall down and skin my knee, the pavement hard beneath my legs. Miranda appears at my side, one hand running sweetly through the length of my hair, petting me as if I am an animal pried from a trap, something to be cradled and pitied. I try not to look at the hole in her head, how it resembles a flower gone wrong, its broken petals cascading down the side of her face.

"Shhhhh . . ." Luke says, his voice as liquid and soft as hot milk, a gentle whisper.

"Shhhhh, Alys."

And with his arms wrapped tightly around me, his voice in my ear, it is then, only then that I finally let go, that I let myself break down and cry.

TWELVE

I wake up startled the next morning, sitting up in bed, my hair sticking to my temples. But when I look around the room, no one is there and the house is quiet. I lean back against the headboard and try to catch my breath, propping myself up on my elbows. If I was dreaming, I can't remember it. The sunlight peeps through the curtains, and there is a feeling of dread in the pit of my stomach when I think about getting up for school. Then I realize that it's Saturday, and I'm free, and relief washes over me in an enormous rush. Until I remember that my father is gone, that he walked out last night, and then the depression creeps back in, obscuring everything.

At the knock on my door, I sit straight up. The door swings open, and I pull the covers up to my chest with both hands. My mother is dressed in a pair of jeans and a gray sweater the color of low clouds before the rain. She sits down on the edge of the bed, and I wonder if she knows that my father is gone, if he told her last night or even left a note.

"I was thinking," she begins, reaching behind her head and securing the low ponytail she wears with a gentle tug, "that we might go to the mall today and get you some new clothes, do a little spring shopping." She reaches over and pushes the damp hair back from my face, her fingertips butterfly light.

I want to go shopping about as much as I want to be sold into white slavery.

My mother hates the mall, hates most girly stuff like shopping, and avoids it whenever possible, so I nod slowly, trying to process the situation, feeling it out like a blind girl, arms outstretched in darkness. Then I remember prom, Riley, and the fact that I have absolutely nothing to wear, and reconsider. The mall, as much as I may loathe every minute of it, might actually be a good idea after all.

"I need something . . . for prom."

I stop, gauging her expression, watching as her face lights up momentarily, then falls slightly, the corners of her mouth turning downward in dismay.

"But . . . you never said anything!" She pulls me close, and I rest my head on her shoulder, breathing in the familiar scent of her perfume, the laundry detergent on her clothes, her skin, fresh from the shower. If I could climb back inside her body somehow, float there in a warm sea of tranquility, I probably would.

"It just happened the other day." I pull back and rearrange the covers around me, suddenly embarrassed. "I was meaning to tell you—I must've just forgotten."

She still looks hurt, her bottom lip quivering almost imperceptibly, so I spill the beans all at once, hoping it's enough to perk her back up.

"It's no big deal—I'm going with Riley. Just as friends," I add quickly.

My mother raises one eyebrow, her lips quivering with amusement. "How did *that* happen?"

I sigh, sitting back against the headboard. "We've just hung out a few times. It was nothing special." I cross one leg over the other, stretching my toes under the covers, hoping that she won't ask me for more details. I look at the ceiling, the crack that runs partway across it, the one my dad said he'd fix when he got around to it, which clearly won't be any time soon.

"I need to talk to you about something," she says, taking a deep breath and picking a piece of white lint off her pants. She waits a beat, as if she's not sure how to say what she needs to tell me, how to find the words. "Your father and I are going to separate for a while—he's going to do some traveling." She exhales hard, the air hissing like a deflated balloon. "I don't know how long he'll be gone—a couple of weeks at least, but we just can't seem to live together right now, Alys."

A tear falls from one eye and plops down her cheek, then another, falling this time onto the stark white coverlet of the bed, and I try to keep my face impossibly still.

"I know this is hard. But it's just for a while. And it has nothing, and I mean absolutely *nothing* to do with you. Do you understand?"

I nod mutely, but my brain floods with the memory of my father last night in the kitchen, the hopelessness and desperation that leaked from his pores like poison.

"I saw him last night," I say, unable to look her in the eyes. "In the kitchen."

My mother freezes for a moment, taking it in.

"Did he say anything to you?"

Every time I look at you, I see his face . . .

I swallow hard, a lump the size of a basketball welling up in my throat.

"Just that he was leaving. Just that. Nothing else matters anyway."

My mother is quiet, her chest rising and falling with her breath, and I can feel her hand shaking as her grip tightens slightly on my leg, holding on.

"Do you really think he's coming back?" I ask, my voice growing smaller, less sure of itself.

"I think so," she says, swiping at her eyes. "I don't know. I *wish* I knew, Alys."

I lean forward, petting her arm, trying to console her. I concentrate on the feel of her arm beneath the sweater she wears. I imagine my hand transmitting some kind of energy, some radiant warmth that will creep deep inside her, healing the most broken bits until she is fixed, until she is whole again.

When we get to the mall, the lot is packed, and we drive around in circles looking for a spot until I am vaguely nauseous. When we finally park, my mother shuts off the engine and we sit there for a moment, just waiting. She checks her eyes in the rearview mirror, then puts her big black sunglasses on. She takes a deep breath, steeling herself, clutching her purse in her lap, and I wonder why she wanted to come here at all.

"Ready?" She turns to me, her face illuminated with false enthusiasm, and by way of answering, I grab on to the door handle, pushing it open even though I am anything but.

The mall is crowded with people, but once we're inside, a calmness falls over me. Maybe it's the elevator music piping through the speakers overhead, or the smell of chocolate chip cookies drifting from the food court on the top level, but all at once I zone out, lulled into a stupor by the window displays featuring spring dresses the color of Easter eggs, the glass atrium shining transparently above us.

Each time we pass a crowd, I dip my head, not wanting to make eye contact. If anyone recognizes us, I can't tell. My mother stares straight ahead, her face half hidden behind her sunglasses. She holds on to my arm, her fingernails digging into my jacket. It's warm inside the mall, and I am sweating. I want to take my jacket off, but it feels like I need it for protection, some kind of armor. Besides, she is gripping my arm so tightly that it would be more trouble to disentangle myself than it's probably worth. My stomach growls loudly, and it slowly dawns on me that, with the exception of those few moments in the diner with Riley, this is the first time I've actually been hungry—with all the physical sensations that go along with it—in ages. The smell of grilling hamburgers, fried chicken, and the fried rice at Panda Express wafting from the food court tantalize me, making my mouth water.

"Can we get some food afterward?" I ask, and without warning, the memories of my old life come crashing in. Me and Delilah eating frozen yogurt with Oreo cookies mixed in, licking the spoon languidly, kicking each other under the table with booted, pointy feet. Ben's face that one summer afternoon when I came out of the dressing room at Dillard's wearing a short black dress, how he kissed me right there among the shoppers shuffling around like zombies.

Suddenly I'm not hungry anymore.

"Sure," my mother says. "But let's find you a dress first, okay?" She makes a sharp right turn, and we are standing in front of a department store, the makeup counters gleaming like caskets full of jewels. Vials of perfume, with their complicated, delicate alchemy, beckon with a whisper of ambergris and musk, the allure of colored glass. *You smell great,* Ben growled in my ear the last time we made out, his hands under my shirt as if he never wanted to find his way out again, my face buried in his neck. There is a sharp pain in my stomach, and I stop, one hand over my abdomen. I try and breathe deeply through my nose, remembering that Luke told me once that you take in more oxygen that way.

Luke told me a lot of things. Not all of them were true.

"Alys?" My mother stops, pushing her sunglasses on top of her head, one hand resting lightly on my back. "What is it, sweetie?"

I exhale sharply and stand up, the pain fading to a distant memory.

"I just had a cramp," I say breathlessly, which I suppose is almost true. A half lie.

"Do you want to eat now instead of later? We can go upstairs and get some lunch."

"No, no," I say, shrugging off her suggestion. "I'm fine. Let's go inside."

In the dress department, I am immediately overwhelmed by the sheer variety of choices. Racks of dresses in daffodil, magenta, bronze, and rose red, lined up like cheerful friends, waiting to go for a stroll. I pull off my leather jacket, holding on to it with one hand as I run the other over yards of satiny material. My mother deftly pulls dresses from racks, draping them over her arm in a rainbow of color. I am pulled, almost magnetically so, toward the black dresses, simple gowns with a whisper of jet beading at the neck and waist, sweeping the floor lightly, without pretense. My mother wrinkles her nose, steering me back toward the light, pulling out a white tea-length dress from the pile and holding it up to my body in front of the full-length mirror. It is the shade of lightly sweetened cream, of day-old snow, the round neckline studded with shimmering pearls. My face glows as if someone's turned on a strobe inside me, highlighting the slant of my cheekbones, the ivory pallor of my skin.

"With your hair up," my mother says, reaching behind me to gather my ponytail, twisting it into a neat bun, "it would be perfect."

"I don't know." I turn to the side, and she lets go, my hair tumbling back down again. "Isn't it kind of bridey? I feel like I should be standing on top of a wedding cake or something."

My mother rolls her eyes at me in the mirror.

"God forbid." She chuckles, pulling the dress away and placing it back on the rack.

"How about this one?"

She holds up a dress of cornflower blue, the blue of spring skies, the bodice nipping in neatly at the waist, the skirt flaring out at the knee. At the neck, there are two rows of discreet blue beading, sparkly and festive without being over-the-top. I take the soft material from her hands and hold it up to my body. The girl reflected in the mirror looks almost happy, her cheeks pink from the impending spring heat. Her eyes shine like the first twilight beams of the night.

"Do you want to try it on?" My mother points toward the fitting room at the back, and I nod. I quickly yank my sweater off, then throw the dress over my head, pulling it down around my waist before stepping out of my jeans, kicking my sneakers off. My mother zips up the back, and her hands are cold, the metallic sound reminding me of my father's duffel bag, a kind of permanent closure. The fit is perfect. My mother's face behind me is pensive, her eyes shining under a glaze of tears.

"Look at you," she breathes, stepping back slightly. "You're almost all grown-up." She smooths my hair with the flat of her palm, cradling my skull for a moment before letting go. I look at my reflection, and a stranger stares back at me. She looks older, a little wiser, a slight wrinkling around her eyes, so tiny that you'd have to lean in close in order to see it at all. I notice for the first time the way my bones have suddenly risen to the surface of my skin, reaching toward the light. Whether it's the weight I've lost or simply the act of growing up, I can't say for certain.

"What do you think?" My mother's voice breaks into my thoughts.

"It's perfect," I say, turning around to see the back, feeling the material swish out and leave my legs naked as I twirl. For the first time since the shooting, since Luke's death, I feel almost weightless. I smile over my shoulder, unable to help myself, and my mother grins back, our faces stretched wide.

At the food court, I choose lemon chicken, fried rice, a cup of frozen yogurt. My mother grabs a diet soda, a small sandwich, an apple—food I know she will look at determinedly but won't really ingest. I, on the other hand, am weirdly hungry again, the smells drifting from my plate making me salivate, my mouth loose and watery. The first forkful is pure bliss, and I close my eyes so that I can better savor it. But a few bites are all I can seem to manage. I push the chicken away and concentrate on the yogurt instead, licking the spoon carefully, making each cold, sweet spoonful last.

"So, how did this thing happen with Riley?" my mother asks nonchalantly, pretending to be engrossed in her sandwich, which looks dry, like it needs more mustard. "Prom, I mean. He was always more of Luke's friend than yours, wasn't he?"

I love it when my mother pretends not to care about my life. It's such an obvious fiction that it amuses me to no end.

"I mean, we've hung out a few times since Luke . . ." That sad look creeps back onto her face, and I can't finish the sentence. "But that's it. I think he just thought it'd be nice to go as friends, since I'm not going with Ben and all."

Ben. I can't say the name aloud without feeling vaguely seasick. I push my cup of Pinkberry away, toward the center of the table, disgusted.

"Doesn't Riley have a girlfriend?" My mother takes a small bite of her sandwich. "Or am I thinking of someone else?"

"No," I say slowly, hoping she changes the subject soon. "He *had* a girlfriend. But she broke up with him."

"Why is that?"

"I'm not sure exactly," I say, which is not really the truth. After all, no one wants to date the best friend of the freak who opened fire on her classmates. No one.

"I'm really proud of you for going, Alys," she says after a moment, taking another bite of her sandwich and chewing thoughtfully. "To prom. I'm not sure I would if I were in your shoes. I'd be too scared, I think. I was always scared at your age."

"Of what?"

My mother takes a deep breath, then releases it, looking off into the distance.

"Of everything, really. What people thought of me. What they might say." She picks at the bread on her plate, pulling off the crust with delicate fingers. "But then I met your father. He made me feel like I could do anything." Her eyes cloud over, lost somewhere in the past. "It's funny how things work out."

Her bottom lip begins to tremble, and I reach over,

covering her hand with mine. I know that whatever is going on between my parents right now, even though the cord that binds them together is frayed, unraveling, it isn't severed completely. Not yet.

"He'll come back, Mom." She looks at me, tears wetting her eyes, then glances off to the side, the line of her jaw so finely etched that it breaks my heart. "I know he will." Her expression changes to one of wariness, apprehension, and it dawns on me that she may not want him to come back, that maybe she's glad he's gone. That maybe, somehow, it's easier.

A group of girls sits down at the table next to us, all wearing some version of the same hideous sweat suit in pastel colors, rhinestones decorating their asses, their laughter ringing out into the air, dripping over us like syrup. If they recognize us, I can't tell.

"It's not that simple, Alys." Her lips move clumsily, as if the words themselves are thick and sticky in her mouth.

"You love him," I say, and she turns to look at me, startled. "Right?"

She nods quickly, a slight dip of her head that tells me that sometimes she wishes it weren't true. That it weren't true at all.

"So maybe it is. That simple. You guys belong together."

And they do. Something that, despite their ever-increasing fights over the last few years, despite my mother's growing bitterness, widening the chasm between them even further,

I've always known to be true. They are two parts of the same whole, one making no sense without the other.

The words hit my mother hard, and her mouth opens then closes again, her face crumpling, tears falling from eyes that she lowers shyly, squeezing my hand tight. I concentrate on the feel of her warm skin and fragile bones. The golden gleam of her engagement ring scratches against my palm like frost scraped from a window, a language that neither of us can decipher or understand.

THIRTEEN

—

AS I'm gathering up our trash, stacking it on top of the trays in preparation for the long walk to the garbage cans, I see Arianne, Ben's mother, across the food court. She's alone, her curly brown hair unbound, falling messily to the middle of her back. She's wearing a pair of faded black pegged pants and a ratty gray button-down. I want to look away, but I can't—I watch helplessly as she searches the food court—for what, I don't know—her gaze drifting over the food stands and out over the room until it comes to rest on my face. Whatever she's thinking, her face betrays nothing. But before I can say anything, she walks toward us, weaving around the crowds waiting in line until she is standing right in front of our table.

"Arianne." My mother's face is white as bone. "Hello."

Arianne looks at my mother, stone-faced, before her attention shifts back to me.

"How are you, Alys?" Her voice is warm caramel, slightly husky. But the inflection in her words is absent, robotic, as if the organs and blood in her body have been stripped out, replaced with rows of gleaming metal screws and springs, pulleys working mechanically beneath her skin.

"I'm . . . fine," I stammer, not sure how we're going to make polite conversation. Everything feels surreal, the plastic trays of food in front of us, the girls lining up in groups at Pinkberry.

"You're looking so . . . grown-up these days." Her tone is wistful, and her eyes sweep over my face and body as if she wants to possess them, consume me whole, leaving nothing remaining but a few random nubs of bone and a pile of dust.

In the silence, Arianne glances at the shopping bag at my feet, missing nothing. The girls next to us have gone quiet, and I can feel them watching us closely, their bodies tensed, waiting for something to happen.

"Doing some shopping?" The question is innocuous enough, but there is an undercurrent that sets me immediately on alert. *We are teetering on the edge of things,* I am thinking. *Teetering on the edge . . .*

"Katie might have gone to prom her junior year," she muses, reaching down into my shopping bag before I can stop her or protest, pulls out my new blue dress, holding it up to her own body, fitting its contours against her frame dreamily, as if she doesn't quite realize just what it is she's doing.

"Of course, as a freshman, she was a little too young this time around. I would never have let her go—even if she was asked." She looks at me, her eyes flat. That cornflower blue of spring, so enticing in the dressing room earlier, now repulses me with its sickly tinge, the indigo of corpses, bodies dragged up from the sea. I look at my mother, pleading for some kind of help, and, to her credit, she leans forward in her chair and tries again, raising her voice this time, determined to be acknowledged.

"Arianne. How have you been?"

With these words, the moment between us is broken. Arianne finally looks at my mother as if she's just noticed that she's seated right there with me at the table. For the first time, a spark comes into her eyes, a smoldering, and at once I am not only uneasy but afraid.

"I've been . . . as well as can be expected, I suppose." She stares at my mother like a stranger, as if she's never seen her before. "Considering your son killed my daughter."

I cannot move. I blink once, twice, hoping that I've hallucinated. My mother could not get any whiter if she were on an operating table. I am aware that the people around us have stopped eating and are now watching us with hungry fascination. The girls next to us begin to twitter again, whispering softly to one another.

"Arianne," I say, jumping in. Everything is slipping out of control, moving too quickly. The elevator music piped through the speakers is suddenly loud and brash, an orchestra out of tune, out of time. Arianne's jaw is set in concrete, and I want to wake her up, to remind her of the driving lessons, the afternoons on the front porch, our eyes closing drowsily amid the sounds of bees droning away in the garden.

She glances at me with a look that immediately dismisses anything I could even hope to say. I am reminded of the futility of words, how they often do more harm than good.

"Did you hear what I *said*?" She leans in a bit closer. I don't like the way she is looming over my mother, who looks small and frail in her chair, but I feel powerless to do anything to stop it. This scene, whether I like it or not, has to be played out. "Your son killed my daughter."

"I heard you the first time," my mother says quietly and without malice. She looks up at Arianne, her gaze weary and exhausted, and I watch as they consider each other for a long moment. I wonder if they remember all those afternoon coffees at our kitchen table, the laughter that used to spring up between them like bubbles in a cold pool. The loaves of bread and bottles of wine my mother brought over when Arianne's mother died, cradling Arianne in her arms like she was her own child.

Finally, after what seems like hours, Arianne straightens up, pulling back into herself.

"That's all I wanted to say."

And with those words, I hear my mother exhale sharply, a long sigh that seems to come from the very center of her being, a moan escaping her lips, and I reach across the table and take her hand, holding on tight. Her palm is sweaty and cold against mine, and I try to tell her with my eyes that it's okay, that it will be over soon, but if she understands, she makes no sign of it. Instead she watches as Arianne walks away from us, her feet a broken shuffle against the dirty floor, just one of a hundred lost souls milling through the wide, empty space, all trying to find our way home.

FOURTEEN

The rest of the month crawls to a close, the days repeating themselves in an endless parade of sameness. I drag myself through the halls, head down, avoiding eye contact, eat my lunch on the stairwell, sometimes with Riley, but most of the time I'm alone, picking at a bag of chips I won't finish, a book sprawled across my lap, open and unread. Riley at least has basketball; long mornings in the gym, where he sweats himself mute; lunch hours spent on the court, tossing endless balls through metal hoops. When people pass by me, sitting there, I look away and try to pretend it doesn't bother me when they begin to whisper, their voices harsh and guttural. When I drive home in the early spring afternoons, the lilac bushes are heavy with blossoms, the rich, heady scent a forbidden perfume, violet petals wet with rain. In my room, it's the same dance every day. I pick up my violin and put it down, only to pick it back up again, hugging it to my chest and closing my eyes. I've blown off my lessons with Grace, let her calls go unanswered, my cell phone going straight to voice mail. Each day I wait for Luke, for Miranda to emerge from the closet, blood trailing behind her on the floor as my fingers pluck nervously at the strings. Mostly I stare into space, the house so eerily quiet without Luke moving around in his room, without my father's ball games on TV, his voice loud and jovial in the halls. My mother down in the basement, the sound of piano drifting through the house like a delicate snowfall, the classical CDs she plays now when she's working, her foot pressed against the pedal of her potter's wheel, shutting everything out. Not that it seems to help her art any. I find pieces of pots in the trash each week, shards of pottery sharp enough to cut open a vein, the glaze cracked and bubbled.

Suddenly, prom night has snuck up on me. I should be excited. I should be jumping out of my skin considering this is my first prom ever. But as I stand in front of the mirror, contemplating myself in the glass, I am full of dread. There are girls standing in front of their mirrors tonight, a dreamy look in their eyes as they pin a creamy blossom in their hair, picturing the good-night kisses or even more, the slow dances, their head on some boy's shoulder, lulled into a kind of slumber by the music, the dim colored lights, the tickling sensation of hot breath in their ear.

I am not one of them.

My mother bustles around me, clucking like a hen, her mouth full of pins as she secures my hair in a neat bun that reminds me of a cinnamon roll. The blue dress shines against my skin, brightening my face, the blush she swept over the apples of my cheekbones earlier heightening the effect, my eyes lined with black pencil, the lashes darkened to a thick fringe. Her diamond studs sparkle in my ears, and as I watch myself twist before the glass in an attempt to see my body from every angle, my mood begins to rise. Maybe in all the excitement, I tell myself, trying to sound confident, they'll all just forget about me, forget I'm even there. Forget that Luke—

(—shot and killed all those people. People who should be there tonight, standing in front of mirrors, feeling pretty for maybe the first time ever—)

The phone rings, and my mother pats me on the head once before rushing out of the room to answer it, yelling over her shoulder as she exits.

"It's probably a telemarketer."

No one calls much anymore, so she's probably right. Still, my body tenses up as I await her return. I am leaning into the mirror, fixing a small smudge under my left eye, when Miranda appears behind me, the dried blood on her face cracking in the yellow light. She fingers the silky material of my dress, a wistful expression altering her features, making her almost pretty again.

"It's *such* a nice dress," she says with a sigh, and her touch burns right through me, my thigh aching beneath her hands, the skin deadened with frostbite. I hold my breath until she lets go.

"My dress was black." She looks into the mirror, fixing the snarls of her hair. "My mother said it was too sophisticated for someone my age, but I didn't care. It made me feel beautiful, like I was almost *finished,* you know? Grown-up."

I nod, and she smiles at me like we're sharing a secret. Since she's been dead, I've never seen Miranda smile, and her teeth are white and even in her ravaged face.

"You look really pretty," she says with a soft hesitancy, smoothing down the back of my dress, pulling the zipper all the way to the top.

I whirl around to face her, the light shining through her limbs like a Chinese lantern.

"Why didn't you save me?" she asks, her eyes tired and sad, the bullet wound on the side of her head pulsing softly with the rhythm of her breath.

I cannot feel myself breathing, though I know there is air in my lungs. If there weren't, I'd look like Miranda. Slightly blue. Transparent. Dead.

"I'm sorry." I swallow hard, my tongue coated with sand. "I didn't know how to. I was scared."

(—her shrieks getting louder with every step of Luke's boots. The

barrel poking beneath the table, her screams rising through the air, a
broken siren—)

"I should've done something."

I say this, even though I don't know what, if anything, I could have done differently. Could I have stopped Luke if I had tried? I've never really thought about it. The idea makes me pause, Miranda's face flickering before me. Could I have walked over to him, placed a hand on his shoulder, spoken softly, persuasively in his ear until he put the gun down, lowering it to the floor? I will never know. And now it's too late.

"Maybe I could've stopped him," I say tentatively, more to myself than to Miranda, a faint muttering. "Maybe I should have tried."

There is a weight that slides off of me as the words leave my lips, and I take a big breath, my chest wide-open, the air moving effortlessly in and out for what feels like the first time in months. There is something freeing in hearing the words aloud, taking responsibility—no matter how small— for what I could've done, the path not taken.

"Thank you." Miranda's face fills with something like relief, a pearly glow emanating from her eyes, her limbs, her very being, and all at once, she disappears from sight, leaving the eggy smell of sulfur and the lush reek of wild roses in her absence.

"Your father's on the phone, Alys." My mother steps

back in the room and immediately begins recapping the bottles and jars strewn across the top of my dresser in a fit of what is either industriousness or anger. "Do you want to talk to him?"

I knew my father would call, but I didn't think it would be tonight. I wonder if this is the first time they've talked since he left, and judging from my mother's jerky movements, I suspect that the answer is yes. "Maybe later," I say, my lips barely moving. I do want to talk to him, and I will. But not yet. I'm not ready to hear his voice, to hear his answer when I ask when

(if)

he's coming back to us. I feel hot and cold all at once, and the air in my bedroom shimmers slightly, as if it's full of handfuls of broken glass. My mother's footsteps in the hall coincide with the ringing of the doorbell. I watch the girl in the mirror, standing there alone, wearing a blue dress that announces the rites of spring.

I've never seen Riley in a suit, but here he is, groomed, bathed, and cologned, his hair slicked back so that the bones of his face stand out beneath the hall light, his cheekbones set at a rakish angle. He takes in my dress, the jewelry sparkling at my wrists and ears, his eyes broadcasting his approval.

"You look great, Alys," he says, sweeping the length of my body. "Really great." We smile at each other as if we are the only people in the room, in the city, on the planet, until I remember that my mother is in the house, walking down the stairs behind me.

"So do you," I say, and I suddenly cannot meet his eyes. I look down at the small black clutch in my hand instead, trying to remember if I've actually put anything useful inside it, like lip gloss or money.

"Don't you two look gorgeous!" my mother chirps, her face bright, holding a camera in one hand. I roll my eyes at Riley, and he smiles, willing to forgive her for anything, to tolerate what I know will be a complete and total photo-op embarrassment. "Let me get a few pictures before you go."

She stands in front of us, raising the camera to her face as I lean into the warmth of Riley's body, his arm draped lightly around my shoulders. We smile broadly, real smiles, and I want Luke to stay away tonight, up in his bedroom, where he belongs, and not out here in the real world, the place where he messes everything up. Even so, I can hear his voice in my ear, a low mumble.

It's so fake. It's like she wants proof that we're all so fucking happy all the time . . .

But why can't we be? I shrug off the echo of Luke's words. Why can't we be—at least sometimes?

In the car, I don't know what to say. Suddenly, it's like we're on a real date—the flower blooming extravagantly on my wrist, our clothes so formal, so unlike the uniform of jeans and sweats we wear to school each and every day, that I'm nervous, my palms itching and sweaty.

Riley turns the key in the ignition, and the engine springs to life, the seats vibrating slightly. Riley drives an old Dodge Dart that his parents helped him buy last year. It's a total muscle car painted cobalt blue with shiny chrome wheels and slightly ripped leather seats. If Riley has a soul, it probably looks a lot like this car.

"Your mom's pretty funny." Riley chuckles, adjusting his rearview mirror. "Where's your dad at?"

I look out the window so I don't have to face him.

"He left," I say, my voice ragged and small.

"On business?"

"No," I say, swallowing hard. "For a while. But I think he'll come back. That's what I told my mother, anyway."

I can see the silhouette of my mother's body framed in the living room window, and I know her brow is knitted in concern, wondering why we're still sitting at the curb, engine idling. Watching her, I ache for the time when we were all a family, when my father would stand behind her, one hand on her shoulder, the other raised in my direction, waving good-bye as I walked into the night.

"God," he says after a few moments of silence. "I'm so sorry, Alys. I don't know what to say."

"There's nothing *to* say." I stare straight ahead, looking at the streetlights above, the slightly pitted moon, the sprinklers across the road popping on one by one. Even though the engine is on, Riley makes no move to pull away from the curb. I look over at him and see that in the moonlight, his profile is cut in two. The places where the light touches his skin make it shine brightly in the dark. I feel drugged, slightly strange, and I wait for Luke to show up, for his restless, heated energy to fill the car, imploding it.

"We should get going."

I say this even though prom is the last place I want to be right now. Despite what I'd hoped for standing in front of the mirror, my flushed, hopeful face reflected in the glass, any dreams of normalcy seem laughable now. The dead show up in my bedroom on a daily basis—what do I know about normal anymore? I want to stay here, headlights on, engine running, safe in the womb of the dusky interior. But now that I've said it, we are on our way. Riley puts the car in drive and eases off down the street, passing my house, my block, turning the corner so quickly that I grab on to the door handle, my heart beating in time with the rattle of the engine.

When we enter the gym after circling the parking lot for what feels like forever trying to find a spot, mostly since a bunch of limos have been triple-parked, I'm stunned by the way it has been transformed. It still unmistakably smells like a gym—sweaty socks and locker rooms—but the lights are dim and blue-tinged, a giant, crashing wave projected on the far wall, an obvious nod to this year's theme: "Escape to Paradise." Sand crunches beneath my heels; white, pink, and red flowers are banked in masses on the sides of the stage; and a DJ wearing a tropical-print Hawaiian shirt spins at the front of the room, silver headphones covering his ears.

When we walk in, all eyes turn toward us, their faces incredulous. Even though I suspected this would be the case, worried about it all last night when I couldn't sleep, it still hurts. Whether they are shocked that we've arrived together or that we've even so much as dared to come at all is up for grabs. Moments before, we sat comfortably in silence, but in here, we are both visibly tense, nervous, eyes darting around the dance floor, not sure if we should sit or stand. I smooth down my dress with one hand, grateful to have something to fidget with, a reason to lower my head and look away. The music is so loud, it makes conversation impossible, and when I glance over at Riley, he shoots me a reassuring smile. I try to smile back, even though I feel like I'm about to jump out of my skin, which is cold and clammy despite the heat in the room.

Riley takes me by the hand and leads me to a round table at the back of the room, which is set for dinner. I've heard that most people don't actually eat the gross chicken or steak but instead spend the majority of the night sneaking off to the bathroom to get high in the stalls or drink whiskey stolen from their parents' liquor cabinets. I'm so on edge that a little inebriation doesn't sound half bad. I would give anything to have the world softened around the edges, fuzzy and blanketed with static, for my thoughts to stop whirling around my brain so I wouldn't be so conscious of the fact that everyone is looking at me, waiting for . . . what?

"Waiting for you to crack," Luke whispers smugly in my ear, and for once, I know he's right.

Leave me alone, I think, concentrating with all of my might.

"Are you okay?" Riley leans into me, his mouth barely moving.

I nod, trying to look cool, normal, like none of this bothers me, when all I want to do is leave, run away and never come back. My palms are sweating, and I don't know why I agreed to this. The music changes from frantic hip-hop to a slow song, couples pairing off on the dance floor, arms wrapped around each other so tightly that it's amazing that they can still take in oxygen.

"Do you want to dance?" Riley speaks so close to my ear that his words buzz through me like a plucked string.

"I don't really know how," I say, embarrassed.

Shouldn't someone have taught me? Luke? My father?

"So we'll fake it," Riley says confidently, standing up and holding out one hand for me to follow.

On the dance floor, I place my arms around Riley's neck, swaying from side to side with the beat of the music. It feels strange to be this close to him, to smell the clean scent of his hair, to feel the taut muscle of his biceps beneath his pressed suit jacket.

"See?" Riley raises an eyebrow. "Nothing to it."

I'm grateful for the fact that the dance floor is packed with people, none of whom seem to be looking at me. Most are too busy making out, leaning in for kisses. Out of the corner of my eye I catch glimpses of corsages resting on shoulders, rhinestone hair bands sparkling in the blue light, shoes sporting a mirror shine. I close my eyes, Riley's body swaying against mine, his hands firm at my waist.

When the song ends, I raise my head from his shoulder, and we stand there awkwardly for a moment, just looking at each other. On the way back to the table, my hand in his, I see Delilah walk over to an adjacent table, her hair pulled up in some complicated arrangement at the back of her head that makes her look so grown-up that for a minute, I don't recognize her. She's wearing a white dress that ebbs and flows in soft peaks to the floor, Grecian-style, a band of small white flowers peeking out from her dark hair, a diamond chip sparkling at her throat, which looks long and bitable with her hair pulled away from it. She's talking to the girls seated there, leaning over their shoulders, smiling, and at that moment our eyes meet and she freezes. I feel a pang in my chest, somewhere beyond my ribs, and I miss her so intensely that it hurts to breathe. She raises one hand tentatively, slowly, to wave at me, and as I'm about to raise mine in return, I see a figure come up behind her, a tall, dark-haired guy who immediately wraps his arms around her waist, burying his face in her neck as if he wants to devour her. When he raises his head, I hear a sharp intake of breath, and realize that it is my own. Ben stares back at me, his eyes catching mine and holding them, the color flooding his cheeks in an avalanche of blood.

The room is stifling, pressing in on all sides. I am vaguely conscious of Riley still beside me, his hand on my arm as I begin to move across the room, pulled toward Ben like a magnet. I know that Riley is talking to me, tugging on my arm insistently as a small child would, but his features have gone out of focus, the room whirling before my eyes, and I cannot tell if it is tears or panic that makes what I am seeing so incomprehensible.

Suddenly, I am standing in front of him. Ben. And he is so very beautiful, his dark hair brushed back from his face, that all the words fall out of me onto the floor, swimming there, mixed up and out of order.

Why? When? How?

He looks at me uncomfortably, his eyes moving restlessly from me to Delilah, and then back to me again, as if he isn't sure where to turn or what to do.

"Alys," he finally says, looking at me, his smile stretched tight and thin. "I didn't think you'd be here tonight."

The music surrounds us, a pummeling beat that begins

ferociously, and I have to raise my voice to be heard over the din, the shrieks and whoops erupting from the dance floor.

"Well, I am," I manage to get out, the rush of adrenaline pumping through my veins. "So, how long has this been going on?" I nod at Delilah, whose face is now as pale as her dress.

"It's not what you think," he says quickly, raising his voice and taking a step toward me. I immediately retreat, needing to be as physically far away from him as possible, while at the same time all I want is to be in his arms.

"I think that it is."

His face flushes again, the way it always does when he's embarrassed or caught in a lie, and I realize that I know him too well to play this game, that we are dancing without music, stepping around each other nimbly.

"Look," he starts, raking his hand through his hair, his expression conflicted. "We didn't plan anything . . . It just happened . . ."

I stare at him blankly, my mind refusing to process the words. People directly around us are also staring, whispering, but I can't, I won't, take my eyes away from Ben's face. The music thunders in my ears, and I wish someone would just shut it off, pull the plug, the world going quiet and still.

"Things don't just *happen,* Ben." My throat hurts from yelling, scratchy and dry, and I lean in slightly so that I'm sure he can hear me. "We *make* them happen. Luke didn't

just happen to stumble past a gun and then kill fifteen people. He *planned* it. He *wanted* it to happen."

Ben flinches noticeably. It's as if I've reached over and
slapped him.

I have never said this out loud. Not in this way, and not
even to Riley. My brother shot and killed fifteen people. And
he planned it. I have always known this, but now it seems
real, here in this gymnasium I know so well, my words falling
like grenades. Luke wanted people to die.

"Well, what about you?" he yells back, his eyes snapping
with anger and defiance, and I remember how when Ben
is pushed up against a wall, he fights back the only way he
knows how—dirty. He points somewhere behind my head.
Riley is still standing there, waiting. "How long has *this* been
going on?"

"It's *not*," I say, my cheeks flushing. "We came as friends."

"*Friends,* huh?" Even partly drowned out, Ben's voice is
nasty, cutting. "Sure you are." He scoffs.

"Was this . . ." It is hard for me to finish, to even contemplate that what I'm about to ask might be true. "Thing with
Delilah . . . going on when you and I were . . . together?" I
swallow hard and look at the floor. The moment I tear my
eyes away from his face, I can feel how close to crying I've
been this whole time.

"No!" he blurts out. He grabs my arm, and I let him, his

grip firm. When I look up, his face is contorted, the anger and sadness twisting his features like so much pulled taffy. His voice lowers, his tone softening. "You know me better than that, Alys."

Somehow I find the strength deep inside to pull my arm away gently, rubbing the place he touched with one hand as if to rub him, finally, away.

"I thought I did."

I stare straight at him, daring him to argue with me, to say it isn't true.

"Now I'm not so sure. There are a lot of things I don't understand anymore—I guess you're one of them."

He stands there, openmouthed, then looks at Delilah, who quickly turns away. There's nothing left to say, so I do the hardest thing I've ever done—I turn my back on him and force myself to put one foot in front of the other. The dance track melds into a slow R & B song, and I think of how happy I was just a few minutes ago, my head on Riley's shoulder, the world falling away. There is glitter in the air, silver clouds of it falling from the ceiling, coating the top of my head, my dress. I keep walking, looking straight ahead as if I am wearing blinders until I am in the front hall, then outside, the night chill descending over my face, the skin of my bare legs. From somewhere far away I hear my name being called, and it is garbled, nonsensical. I rub my ears, trying to make it all go away. There are hands on my shoulders, and then Riley is in front of me, breathing hard.

"I want to get out of here," I say. "I want to get out of here now." My voice sounds harsh out in the open air, and I remember that I've left my black clutch sitting on the table, my phone tucked inside, but I couldn't care less. There's no reason to stay here, not anymore. Ben and Delilah, the look on their faces, caught red-handed—it all reminds me that there's no going back, that there's nothing left for me here. I should've gone to my grandmother's when I had the chance, moved in with Grace—anything but stayed here, the place I will always be known as Luke's sister, the guy who murdered fifteen people, gunning them down like animals. I've been holding on so tight that I've barely noticed that there's nothing left to hold on to at all, my fists closing around miles of empty air. I've fought so hard against the idea of running away, starting over, and now, standing here in the parking lot, stars hidden by thick clouds, it's hard to remember exactly what I've been fighting for. If I leave here, no one besides my mother will care, no one at all. I'll become a faded memory, a ghost haunting the town when the nights are long and cold.

You know whose sister she was, right?

"Okay," Riley says, his body stiffening slightly, fishing his keys from his pocket. I don't know what he's thinking or if he's angry with me, Ben, or just the whole world. "I'll take you home." He begins to walk toward the parking lot, and I call out, glitter shining on the shoulders of his jacket.

"Riley!" He stops, turning around. "Not home. I don't want to go *home*. I want to get *out* of here."

"What do you mean?"

"Out of this crappy town, out of this state, maybe even out of the fucking country." I can feel the desperation seeping out of every orifice of my body, out of the follicles of my hair, the pores of my skin.

I take a step toward Riley, then another, the ground shaky beneath my feet, and then I am in his arms, breathing deep, his hand coming around to draw me closer. We are holding on to each other as if we are lost at sea, our bodies the only thing keeping us afloat. I need him right now, need something, his hair soft in my hands. *Lost.* I close my eyes and think about disappearing into the darkness inside Riley's car, his hand on the gearshift, the heavy purr of the motor drowning out the possibility of thought.

We are lost.

"All right," he mumbles, pulling me against him more tightly now until I can barely think, barely breathe. "Let's go."

FIFTEEN

The road stretches out before us, black as licorice. Dark candy. Outside Madison, we stop for gas, and Riley takes off his jacket, rolling up his shirtsleeves. On the freeway, he drives with one hand, sitting back as if he's parked on a beach somewhere, all the time in the world at his fingertips. The headlights illuminate only patches of the interstate at a time, and I'm transfixed by the crimson swirl of taillights, the smell of cold air and exhaust, how the pavement looks shiny, almost wet, in the absence of daylight.

"Where do you want to go?" Riley turns down the music, his iPod playing old blues tunes, low-pitched growling amid the plucking of guitars, strings vibrating through the speakers.

I watch the exit signs as we pass by, the turnoff to Chicago looming up ahead. The freeway will fork in two—just like my life. There will always be the memory of my life before the shooting. And after. My whole existence reduced to two separate, distinct spheres that have little to do with each other.

"What about Chicago?" he suggests before I can speak. He puts on his blinker and changes lanes effortlessly, barely looking in the rearview mirror. "I've never been there," he admits, glancing at me briefly. I can't tell if he's worried about the fact that we're leaving or if he's as relieved to be getting out of town as I am. I don't dare ask when we're coming back, what we'll do for money after tonight, or even where we'll stay. It's enough to be here in the car with him, the green glow from the radio, the heat pumping from the vents wrapping us in a cocoon that sways in the dark.

"Me neither," I say, although I think I was there once, with my parents and Luke when I was super little, but since I can't remember the trip or what we did there in detail anyway, I decide that it doesn't really count.

"Chi-town it is," Riley says decisively, switching lanes again to follow the exit. "Do you want to call your mom?" he asks lightly, trying not to make a big deal of the question. I picture my phone tucked inside my purse, sitting innocuously on the table draped with cloth and crepe paper, ringing intermittently beneath the heavy thump of the music.

"Not really," I answer, because I don't. "Not now."

I imagine her panic rising through the phone, latching

on to my body, my brain, my heart beating faster. I know that she is waiting up for me, a book in her lap, unread. To-morrow will be soon enough.

"What about you?"

"Don't worry about me," Riley says briskly, an edge to his voice that makes me sorry I asked.

I watch the speedometer as it creeps up to seventy-five, then back down to seventy with the release of his foot on the gas. Riley is a pretty good driver, and for that I'm grate-ful. I may be seeing dead bodies come to life on a regular basis, but I have no desire to go spinning off the earth any time soon. We drive for a while without speaking, the silence between us a quiet lull, and I watch the way the headlights from the adjacent lanes of traffic sweep over the planes of his face, lighting it up like a strobe. There is an exit coming up, gas, food, lodging, and without warning, he eases the car over and onto the off-ramp, the wheels following the gentle curve of the road.

"I'm pretty beat," he says, and now that I'm looking for it, I can see it in his face, the exhaustion hanging over his fea-tures, sharpening them to a fine point. "The thing is, we've still got a ways to go, and I don't like to drive when I'm tired." He rubs one eye, digging his fingers in roughly, and I want to grab his hand, tell him to stop. "Okay if we find somewhere to crash for tonight?"

"You mean like . . . a motel?"

The thought of being alone in a motel with Riley makes my mouth suddenly dry, the car slowing as we exit the freeway.

"Unless you want to sleep on the side of the road somewhere." Riley laughs, and I watch out the window as we pass fast-food restaurants, a gas station. At the end of the block there's a Motel 6, the sign glowing like a neon savior.

We pull into the parking lot, driving up to the office. Through the window, I can see a tired-looking woman seated behind the desk, engrossed in a magazine, her long fingers turning the pages idly, a mass of blond curls tumbling down around her face. When Riley walks in, she looks up and pushes a sheaf of papers toward him, pecking blindly at her computer.

The room is like every nondescript motel room scattered across the country: drapes the same unremarkable shade of dirty-looking beige, plastic-wrapped water glasses in the bathroom, the caustic smell of bleach emanating from the sheets and towels, washed to a shade stark as bone. I sit on the bed and wait for Riley to return from the gas station with supplies, flip the TV on to a talk show, then flip it off again, too restless to pay attention to anything.

I hear a jangle of keys and sit up as Riley pushes the door open, a bulging paper sack in his hands, a bag of salt-and-vinegar potato chips sticking out of the top. He grins, dumping the bag onto the bed, kicking his shoes off one after the other, and tossing his crap around the room in that special way that only boys can do, marking his territory.

"Hardly anything was open," he says, sitting down on the bed and facing me cross-legged. He reaches into the bag, pulling out the chips, some candy, a bag of popcorn—and, last, he yanks out a six-pack of beer with a ridiculous flourish that immediately cracks me up.

"How'd you get that?" I say through my laughter.

"Please." He rolls his eyes, feigning irritation that I would even ask, twisting the top off of one of the bottles and handing it to me. I take a long drink, tilting my head back, and the coldness of it, the bubbles tickling my dry, scratchy throat, feels so good that it's everything I can do not to drain the entire bottle in one long gulp. I watch as he tears open the bag of chips, popping a few into his mouth and moaning with exaggerated pleasure. "Mmmmmm . . ." he mumbles, "I didn't realize how fucking hungry I was until I got in there."

We sit there munching in unison, fingertips crusted with salt, knees touching. The room is warm, shielding us from the early spring chill, the curtains drawn. It's almost cozy, being here with Riley, the door locked and bolted, the lamps casting a soft glow over the bed, the sheets, the white marble slabs of the pillows awaiting the insistent crush of our heads. I finish my beer and Riley opens two more, passing one to me.

"Are you trying to get me drunk?" I grin at him, the malty scent hanging between us.

"It's prom night," Riley says, taking a long drink, wiping

his mouth with the back of one hand. "It's a goddamn *tradition,* or haven't you heard?"

I think of the gym, the dim blue lights sweeping the dance floor, Ben and Delilah wrapped in each other's arms, her dark hair pinned up so the back of her neck is exposed, vulnerable and defenseless. I close my eyes for a minute, sickened.

"I wonder what it would've been like if everything hadn't happened the way it did," I mutter. Maybe it's the alcohol flooding my system, maybe it's being in a strange place, an anonymous room so far away from my real life that I can say anything. I open my eyes, one thumbnail absentmindedly picking the label off the bottle in my hand. Riley takes another swig of beer, tilting his head back. "I mean if I had gone to prom with Ben. If none of this had ever happened. Would you be there with Janelle right now? Would we be happier?"

There is a stabbing sensation in my head, a constant reminder of all that has been taken from me, the wound raw and bloody, refusing to heal. I can almost *feel* Ben and Delilah together, see the way he takes her by the hand and leads her to his car, the place we spent so many hours, our mouths moving against each other's bodies, the windows fogged and steaming.

"I guess we'll never know, will we?" Riley's expression shifts slightly, and I can see the anger and sadness rising in him, making its way to the surface. He shoves the bag of chips to one side of the bed so that there's nothing between us now but a few paltry inches of air. "Luke made sure of that."

A wave of shame sweeps over me, and I want nothing more than to vanish. I wonder if it will always be like this, my brother and I so intricately connected that, like Siamese twins, we will never again be separate entities.

"Maybe it's better this way," Riley says flippantly, breaking into my thoughts.

"How can you say that?"

The idea is inconceivable to me. Monstrous.

"Think about it. Maybe we'd be at prom right now, having a totally miserable time. Maybe you'd be hiding in the bathroom wishing the night would just hurry up and be over because Ben turned out to be an A-hole anyway. Maybe I'd have gotten totally shitfaced just so I could deal with Janelle's endless bullshit, just so when I woke up tomorrow morning, I wouldn't remember anything at all."

I smile, despite myself.

"This isn't so bad, you know? Me and you here together. We've got beer." He points at the bottle in front of me. "Snacks. What else do we need—bad music?"

"True," I say grudgingly, laughing a little. "Still, I wish it had never happened. Any of it."

"Even being here with me?"

He is staring at me intently. If I reached over and touched

his leg, the bare skin of his forearm, we would tumble into each other, falling backward onto the bed and inhaling each other's breath, drunk on it. *Dangerous*, I am thinking as I look at him, fighting the urge to turn away. *This is very dangerous . . .*

(—*"Don't," Luke said, his annihilating heat permeating the room—*)

"What do you think Luke would've thought of . . . this?" I say, the tension in the room like so many pounds of air crushing my chest.

"What," Riley asks. "You and me?" He smiles a funny half smile, full of pain, pointing in my direction, then at himself. "He would've hated it." He laughs, a short, rough sound that comes out more like a yelp, nothing expressing happiness or mirth. "He probably would've killed me."

I can feel the warmth draining from my body as soon as the words leave Riley's lips.

Killed. Because that's what Luke is

(was)

A killer. A liar. Someone who fooled us all expertly, so seamlessly, that we didn't know we were being fooled at all until it was way too late. Until there was blood streaking the floors of the library, the hallways, the asphalt in the parking lot.

I must look terrible because Riley stops, taking my hand gently, carefully, in his own, and holds on tight. I feel queasy, and I lean over and put my beer bottle on the floor without breaking contact.

"I miss him," I say, my voice barely audible. "Most of the time I wasn't sure he even liked me." I am ashamed to admit this somehow, and I drop my head, afraid of Riley's reaction. "I mean, it's not like we were close anymore. Most of the time he barely spoke to me, and I just pretended that everything was fine because that's what we *do* in my family. And even though I'm so mad at him for what he did, I can't help it—every time I walk into that house, I miss him so much. I miss hearing him come home at night, the sound of the door closing behind him, knowing he was in the next room, right where he was supposed to be. I miss the way he'd listen at the door of my room when I practiced sometimes, so quiet I didn't even know he was there until he clapped, and we'd just crack up together. I miss watching him argue with my mom at breakfast, the way he wouldn't eat a goddamn thing in the morning. I miss his stupid fucking sugar packets in his stupid fucking Cokes."

I break off. Unable to find the words to go on, staring at the bedspread, the pattern of leaves and vines crawling across the rough fabric.

"Hey, Alys." Riley lets go of my hand, tilting my chin up to meet his eyes, wet with tears I know he's too proud to spill. "I know," he says, almost resigned now. "Believe me, I know. He shut me out," he says bitterly, "just like he did everyone else." We sit there for a long moment, just looking at each other, and I'm trying to hold it together, trying not to break into a million pieces when Riley speaks again.

"And he definitely liked you—I know he did. Hell, he *loved* you. You were his *sister.*"

I want so much to believe him. It's hard to keep looking at Riley, like staring straight into the sun, the force behind his words, the insistence and surety of them making me dizzy.

"I see him sometimes."

My voice shrinks down even further, a murmur, and Riley leans in closer.

"You see him? Like in a dream?" Riley looks first confused, then worried when I don't answer right away. "I have those too. I told you, Alys. They're not real."

It takes everything I have to keep talking, to get out what I need to say, what I need somebody, anybody, to hear.

"No. I mean, I *see* him. In the house. In my room. Even at school, sometimes. He just shows up. He won't leave me alone."

I am racked by sudden sobs, the air stopped in my chest, syrupy and thick. I keep my head down as tears run over my face, scalding it, and Riley pulls me to his chest. The sounds I am making are incomprehensible, my body shaking violently. Riley holds on tight, drawing me into his lap. He moves from side to side, rocking me, my face buried in the salty folds of his neck.

"Shhhh . . . Alys," he says quietly. "It's okay. It's not real. It's going to be okay."

I lift my head, aware that I'm a mess, makeup streaked across my face, hair coming down from the bun my mother fixed so many hours ago.

"What if it *won't*?"

Outside, a car pulls up and a door slams shut, and the lamp on the table buzzes and hums, a moth flitting around inside the shade, wings beating heavily. Riley looks at me, his face crumpling slightly as he begins to cry, and the very sight of his tears, his face so open and vulnerable, strikes a sharp chord inside me, moves me in a way I can no longer deny.

I kiss him, pulling him down on top of me, my hands in his hair, his mouth sucking avidly at mine as we press our bodies together, trying to destroy the space between us. From somewhere far away I'm aware that I'm still making noise, desperate moans, and Riley pushes up on his elbows for a minute, his fingers scrabbling against the buttons of his shirt before he pulls it off. His hands are underneath my dress, thumbs hooked into the sides of my panties, and I pull him harder against me, wanting to get as close to him as I possibly can when my eyelids flutter open, and over Riley's shoulder I see Luke, looking at us from the side of the bed.

There is a burning smell in the air, a reek of hot, dripping wax and charred blossoms. Riley is kissing my neck, oblivious, and I stare at my brother's face, too helpless to move, to say anything at all. But for the first time, there's no anger, hostility, or sarcasm in his expression. He shines in the lamplight, flickering like a candle on its way out.

It's okay, he mouths. His lips barely move, but I can hear his voice in my brain, as if he is already a part of me, inside me forever. *It's going to be okay, Alys. But this isn't what you need right now.* He smiles at me once, so sweetly, and so unlike the half-cocked, sarcastic grin I know so well that I want to beg him to stay here with me. But as quickly as he arrived, he begins to fade, and it takes all of my strength not to cry out as he slowly blends into the walls behind him, the light, the very air in the room until nothing remains but Riley and me, locked together in an embrace that could beat back death itself, banishing it from the premises.

"Wait," I say, my voice guttural, scorched. "Wait."

Riley stops, his face full of concern. I'm crying again, turning my head to the side, unable to really look at him.

"What's wrong? Do you want to stop?" he asks, stroking my cheek, his voice tight. "Did I do something wrong?"

"No," I say, pushing him off of me and sitting up. "I just..." I'm not sure how to explain, how to make Riley understand.

"Are you just not... into this? I mean, *me*?" He looks away, sitting back on his knees and running one hand through his tangled hair.

"No." I put my hand on his thigh, and he looks at me, waiting for what I will say next. "I *am*. I mean, *obviously*!" His smile is uncertain as he covers my hand with his. "But I'm not sure we're . . . doing it . . ." My face flushes with embarrassment. "For the right reasons. I think we miss him. Luke, I mean." Riley nods, his face tight. "But we can't bring him back . . . by being together. I don't think it works that way."

"You don't feel . . . anything for me, then?" Riley looks right at me, and he is more beautiful than I have ever seen him, shirt off, his bare chest gleaming in the lamplight, the crystalline blue of his eyes fixed on mine.

"I do," I say slowly, "but I don't know *why* I'm feeling it, or if it's really real. I mean, you are the closest I can get to him now. You were his *best friend*."

"I thought I was." Riley's voice breaks jaggedly and his eyes fill with tears again. I can tell that he hates it, this loss of control, that he's trying desperately not to cry again but is forfeiting the battle with his own emotions, giving up.

"You were." I rub his palm softly, curling my hand around his until our fingers are entwined. "Riley, nothing that . . . happened was your fault any more than it was mine. It was *Luke's*. But I can't run away . . . from everything—no matter how much I want to."

Riley nods slowly. "I get that," he says. "I do. I just wish things could be, you know . . . different. With us."

We stare at each other, and even though we're so close that I might fall into his arms once again, run my hands over his warm, bare skin and feel his breath in my mouth, it is as if a wall has come down, cleaving us in two. I want so badly to change my mind, to keep going until we reach Chicago, the Dodge gliding through the warm spring streets, carrying us along in its metallic blue haze, but I know in my heart that it won't solve anything, that it will only delay the pain waiting for us back at home, the healing that we both need to go through.

"I know," I say, breaking through the wall one last time and pulling him toward me, wrapping my arms around him. The heat from his body melts into mine, and we stay like this for a long while, listening to the silence in the room, the numbers clicking on the cheap digital clock on the bedside table, the light fixture buzzing in the bathroom. I close my eyes, grateful for this one moment where I feel small, where I feel almost loved. "I do too."

After a while, Riley lies down on the bed, spent, and I switch off the lamp and lie down next to him, his tears hot on the back of my neck. We are both shaking slightly, and I hold on to his arm, rubbing the smooth skin in order to soothe him, to soothe myself. We drift off into sleep, comforted by the closeness of our bodies, the only beacon in the room the sound of our breathing. One by one, the stars dissolve in the sky and light, pure light, with all its clarity and wisdom, peeks through the crack in the curtains, falling across the wide, white confines of the bed.

In his sleep, Riley whispers my brother's name in my ear, turning over once, his feet kicking the covers like a drowning man.

SIXTEEN

In the morning, everything looks different. Harder. Uglier. My eyes are ringed with dark makeup, and in the bathroom mirror under the buzzing fluorescent light, I resemble a pale, slightly rabid raccoon, my lips chapped and peeling. I'm still wearing my dress, the color too bright and bold in the harshness of the bathroom light, too vivid for daylight itself. I grab the little bar of soap and unwrap it, scrubbing at my face while steam clouds the mirror, the sound of the running water soothing my frayed nerves.

When I walk back into the room, Riley is stretching like a cat, arms overhead, his face splitting into a wide grin.

"How'd you sleep?" he asks, sitting up and running his hands through his hair, naked to the waist. The sight of him still makes me weak, the breath catching in my throat, so I distract myself by putting on my shoes.

"Like crap, pretty much. You hog the covers, by the way."

I'm smiling as I fasten a thin strap around one ankle. He throws his legs over the side of the bed, searching around on the floor until he finds his white dress shirt, pulling it on, his fingers languidly working the buttons as if we're never leaving this room, this town, the rumpled bed, the covers kicked to the floor in a heap of white cotton.

"Well, I may be a cover hog, but you *snore*," he retorts in protest, and I can't help but laugh at his face, the mock outrage I see there. But our smiles quickly fade as we stare into each other's eyes and the room becomes hushed and somber.

"We need to go back," I say, wrapping my arms around my waist, my bare arms chilled, covered in tiny pricks of gooseflesh.

Riley stops midbutton, his expression grave—a sharp contrast to his usual carefree attitude and ready grin. There's a moment when I know it would be possible to stuff the words back inside me, but I know that we can't, that in some ways we're already back in Plainewood, the orderly rows of tree-lined streets calling our names, the leaves rustling together in the breeze, whispering our secrets.

"I know," he says with a sigh, his fingers fastening the last button with a finality that makes me want to erase it all, to get in bed with him and stay there forever, living on stale chips, my lips stinging with salt and drunk with the heat of his mouth on mine. But I know I can't.

"We will," he says after a long moment. "We are."

I grab Riley's jacket, pulling it over my shoulders like a shroud.

The car ride back seems to fly by, moving too fast, the roads clear of traffic, the speedometer creeping toward eighty. Sunlight fills the interior, warming us without our having to run the heater, and Riley stares straight ahead, quiet, pensive, as if he's by himself and I'm not really there at all. At a gas station, he buys two cups of coffee, and the car fills with the rich scent of roasted beans. I hold my cup between my hands, grateful for its reassuring warmth even though the coffee itself is beyond atrocious. Riley turns the music way up with a flick of his wrist, the screeching guitars and ponderous drumbeats eliminating any possible hope of conversation.

When I see the exit for Plainewood, my heart starts to skip, and I wonder if it's the caffeine in my system or my trepidation at being right back where I started. We drive through the center of town, the noise of the day bustling just outside of the windows, a typical Sunday morning, people coming in and out of the bakery on Main Street, church bells ringing intermittently with ecstatic, joyful chimes. As we pass the cemetery, I see Luke walking beneath a tall tree, his fingers trailing the metal fence, and my arm reaches out involuntarily, grabbing on to Riley's wrist, squeezing it tightly.

"Stop," I say, suddenly frantic for him to pull over, to let me out. "You can drop me off here." Riley looks at me, confusion blanketing his face, and pulls the car to the curb, the engine still idling in a slow growl.

"You want to get out *here*?" Riley asks, taking in the rows of tombstones, the tall oak trees sprinkled throughout the cemetery, their wide arms outstretched.

I nod, one hand on the door, the metal cold under my palm.

"Are you going to be okay?" He reaches over, pushing my hair back with one hand, and the tenderness of his touch almost brings me to tears, makes me want to crawl across the seat and bury myself in his arms.

"I think so," I say, and for the first time the words feel like a little less of a lie. Not much less, but a start. I push open the car door, and shiver, the morning air still chilly. I turn back to Riley, and he's staring out the windshield, not watching as I leave.

"Are we still friends?" The words leave my lips before I can second-guess them.

"You bet," he says, grinning broadly, his eyes shockingly blue in the morning light. "Always."

I look at him for a long moment, memorizing the lines of his face, the way the sunlight turns his hair to spun gold, how its rays wash everything clean. I get out, closing the door gently behind me, and stand there at the curb as Riley pulls away, exhaust pumping, a trail of vapor hanging in the air long after he turns the corner and disappears out of sight.

SEVENTEEN

The ground under my feet is damp, my heels sinking into the grass, and by the time I make my way across the wide expanse of lawn to Luke's grave, my shoes are soaked, ankles dotted with droplets of dew. I crane my neck, twisting my head all around, but I don't see my brother anywhere. My heart dips in disappointment, but I keep going, trudging across the grass until I am right in front of Luke's headstone, throwing Riley's jacket to the ground. What I see there makes my hand fly to my mouth, my eyes wide pools of disbelief. I sink to my knees in front of the white stone, MURDERER scrawled across the smooth surface in some kind of thick red marker, the letters jagged and ominous. The stone is cool under my fingers, and I trace each letter as if by doing so I can erase it, dissolve the stain from the pure white surface until nothing remains but the letters of his name.

Lucas David Aronson.

I grab a handful of grass, ripping it up angrily, my face hot and stinging, and scrub the grass against the headstone, using all of my might. When that doesn't work, I search the perimeter, picking up a rock with a sharp edge, digging it into the stone, scraping the side of it against the letters. I work hard, pushing my hair back with one hand, my shoulders aching, sweat beading on my brow, but the word remains, damaged now, but still staring up at me defiantly, mocking me.

"I wouldn't knock myself out if I were you."

When I look to my right, Luke is sitting there, a blade of grass in his mouth, watching me with amusement. Just looking at him, I am angrier than I've ever been. I can feel the rage building inside me, a kettle giving off clouds of steam, ready to shriek, ready to make its presence known.

"And why is that?" I say nastily, continuing to scrub at the unyielding stone. "Maybe you don't care anymore what people think, Luke, but I do."

He tosses the blade of grass to the side, stares up at the sky, squinting into the sun. I wonder if he can feel the rays on his skin, warming him from the outside in, or if they simply shine through him. "That was always your problem, though, wasn't it? You cared too much—about everything. I used to hear you practicing your violin at night, playing the same piece over and over, working on it until you got it exactly right. I could almost see you patting yourself on the back afterward." He lets out a short, dry laugh. "As if getting into some dumb summer program was going to really change your life."

I put the rock down on top of his grave, stone on stone, and look him in the face, smarting from the meanness of his attack, tears springing to my eyes. *I will not cry for you anymore,* I tell myself. *I will not.*

"Well, if we're really talking now, I guess your problem is that you didn't care *enough*. About anything."

He looks at me, and I can see the outline of the trees directly behind him through the slightly transparent parameters of his head. His eyes are filled with an otherworldly radiance and examine me as coolly as if I am a science experiment, not a real flesh-and-blood human being sitting in front of him. Not his sister. Not anyone who counts. I think of the gun, how he held it so nonchalantly in front of my face. *Hey,* he said, his face expressionless.

Hey.

"Maybe we just care about different things," he says, his hands pawing at the grass, ripping it out by the handful. "But I guess you never thought of that." His face is full of sadness now, and I want to reach out and touch his hair, his shoulder, but something stops me, an invisible force field surrounding his body, a warning.

"When did you start hating me, Luke?" I ask, my voice

swallowed up by the words themselves, not sure that I really want to know.

"I don't hate you, Alys." His fingers are still full of grass, but he stops ripping it momentarily, holding very still. "I was jealous of you, if you want to know the truth."

Jealous. Of me. His little sister. The girl who followed him everywhere, diaper sagging at her chubby thighs.

He glances up at me, his features distorted by pain. "You had something you were good at, something you cared about. I had nothing. I was ordinary. Boring. Even Mom and Dad thought so."

"That's not true, Luke," I say, protesting. "You were great at science! At math!"

He looks at me skeptically, but I press on, wanting him to see how wrong he was, how stubborn he's being.

"And you were never boring," I say. "Never."

"Well." His expression shifts to a smirk, Mr. Sarcasm entering the room with a flourish. "*Now* I'm not." He lets out a small, dry laugh, and I shiver, picking up Riley's jacket and wrapping it around my shoulders.

"I don't want people thinking you're a killer," I say quietly, unable to look at him.

He laughs again, bitterly, and even though I can't see his face, I know he's looking at me incredulously, that once again I've amused him without even trying.

"Why not? It's what I am."

I look up as he shakes his head from side to side as if he can't believe my stupidity, then closes his eyes, his head tilted back as if he's drinking in the sunlight.

"It's not *all* you are," I mumble, staring over at those red words splashed across his tombstone, the sad brutality of them.

"Don't you mean 'were'? I'm dead now, Alys, in case you haven't noticed." Luke snorts in that practiced way of his, and I wonder how long I can keep the conversation going without him tearing what's left of my heart to shreds.

"That day in the library . . . did you want to . . ." I can barely make myself say the words. They stick in my throat, and I have to cough once, hard, to get them out. "Would you have . . . Did you want to . . . shoot me?"

His gaze is steady and without malice. I can almost hear him thinking, the gears in his brain clicking through their delicate circuits.

"I don't know," he says finally. "Maybe. I can't remember."

I am stunned for a moment, his words pinning me to the earth.

"Why?" I ask, when I can finally speak, because in some way I've needed to ask ever since he put a gun to his forehead and pulled the trigger, leaving me here to clean up his mess. My voice is scratched and faded as an old record, the needle skipping. "Why, Luke?"

"Why what?" he answers, perfunctorily as a machine.

"Why did you do it? Hurt all those people?" The words spill roughly from my lips in a torrent of bitterness. He doesn't answer me right away, so I go on. "Why were you building a bomb, Luke? What the hell were you thinking?"

"You still can't say it, can you?"

Luke crosses his legs beneath him, resting his elbows on his thighs, his chin in his hands.

"I didn't just 'hurt' them—I shot them. And, as usual, you're asking the wrong questions."

There is a pause as I rack my brain, trying to figure out what he means, but come up blank. Aren't these the only questions? The only questions that count? Sensing my confusion, he tries again, patiently, and all at once I am six years old, sitting on his bed, a book on deep-space travel spread out across my knees, Luke's voice filling my ears, explaining the world, the universe, the way things work.

But they don't. They don't work. Not like this. Not without him.

"It doesn't matter why I did it. Everyone will just make up their own reasons anyway. They'll never forget me now, after what I've done, but they'll never have all the answers either. Why doesn't matter, Alys. Why won't make you—or anyone else—feel any better. It won't give you closure. And it won't bring me back either." His face suddenly softens, the anger melting away. "No matter how much you want it to."

"I know that," I say, and the sudden openness of his

expression, the absence of all meanness, disarms me momentarily. Sitting there across from me, he is my brother again, the Luke that I know, the one who put Band-Aids on my scrapes when I fell roller skating in the driveway, who taught me to play cards, reaching over to tousle my hair when I showed off a good hand. The one who protected me from the monster under the bed, from the ever-shifting, unsteady ground outside the front door. "I know it won't. I just really miss you. I miss you, Luke. And I feel like I can't, like I'm not allowed to because of what you did, and it hurts. It feels like crap." The past hangs there in the distance, shimmering but rapidly fading from view. Our arms entwined in an old photograph, chins jutting toward the camera, the weight of his body leaning into mine. I drop my head, crying openly now, unable to stuff my emotions back inside. There is, it seems, no limit to the tears I will cry for him, no end in sight.

"I miss you too, Alys." It's getting hard to hear him, and when I look back over, I notice that he's getting more transparent by the minute, his body blurring wildly around the edges. "So much." For the first time since he's been gone, there is something ragged in his words, his expression, a kind of tearing, and I notice that his face is contorted as if he is crying, though no tears fall from his eyes. "And that's the truth. But you have to let me go."

I nod, not wanting to agree out loud, to say the words that will make him, like a magic trick, disappear from the world forever, and it dawns on me that as much as he's frightened and annoyed me in equal measure, that all this time I've invited in his spirit. That having his ghost roaming around the house was better than not having him here at all. I've clung to his memory, refusing to let go, unable to let him rest.

"You need to get on with your life," he says, fading in and out, so close, then so very distant. "I need you to do that for me."

"How?" I say, watching as his feet begin to dissolve, then his legs, then his torso, until all that remains is the spectral glow of his face. "How am I supposed to do that?"

He smiles, his eyes shining brilliantly, so full of unbridled love and compassion that it threatens to take my breath away, his face half gone now, the rows of tombstones growing increasingly sharper behind his skull. He winks at me, that old mischievous Luke I lost so long ago.

"You'll find a way," he says right before he vanishes completely, leaving me alone with his grave, his body buried six feet under, dissolving into the dark soil of the earth with each day, each hour that passes, until nothing of him remains.

There is the smell of hothouse roses drifting through the air, the first breath of summer, and I run my hands over his headstone, then lie down so that my head is on top of it. I want, at this moment, to get as close to him as I can, to make sure that wherever he is, he can hear me, can hear my voice clearly when I tell him what I've wanted to say for so long now, the words that have stayed stuck inside me, unheard by anyone at all.

"I loved you," I whisper to him through the stone, picturing the words echoing all the way down to his coffin. The past tense sounds funny to me, not quite right, so I try one more time.

"I love you, Luke," I whisper, hoping with all of my heart, cracked and patched in places but still beating, that he can hear me, that he understands, and all at once it hits me that just because he's gone now doesn't mean the love is too—I can love my brother even though he's dead. I can love him in spite of the fact that he's done terrible things, even though he's hurt people inexplicably. Me among them.

I lie back, staring at the blueness of the sky, my arms outstretched in a cross, wet grass tickling my bare legs. I'm cold, but I don't want to get up and move, don't want to go home just yet. I know that in less than a week, whether I'm ready or not, I'll get in the car and drive to Madison, traveling down the long road, so familiar that I could navigate it blindfolded, taking the exit for the university. I will drive onto campus, marveling at the beauty of the oak trees lining the long paths, the redbrick buildings, so stately and somber. When my name is called, I will stand on the stage in front of the judges and raise my violin, nod to the accompanist seated behind the black, gleaming piano, and bring my bow down onto the strings, my body trembling with excitement and fear, the lure of possibilities wide open. My mother will be in the audience, clutching her purse in her lap, hugging it tightly in her nervousness, Grace seated beside her, muttering softly under her breath, urging me toward the finish. Maybe even my father will be there, nodding his head, one foot tapping the floor, keeping time with the music that fills the womb-like theater: the sweet, high wail of the strings, his hand reaching for my mother's, their wedding rings crossing in the dim light of the auditorium. And whether or not I drop a note or two, my fingers tripping on the strings, even if the bow falls clumsily from my hands, I know that whatever happens next, life, in all of its wonder and grace, will open up again when the first pulses of light hit the morning sky each day, painting it indelibly—even if I don't make the cut.

Or maybe that's just what I want to happen. I'm not innocent enough anymore to believe that my life will change overnight, simply from one well-played piece of music, one moment of beauty lighting my way out of the darkness. This is not that story, and I am not that girl. Not anymore. But I hold on to the thought nonetheless, cradling it in my chest like the first spring flower, like a poem or a sonata.

A song.

The sun peeks its face from behind a cloud, and I close my eyes, taking in the feel of the rays on my face and arms, the cool, damp lawn under my dress, the moisture soaking through. I know it will be ruined, the silk grass stained and wrinkled, but right now I don't care. I breathe deeply, in and out, and I know that when I'm ready, I'll get up and brush the grass from my skirt, slapping my thighs briskly, my stinging skin alerting me to the fact that I'm here, I'm still here, I'm alive, and when I walk out of the cemetery, I will leave behind an infinitesimal pinch of the sadness I've carried with me for the past few months, the tiniest fraction of it, even though I know all too well that there will never be a time when I will forget completely, when the memory of that day will fade from the fabric of my dreams. The imprint of that sadness, that regret, still colors me like a stain, but one that someday I might learn to live with, one that, if I'm lucky, will grow lighter with each passing year, each day that ends with my face turned upward to take in the pinpricks of stars, light-years away, the beauty of the known universe, the miracle of another day, another chance.

Something Luke will never have.

And even as I lie there hoping, hoping with everything I am that somehow I have the right to go on, to make a life for myself apart from what Luke has done, I also know that it might just be a fantasy, a moment of wishful thinking. A story I tell myself in moments of quiet contemplation, when the wind outside shifts through the trees in a whisper, rustling the curtains, and lulling me into sleep.

But, in spite of everything that's happened, I would like to believe it.

RESOURCES

Silent Alarm is a work of fiction, but, sadly, events like those depicted in these pages have become all too common. If you or someone you know is suffering from depression or anxiety, contemplating suicide, or talking about committing a violent act, please reach out for help. There are people who will talk to you, who will listen.

SPEAK UP
1-866-SPEAK-UP (773-2587)
www.speakup.com

Thursday's Child National Youth Advocacy Hotline
1-800-USA-KIDS (872-5437)
www.thursdayschild.org

National Suicide Prevention Lifeline
1-800-273-TALK (8255)
suicidepreventionlifeline.org

National Hopeline Network
1-800-SUICIDE (784-2433)
1-800-442-HOPE (4673)
www.hopeline.com

Crisis Call Center
1-800-273-8255 or
text ANSWER to 839863
crisiscallcenter.org

National Institute of Mental Health Information Center
1-866-615-6464
www.nimh.nih.gov/site-info/contact-nimh.shtml

Mental Health America
www.nmha.org

ACKNOWLEDGMENTS

My agent, Lisa Grubka, and my editor, Stacey Barney, for their belief in me. Kate Meltzer, for her careful work on the manuscript throughout the editing process. John and Deirdre Cadarette, who generously provided me with a place of dreams and inspiration in which to work. Bob Cooke, for answering my myriad questions on school policy with aplomb and grace. Lee Anne Blackmore, for providing crucial insights into Alys's musical life, and the study of violin in general. Willy Blackmore: my champion, my heart, my life.

And for Story, with the hope that by the time you are grown, my love, school violence will be a relic of the past, only found in the pages of books.

JENNIFER BANASH

lives and writes in Los Angeles, California, with her partner, Willy Blackmore, and their daughter, Story.

You can visit Jennifer Banash at
www.jennifer-banash.com

She's living the teenage dream, but her life is more like a nightmare

WHITE
LINES

JENNIFER
BANASH

ONE

I REACH ONE HAND OUT from beneath the warm dark of the quilt and turn off the alarm, the shrillness breaking the early morning silence. I open one eye and the face of Mickey Mouse grins back at me, his hand held up in a jaunty wave, his red lips parted in a grin so cheerful it borders on psychotic. When Giovanni gave me the clock a few months ago for my seventeenth birthday, he laughed, tossing his shoulder-length ringlets away from his face before throwing the box in my lap.

"Darling, it's purrrrrrfect. It's better than Prozac! Think of it—not only will you be able to make it to school on time for a change, but you'll never wake up in a bad mood again!"

Famous last words.

I swing my feet around and tentatively place them on the wooden floor, waiting for the inevitable spins, which I know will be followed by a bout of nausea so intense, I will wish I were dead. Even though I should be used to this schedule by now, it's still a struggle to force my eyes open after four hours of sleep—sometimes less—to move my lethargic body through the morning rituals of teeth brushing and toast. For the next twenty minutes I'll stand in the shower trying to lather my hair with one hand while simultaneously holding on to the wall with the other so I don't fall and crack my skull open. Girl Dies While Scrubbing. News at eleven.

I run a brush through my shoulder-length hair—dyed black this week—flicking droplets of water all over the floor and my feet, and stare at my reflection in the mirror. The circles beneath my eyes the color of bruised plums. The bangs plastered straight across my forehead, glossy as a helmet. My face has all the required features—nose, eyes that are a blue so dark, they look almost black unless you look very closely, and a wide, full mouth that made me the subject of various insults throughout elementary school. But somehow, without makeup, nothing really seems to come together. Even though my complexion is a light shade of olive, without added color I'm as pale and indistinguishable as a ghost. If you walked past me on the street when I wasn't wearing makeup, you might ignore me completely. And most of the time—during the daylight hours at least—it feels like a relief. The only time I'm really comfortable with the feel of eyes gliding over my skin is at night, hidden behind a veil of powder and paint.

I look around the living room, at the clothes I wore last night draped over the back of the green thrift store couch I bought when I first moved in six months ago. It has a few busted springs that squeak when you sit down, but it's comfortable enough. The ceiling in the living room slants down at a sharp angle, forcing anyone over five foot eight to stoop a bit when they walk through the front door, but I love the slightly cramped space. The narrowness of the rooms, the way they're laid out railroad style, one opening onto another like a story unfolding in perfect rhythm—living room, bathroom, and straight back to my bedroom—makes me feel tucked in for the night and safe.

In my bedroom, the windows are covered with heavy black fabric. A huge Joy Division poster hangs over the bed, emblazoned with the image of a marble angel in black and white, wings outstretched, the words LOVE WILL TEAR US APART written in bold lettering across the top. I open my closet, grabbing a black tunic that falls to my knees, and pull on a pair of neon-green tights that bag a little around the ankles, signaling that I've lost weight recently. Stuffing my feet into my favorite pair of motorcycle boots, I grab my leather jacket and shrug it on, throw my backpack over one shoulder and I'm out the door.

I attend Manhattan Preparatory Academy. It's basically a school that caters to rich kids (read: *troubled*) who don't like high school and would rather be doing anything else—which is what I suppose I am. I usually do my homework during lunch, sitting by myself on the front steps of the school, or on the subway, my notebook sliding over my knees. As rigorous as the school is purported to be in the glossy brochures that feature girls smiling wide, their teeth sharp enough to devour the city itself, it usually takes only around forty minutes to finish everything. But it's not like I do the best job, either. Who really needs to know how to do advanced algebra in everyday life? It's not like I'll be at the supermarket someday and suddenly need to solve some complicated algorithm just to figure out whether or not I have enough change for a box of Fruit Roll-Ups.

I turn the corner, walking quickly up Third Street, past the brick façade of the local Hells Angels headquarters and the collection of motorcycles parked outside, and turn onto First Avenue. I stop at the ATM and check my balance, green numbers illuminating the screen. From the looks of it, I'll have to call my father's secretary for the second month in a row to ask for more money. I don't have a set allowance, but my father usually puts enough in my account to pay the rent, buy food and drag my laundry to the Laundromat on the corner once a week. But over the past couple of months the amount has been slowly dwindling. I wonder if this is his usual passive-aggressive way of wanting to talk to me—denying me something until I'm forced to make contact. Of course, it would be so much easier to just call me up on the phone, but my father has never been good with being straightforward. Or with confrontation, for that matter.

I stop at the bodega on the corner. Inside it's almost steamy, the smell of toasting bread and frying eggs sliding seductively under my nose. The shelves are stocked with canned goods, loaves of Pepperidge Farm and Wonder bread, boxes of Entemann's cookies stacked alongside bottles of Tylenol and rolls of toilet paper. A small glass case at the front of the store holds empanadas, the pale crescents crimped at the edges. Rows of candy bars line the register along with packs of batteries and a glass jar of tough-looking beef jerky. Merengue music plays softly from a boom box behind the counter, and the sound soothes my tired brain, lulling me back to sleep.

The same Dominican guy who's usually working in the morning stares down at me, licking his lips.

"Whatchu wan' today, mami? The usual?"

He's wearing a pressed white T-shirt, sleeves rolled up to expose his biceps. I see a tattoo of a heart on one arm, the anatomical kind, the valves and meticulously detailed chambers pierced with what look like thick metal spikes. He grins at me, pouring a small coffee before I even ask for it. I don't come in here often enough to be considered a regular, but I force myself to smile, my face stretching uncomfortably, and order a toasted sesame bagel with cream cheese. In the club, dressed in yards of satin or tulle, witty remarks slide effortlessly off my tongue, but here I'm unsure, hesitant and tongue-tied. In real life, daylight steals my words like a vampire running from the sun. Which is probably why I've pretty much given up on trying to communicate with anyone at all. As he wraps up my bagel in shiny tinfoil, placing it in a brown paper bag, my stomach growls loudly.

When I was very small, my mother would lean across from me at the dinner table and cut my meat, her silk blouse whispering against my skin, the musk and spice of her perfume overwhelming me. This was before the divorce, when we were still a family. My father drank intermittently from a glass of red wine, his face lit with a gentle smile as if the very sight of me gave him pleasure. When I think about the way he used to look at me, my throat swells with emotion, cutting off the supply of air. Tightening my grip on the brown paper bag in my hand, I blink my eyes quickly to chase away the tears and head back out into the street.

Stupid, stupid, stupid, I hiss to myself as I reach into the bag. *Stop feeling fucking sorry for yourself.* I rip off a piece of warm bread and shove it into my mouth, chewing in time with the slap of my boots against the pavement.

At the corner, I duck into the subway station to catch the train uptown. I drop a token into the turnstile while simultaneously ignoring that same bum who's always begging for a free ride, his big, blackened toe protruding from one of his ripped Nikes.

"Just let me get in behind you," he pleads, grabbing on to my jacket, and I shake my body hard until he lets me go. Last week I gave him a dollar as I slid by, which was clearly a mistake, because he's been lighting up like a Christmas tree at the sight of me ever since.

"Leave that girl alone now," an ominous voice booms over the loudspeaker. I turn around and lock eyes with a small man with white hair working the token booth. His face is weathered, and he stares out at me with concern. He raises his chin in my direction ever so slightly as the train thunders into the station, the cars streaked with black and silver graffiti. The platform smells like days-old urine and the peanut-scented belch of hot exhaust. The crush of schoolkids on the platform reminds me of last night, the crowds of brightly dressed partygoers that pushed at the velvet rope, willing me to let them inside.

I clutch my bagel and coffee tightly as I enter the train, the doors closing loudly behind me. It's crowded, and I hold on to the silver pole with one hand, trying my best to shove as much bagel into my face as I can with the other. Since I moved out of my mother's apartment, my eating habits have been random at best. With no set mealtimes, I'm either ravenous or totally disinterested, with no happy medium between the two. What's the point of throwing food into a pot or setting the table when I'm the only one eating?

"You're so effing lucky," Sara moaned when she first found out I was getting my own apartment, throwing her lanky body down in protest onto the oversized white leather sofa that took up half of my mother's living room. Sara is basically one of the few girls I can actually stand. She always says exactly what she thinks, and her level gaze behind her black rectangular-shaped glasses is unflinchingly honest. She's got this huge shock of white-blond curls that seem to spring uncontrollably from the depths of her skull, and there is nothing in her wardrobe that isn't some washed-out shade of black or gray. When she moved across the street from me in the fourth grade, I wanted to meet her so badly that I stole her bike from in front of her apartment building, hiding it in our basement storage, then watched from the plate-glass window of the lobby as she stood there on the pavement looking confused, hoping she'd come across the street asking if I'd seen it. She never did, and I sheepishly wheeled it back a few hours later and left it with her doorman, taping a pack of M&M's to the handlebars along with a note.

With the exception of Sara and Giovanni, I really don't have any close friends. I'm part of a huge circle of kids who are paid to throw parties—club kids, they call us—but I wouldn't consider any of them real friends. We're more like a bunch of loosely associated lunatics who throw parties with themes like Dante's Disco Inferno! or Iron Curtain Chic! The club-kid scene isn't about forming everlasting friendships or getting real; it's not about having money, though I do make decent cash as a promoter, which comes in handy when I squander away my father's money on magazines, dark chocolate, and records. It's about being on top, where I rarely belong.

"You'll move downtown and I'll never see you again," Sara whined, hurling herself abruptly to the floor, where she collapsed in a fit of fake sobbing. "Good-bye, cruel world!"

Sara goes to Nightingale-Bamford, the school I also attended until last year, when I was "asked to leave" by the headmistress. This may have been because I was basically showing up one day out of five. It also might have been because I was found in the girls' bathroom at the start of the school year, chopping a line on the smooth, granite countertop, a rolled-up dollar bill in one hand. When the door swung open, I looked up at the girl framed in the doorway, her auburn hair the color of burnished strawberries, her legs wrapped in pale pink tights that made me think of pirouettes, a haze of tutus, feathers drifting slowly across a darkened stage. Her rose-colored mouth opened in a wide O, and as she stared at me, her eyes blinking slowly, I froze, gripping the bill tightly in my hand, her face blank and unreadable as the door slowly swung shut. When I was summoned to the headmistress's office the next period during French, I placed my pens and pencils and textbooks carefully into my backpack, my movements slow and deliberate, masking the sinking sense of failure that crept over me like a bad dream.

Even though Nightingale is only fifteen blocks from Manhattan Prep, it might as well be at the other end of the universe, as Sara is in all honors classes and basically lives in the publications lab as coeditor of the yearbook. That's the weird thing about Sara: even though she looks like the bastard offspring of Madonna and the Cure's Robert Smith—all black rubber bracelets, dark eye makeup that she basically sleeps in until it smears artfully and her mane of wild blond hair—people like her, seek her out and want to be her friend. She manages to exist in a space where she cannot be clearly labeled or defined, moving seamlessly from clique to clique, belonging to none of them. If I had even one ounce of Sara's self-confidence and charisma, her solidified sense of self, I could probably rule the world. Instead, I'm the weird girl who goes to a school for "special" kids, that even the other special kids avoid.

"Oh please," I said, smiling at her antics. "Like I won't see you all the time anyway."

"True." She sat up, her eyes sparkling with mischief before her face grew pensive. When Sara shifts gears, it's like watching a wall come down—or go up, depending on what she's feeling at the moment. "Is it because of . . . you know . . . parental stuff?"

The smile faded from my face, and I stared out the window at a garbage truck clanging down the street, not wanting to look her in the eye. "You could say that," I mumble, my voice tight in my throat as if I'm being strangled by my own words.

"I thought things had gotten worse when you showed up with that black eye," Sara said quietly, her eyes on the rug, "but I didn't know what to say. I *never* know what to say."

"No one really does." My voice broke on the last word to leave my lips.

When I think about my mother, I have to stop what I'm doing and just breathe, my brain flooded with images: shades pulled down like eyes slowly closing, the windows shut tight. Wiping the blood and snot from my nose and cleaning the cut that splits my upper lip with hands that won't stop shaking. That feeling of invisibility, the noise of the city closing in around me like a noose.

"What about your dad?" Sara put her arm around my shoulders, leaning in. I could smell her strawberry shampoo and the patchouli oil she always dabs on her neck and behind her ears. It made me think of the industrial-strength cleaning products our maid, Jaronda, used in the kitchen once a week to clean the floors and countertops, that faint medicinal smell she left in her wake.

"What *about* him," I sighed, untangling myself from Sara's embrace. "He's the one who signed the lease on my new place."

When the social workers called him last spring, stating in no uncertain terms that I could no longer live in my mother's penthouse apartment on Eighty-Third and Park, he'd signed the lease on the East Village apartment without comment, except to mention that at six hundred dollars a month, the rent was more than reasonable. A steal. But never once did he suggest that I live with him, that maybe it wasn't a good idea for a seventeen-year-old to be fending for herself in the heart of Manhattan's Lower East Side, just steps from Alphabet City, where gunshots popped in the night air like a string of firecrackers and junkies routinely nodded out in doorways.

I take the train seven stops each way, and I usually like the ride, the narrow series of dark tunnels, the flashing lights that remind me of the strobes that shine down on me in the club, my body illuminated like an X-ray. But today, I'm too nauseated, the whiskey sours I drank last night tumbling around in my stomach like a team of trapped, acidic acrobats. Of course it would help if I could sit down, but there are never any seats during morning rush hour. A man sits across from me reading the *Post,* his face set in grim concentration. The headline for today rises above a large picture of Mikhail Gorbachev and shrieks IS THE COLD WAR OVER? Gorbachev's expression looks worried, his bushy eyebrows knitted together in what might be concern or fear, and I wonder if he knows something I don't. I hang on to the metal pole and close my eyes, wondering how long I can go on this way, how long I can maintain, my blank eyes reflected in the mirror each morning, red-rimmed and wasted. As the train lurches out of the station, I sway back and forth, my fingers burning like icicles, my body frozen to the core.